HIGH LIFE

A laugh-out-loud and utterly feel-good romance

HELEN BRIDGETT

The Mercury Travel Club Book 3

Choc Lit

A JOFFE BOOKS COMPANY

Choc Lit
A Joffe Books company
www.choc-lit.com

First published in Great Britain in 2024

© Helen Bridgett 2024

Cover art by Dee Dee Book Covers

ISBN: 978-1781897270

For Angus, my constant writing companion, xx

CHAPTER ONE: BACK FOR GOOD

'I'm back.'

My best and oldest friend Patty blasts into the Mercury Travel shop like a rock star exploding onto a stage amid dry ice and pyrotechnics. She's wearing huge oversized sunglasses, so I won't be surprised if her next words are, 'Hello, Glastonbury!'

'You couldn't have scared me more if you'd had an axe and shouted, "*Here's Johnny!*",' says my business partner Charlie as I scrape him off the walls.

'You know me — I do like an entrance,' Patty says. 'What are you all staring at?'

We'd been closing up after a busy Thursday's trading when Charlie, Josie our assistant manager, and I noticed people in hard hats carrying clipboards and tape measures arriving at the empty shop across the road. An estate agent — or at least the only one of the group not wearing a hard hat — is now changing the sign from 'TO LET' to 'TAKEN'.

'The builders over there,' I tell Patty, pointing at them.

'Ooh, yes. Not bad at all, but I am taken too.'

'We're talking about the refit, not the workmen,' I scold. 'Wondering what it's going to be.'

'I'm hoping for a gin palace,' says Josie. 'That's definitely what this town needs.'

1

We all nod at the wise words emanating from this young head.

'Maybe one with detoxifying doors,' adds Patty. 'They'd look like normal revolving doors but one spin in them and your body is a temple once more.'

It isn't unusual for the shops on the high street of this leafy Manchester suburb to change hands, but normally we'd have heard something about it. Chorlton has extremely efficient jungle drums. However, I'm not even bothered what it might become at this precise moment in time because the idea of detoxifying doors has me very excited.

'That would be absolutely brilliant,' I say. 'Amazing. Can you imagine? Every new year — no fasting for a month, we'd just take a swing round the doors and our bodies would be pure again. It would put Gwyneth Paltrow and the rest of the clean-eating brigade out of business but I think everyone else in the world would be delighted.'

'We could get my man Dyson to give up on the vacuum cleaners and invent something women really want. It must be the same technology — sucking the crap out of things,' adds Josie, her Aussie accent really going for the word *crap*. Josie has real disdain for a man with a brain the size of a planet who then uses it to invent cleaning products. She keeps a mental list of things that would be a better use of his intellect. Before today, a cellulite attachment for the Animal V8 was top of her list.

'Sounds gruesome,' says Patty, 'but if this was *Dragon's Den* I'd definitely be in. Now who wants to make me a cup of tea?'

Patty breaks our fantasy and heads into the kitchen. As it's past closing time, Josie signals that she'll head home. She knows that with Patty on the premises, it could be hours before she escapes if she doesn't go now.

I lock the shop door and join my best friend in the kitchen. I watch with amusement as she makes herself completely at home boiling the kettle and grabbing some mugs as if we'd invited her to — not that she ever waits for an invitation. Patty has been singing in an eighties tribute group on the cruise ships for around six weeks, and it shows. She's definitely a little rounder and her skin has the glow of a person who is both content and very well fed.

'Where've you hidden the bikkies?' she asks, pulling open every cupboard. 'It would be afternoon tea time if we were still aboard.' I hand her the hidden stash of chocolate digestives. 'Mind you, I could probably do with losing a couple of pounds now.'

'You're still gorgeous,' says Charlie who's joined us.

'You're right and at least there's more to hold on to.' Patty simultaneously sinks her teeth into the biscuit and her butt into one of the kitchen chairs. One or maybe both results in a loud sigh of pleasure and relief. I can't help but smile at the sight of her making herself comfy. It may only have been a matter of weeks but I have missed this woman so much and am suddenly overwhelmed with the sheer joy of seeing her again.

I give her a big kiss on the top of her head and wrap my arms around her as tightly as I can. 'It is so good to have you back. I was afraid you might end up sailing the seas for ever.'

Patty clamps the digestive between her teeth, gets up and hugs me back, one of her all-consuming unabashed hugs. It feels just as good as it looks, so Charlie gets up and joins in. Who doesn't need a hug every now and then?

'It was really great fun,' Patty says when she releases us from her grip. She swallows the biscuit then continues. 'And I'm glad I did it but it made me realize that I can't do it for ever. Even I can't spend my entire life dressed up as Cyndi Lauper. I think only the woman herself would be happy with that. No, my darlings, it is time for a new adventure.'

'Any idea what that'll be?' asks Charlie.

Patty shakes her head. 'I've no idea. To be honest, I was quite fired up about coming home and doing something new but now I'm here, with the exception of seeing my most fabulous friends again obviously, it feels a bit flat.'

The room goes quiet. Patty was marvellous on stage and I can imagine her genuinely missing all that applause. Reality doesn't tend to come with adulation, except on reality shows and they're not really real.

'Well, we can certainly do something about that.' Charlie claps his hands, banishing the contemplative silence. 'Come to dinner at mine this Saturday night. Peter and I will host a reunion for our nearest and dearest. Is Dr Lurve on shore, too?'

Patty laughs at the nickname she gave her partner when she first met him. Jack was the ship's doctor who tended Patty when she took a fall on the dance floor. She likes to tell us she was under him for weeks after that. Seeing her looking like her old self again brings a sense of relief to the room. I love my friend's ability to just cheer up everyone with one dirty laugh.

'Don't worry,' she says, 'I haven't left him behind. How could I deprive any man of all this now he's used to it? Actually, we've both decided this is it. We're leaving the cruises and joining you landlubbers permanently.'

'Is he looking for something new, too?' Charlie asks, but Patty shakes her head.

'Jack already has a great offer in a local children's ward. He's a bit sick of tending sunburn and overindulgence dressed up as gastroenteritis. He starts the new job next week.'

'Well, all the more reason to celebrate before he has to do the whole *Grey's Anatomy* thing. This weekend your new life begins with a glorious dinner party,' gushes Charlie. He loves to entertain and I can see him getting into the mood already.

'All of us together with our menfolk. We've never actually had everyone together at the same time,' he adds

And we haven't. Although Charlie, Patty and I have known each other for many years, we've each started a new relationship over the past year and the only time we've ever had even the majority of the group together was to celebrate New Year. I'd just met my other half, Michael, that very day, so it was hardly a friendship, never mind anything else, and Jack wasn't in the country. Him and Patty had a very different start to their relationship to Michael and I. Although they've only known each other a few months longer, living the whole time in the cocoon of a cruise ship positively nurtured their romance. The frequent emails from Patty are always laced with loved-up innuendo. They both seem completely smitten.

After agreeing the time and dress code, which, let's face it, was always going to be glam and gorgeous with Charlie in charge, we say our goodbyes and head home.

'Is it OK if I come round in an hour or so to collect some things?' asks Patty as we're about to get into our cars.

'If you bring wine.'

'Never go anywhere without it.'

CHAPTER TWO: GIRLS TALK

I've been house-sitting Patty's home while she's been on the cruise ship. I phone Michael and tell him about the dinner party on Saturday. He takes absolutely no persuading and says yes to coming along. He doesn't know Patty well as she left for her cruise contract just as we were properly getting together. He's very curious to meet my best friend and her partner properly. He's heard the tale of how they met several times and there's the added bonus of a decent meal to look forward to. My culinary skills are legendary for the wrong reason.

'Someone who can cook is making Saturday night's meal,' I tell him.

'Praise the lord. I haven't replaced the battery in that fire alarm yet. It's worn out.'

'Ha, ha very funny, that's the last time I cook for you.'

'Good God, all I need now is a brand new Jaguar to appear on the drive and I'll have had all three of my wishes.'

I admonish him then tell him he must find something glam and gorgeous to wear. Knowing his wardrobe, I cannot imagine what he's going to conjure up. His job rarely calls for glamour. Michael runs a property maintenance company, so the dress code is generally overalls of some sort. I was delighted to discover that he's one of those really practical men. Whatever he finds — lawnmowers, cars, remote controls — you name it, he can fix it and he loves doing so. If Michael ever goes missing or doesn't answer his phone, I know I'll probably find him in the garage or garden completely absorbed in some repair with a screwdriver in his hand.

'And a proper screwdriver, not the cocktail version,' I often tell people, in case they assume he's more like me.

As I'm tidying up Patty's house a little before she arrives, I think ahead to the group of people who'll be getting together this weekend and wonder how they'll get on. It can be a little strange when other halves meet, as even very close friends pick very different partners. Charlie picked his perfect match in Peter: he always wanted to marry a guy who'd be the perfect host and that's what he is. Peter makes it his mission to put everyone at ease the second they walk into their home.

Michael isn't too hard to imagine. He seems to have one setting — permanently laid-back and at ease. We met when I reversed out of my drive and hit his cat. The cat was fine but I was terrified at having to explain myself to a complete stranger. I needn't have worried, Michael was just lovely. He was so completely concerned for me and the shock I'd had that I'd taken a gamble and asked him to that evening's New Year Eve party.

The doorbell rings and I rush to open it, surprised that Patty didn't just barge in.

'What's with all the plants?' she asks, noticing the key change to the house as she looks around and is greeted by a jungle of foliage. She feels the leaves to check they're not plastic. Neither of us could ever be described as green-fingered, so the rainforest of healthy-looking houseplants is rather out of place.

'Michael's starting bringing plants every time he comes to dinner,' I explain.

'He comes a lot then.'

'Well, he has to visit so they get watered. He realized that fairly quickly.'

'So what else does he tend to when he's here? Do the mattress springs need replacing?'

'Patty! You could be just a little more subtle — ask me how things are going like a normal person would.'

She just shrugs.

'Open that wine,' I tell her, hoping to change the subject. 'Tell me all about the cruise.'

Patty is more than happy to have the conversation turn to her adventures and we get through three-quarters of the bottle before the conversation turns back to me.

'The business is still going well and all the Mercury Travel Club trips sell out quickly. I couldn't imagine doing anything else. I'm really happy,' I tell her.

'And how are your parents and Zoe?' she asks.

'Mum was devastated that she wasn't picked to appear on *Catchphrase* but has decided the producers must have known she was too intelligent and would have won too much money. I think Dad was relieved though — he was dreading her believing she had celebrity status when they went shopping.' I giggle.

'Can you imagine the freebies she'd try to blag?' Patty laughs.

'I try not to. And as for my wonderful daughter — well as you arrive then she leaves. She apparently applied for a secondment to the hotel's New York chain a few months ago, not expecting to get it but she has. And James got a contract out there too. It all happened incredibly quickly but they're both living the dream in the US of A and still totally besotted. She said to say she's sorry to have missed you but hopes to catch up soon.'

'Good for her,' Patty says. 'So come on, it's just us. Tell me about Michael — are you besotted too? How's the love life going? Jack and I . . .'

I let her delight in the details of their love life and open another bottle in the hope that she forgets she's asked about mine. No chance. As soon as she's finished the tale of their last night at sea, she takes a gulp of wine and asks again.

'For some people these things are private, you know.' I sound more prudish than I'd intended. 'Anyway, if you must know, we haven't got that far.'

Patty sinks onto the sofa, eyebrows raised in disbelief.

'You're kidding? It's been at least a couple of months now hasn't it, since you finally got your act together and started dating?'

'That's not so long is it? It's flown past. Anyway, we're taking it slowly, getting to know each other first. We get on so well.' I take my own gulp of wine and decide to get it off my chest. 'And I really don't want to cock it up like I did before.'

The first relationship I attempted after my divorce was just awful. It hadn't been long but I'd thought I should be 'getting back on the bike', as people kept telling me. After all, my ex had no problem in bedding someone new. I wanted to show him that I could move on, too. In the end, I rushed things and it was a complete disaster   in fact quite humiliating.

'I still cringe when I think about that now,' I tell Patty. 'I think I'd give up on sex completely if I ever had a session like that again.'

'Oh, girl, it won't be like that.' She puts her arm around me. 'You weren't ready back then but you really like Michael.'

I nod. I really do and that's why I don't want to cock things up. So, yes, I have taken my time with Michael. Maybe it seems a long time to others but I have a picture in my head of how our first time will be and that's what I'm holding out for. It will be wonderful — I am determined it will be.

'Then there's this place,' I say, trying to lighten up the conversation. 'Everywhere I look, I imagine you still here shouting out instructions. I half expect you to jump out of the wardrobe shouting 'Surprise, Surprise'. And then there was your parting joke about the nanny-cam, it's hardly conducive to romance.'

Patty guffaws then asks, 'What about his place then?'

'You mean where his wife died?'

9

Patty nods in understanding.

'No, I've decided to wait until I move into my new place,' I continue, 'where hopefully there'll be no one to haunt me and tell me I'm getting things wrong.'

In a few weeks, I move into an apartment of my own. It'll be the first place I've owned alone.

'Going to christen every room then?' Patty teases and gets a friendly thump.

'Stop ruining my romantic vision with your smut,' I tell her. 'Now get your things and I'll see you at Charlie's. And if you dare mention christening rooms . . .'

'Cross my heart.' She does a tiny little x across her chest.

I hug her again as she leaves. Deliriously happy that the people I love most in the world are back together again, I head upstairs and turn the radio up full volume. Jefferson Starship's 'Nothing's Gonna Stop Us Now' fills the room and I dance along as I flick through the wardrobe deciding what I'll wear this Saturday. Glam and gorgeous calls for a cocktail dress with masses of bling. I root through my jewellery box and pull out every costume piece I own. I'll probably end up looking like Zoe when she used to dress up as a little girl but, hey, I'll probably feel just as good too. I find an old lipstick that I never wore because it was just too glossy and leave that out too. I doubt anything will be too glossy at Charlie's. Jefferson Starship are now telling me that they built a city, and as I bellow along with them, I feel invincible. With the business going well, my best friend back and the perfect moment yet to come, this is going to be a good year. I can just tell.

CHAPTER THREE: SUMMER RAIN

When I wake up, I'm still high on life and the prospect of tomorrow night's party. These things alone would have had me leaping out of bed with the gaiety of a Disney princess anyway but when I open the curtains, the change in weather delights me just as much and I'm giddy with excitement.

'Rain, hurrah!' I cry out to no one at all.

Good old Mother Nature has blessed all travel agents by giving us the cold, wet Manchester we know and love just before the May bank holiday. I get dressed quickly and head straight for the shop, picking up a coffee en route. Weather like this reminds people that they need to go abroad for their sunshine guarantee and will mean an absolute bumper day for sales. I positively skip up the high street and see that the shop over the road now has posters up declaring: '*LAUNCHING SOON*'.

I must let Charlie know. He's out visiting some hotels this morning, so I get into the shop as quickly as I can and fire up the computer screen. Josie walks in, flicking the raindrops off her brolly.

'Knew you'd be in early with this weather,' she says. 'Have you seen the sign over the road?'

I nod, not being able to talk through a mouthful of cappuccino and a foamy moustache. I lick the chocolatey milk off my lips and then say, 'It sounds quite exciting, doesn't it? I can't wait to find out what it'll be.'

I swirl my computer screen round to show her what I've been doing — reviewing all the last-minute break options that are still out there. When customers arrive looking to escape the wet conditions we'll give them enough ideas to get the sale, but not so many that they still keep shopping around — people like easy decisions.

'Lisbon or Marrakech for city breaks, then—' Josie reads the availability — 'and maybe still the Canaries or Greece for a week of lying on the beach?'

'Of course, you know where the best beaches are,' says a voice. I look round and see Michael entering the shop with some coffees.

'Northumberland,' he continues, 'remote and beautiful.'

'I agree but we're not going to sell many north-east breaks when it's like this.' I'm very happy to see him and smile at his idea of a good holiday. He does have that wild Heathcliff vibe and I can really see him on the windswept coast even if I can't see my customers there. 'What brings you here?'

'I came round to the house to take you out to break-fast but you'd already left.' He holds out bakery bags. 'So I brought breakfast to you   both of you obviously.'

'That's so sweet,' says Josie, taking one of the pastries.

'It's lovely.' I get up and give him a peck on the cheek. 'I might have to keep you.'

He blushes then sits on the edge of my desk, sipping his own drink.

'So how's the cricket season going?' asks Josie, knowing that he loves the sport but also knowing full well that the England team is being tanked by Australia this year — or so they both keep telling me.

Michael perks up ready for some banter about his favourite subject. No matter how lovely the gesture, I can't have Josie distracted and risk missing this morning's poten-tial sales. I invested in Mercury Travel last year and became a partner alongside Charlie, but it's not just my livelihood:

it's my absolute passion. As I told Patty last night, I do love this business and I know we're going to have a bumper day, selling lots of trips and having a good laugh with all our customers. I'm on a high just thinking about it.

'Guys, we really need to get on. This is going to be such a busy day.'

Michael jumps up, apologizes and starts clearing up the paper bags and cups.

'I'm sorry,' he says, 'and I have to be getting to work, too. See you tomorrow, gorgeous.'

He's too nice and I instantly feel like the wicked witch of the west. Nevertheless I really need to get on. I blow him a kiss and get straight back to my screen.

The day is every bit as frantic and fantastic as we imagine, with customers coming in wearing big coats and weary looks. We've turned up the heating so they don't want to leave. We've got hot chocolate on the go and a little bit of music in the background. The shop is oozing charm today. Charlie taught me all this. Customers aren't just booking a trip — they're taking a break from the stresses of the day. If today's stress is extreme cold and wet, then we have to be the antidote. I make them comfortable and then take time to understand what they'd like — culture, luxury, great food — there's always something that would just make the trip perfect and if you listen to people, they'll eventually tell you. Josie always says she can look at a couple and tell what sort of trip they'd like even before they know it themselves. I've heard her wheedle information out of people on many occasions.

'Is that the new Apple? Wow, you're ahead of the curve,' she might start off like a would-be mentalist. 'You must like a great buzz then? Well I'm telling you, South America is THE place right now, especially Lima. Not many people going there yet but come next year, everyone will want to go. You should get in first while it's still pretty raw.'

Whether customers book up just to get her to stop talking or because Josie has been spot on in her analysis, I couldn't say, but she's got a great hit rate. She's at it now selling Lisbon as a destination, not that it needs much selling — culture, wine, sun and sea — what more could you want? I notice the customers who are waiting to be served listening in on the sales pitch and sure enough, when it's their turn to be served, they ask to hear about the same trip. If the whole of Manchester turns up in the Portuguese city next month, I think it may be our doing.

The morning is every bit as lively as we expected and after lunch, as the early afternoon rolls in at a more sedate pace, we relax a little. Charlie returns and starts telling us about all the deals we've been offered. They look fabulous, so later this afternoon we'll get back on the phone to let people know about them. Today is a good day. Charlie puts on his happy music (he actually has a list on Spotify called Charlie's Cheery Chunes — we're currently being serenaded by Bill Withers doing 'Lovely Day') and we have a little bop around the office.

We're stopped in our tracks by an extremely smart-looking man who walks through our door and stands in the shop taking in the décor without uttering a word.

'Oops, sorry. Can we help you?' Charlie asks, gasping for breath.

'I'm Lorenzo.' He holds out his hand. 'I'm opening the shop over the road.'

'Oh, hello,' says Charlie, genuinely happy and welcoming. We each take turns to shake Lorenzo's hand. 'Good to have you aboard. We've been trying to guess for weeks what kind of shop it'll be.'

'I'm surprised you haven't heard by now. I'm opening a travel agency.'

CHAPTER FOUR: MERCURY BLUES

Lorenzo is midway through a handshake with me when he makes this announcement. I swear as my hand goes limp, that he tightens his grip as if he's performing some mind-reading act.

'This place is nice. I love what you've done with it.' It's as if he hasn't just told us we're fair game in his mind. 'You've really ignited independent travel around here.'

'Thank you, we're doing really well,' I croak, trying to sound elder-stateswoman-ish and failing completely. I can see that the others are still dumbstruck. For some reason I need to assure him of our success. It's as if he's the school examiner and we're getting a performance report. I look him up and down. He's one of those men with an impossibly slim body. From his chest to his pointed shoes it's just one straight line of black jeans and black shirt, only interrupted by a slim snakeskin belt.

'We may even be doing too well.' Charlie laughs. 'We didn't plan to attract any competition.'

'Don't worry,' Lorenzo says, nodding at our racks of brochures. 'From the look of things we're going for rather different target markets, and anyway, I firmly believe there's plenty of business for both of us otherwise I wouldn't be here.'

'So when do you think you'll be opening?' I'm trying to work out whether he's mocking our shop or being genuine.

'I'd hoped it would be this weekend, but the builders tell me what I want is impossible in that timeframe. So it's looking like the end of the month if you can believe that. Still, you have to trust the experts, don't you? I'll pop in with an invite to the opening when I know.'

With that he leaves. Charlie's smile is far too broad to be convincing as we watch Lorenzo slither off the premises. As soon as he's out of sight, Josie declares that she needs to go and wash her hands. I join her. Charlie huddles us all together when we get back.

'What do we think?' he asks.

'He seemed quite harmless,' I offer half truthfully and half hopefully. It's beyond any level of comprehension that I can muster up that he'd actually try to compete with my magnificent Mercury.

'Bollocks,' says Josie, having no problem expressing her views. ' *"Going after different target markets"* — garbage. I know his type and he'll be out to get us all right. So if that's what we're up against, we have to make damn sure he doesn't nab any of our customers.'

Charlie nods. 'I hate to say it but I think Josie's right. We have to make sure our customers never want to travel with anyone else, starting with these hotel offers.'

I think they're overreacting but I'm now fired up by the thought of working with the other two musketeers to defeat the new upstart. We're on fire, certain to emerge the unequivocal champions of travel — we email the hotel offers that Charlie has just secured to customers we know can take advantage of last-minute breaks, and we post everything on our social media channels. The office is buzzing and, as expected, within the hour our phones start ringing. Yep — we certainly know our customers.

I answer mine cheerfully. 'Hello, there — Mercury Travel, where can we take you?'

Josie always cringes at this cheesy line, which is probably why I still use it. I look over at her as I'm saying it but she's deeply engrossed in her own call.

'I was just wondering if there's any chance of cancelling my booking,' says the person on the end of my phone. 'Or if not, could you match this offer?'

The caller tells me that immediately after our email he received another with a voucher. Lorenzo's new travel agency is offering new customers £100 off any booking in their launch week. And by the way, that's what they're going to be called: *Launch*. Funny, he didn't mention these vouchers as he was standing in our shop.

My inbox starts filling up with similar requests. It seems that the whole town has received these vouchers and, because of them, all the good work of this morning looks set to unravel. Josie has her hand over the receiver and I can see from her expression she needs me to make a decision.

I respond to my caller loudly enough for her to hear and copy: 'We really want you to stay with Mercury, so we'd be happy to match that very short-term offer. And we're sure you'll have a fabulous time.'

I'm not sure that giving so much money off is the best thing to do but it feels as if my beloved Mercury is undergoing a surprise attack and I have to do something. Just then, a customer comes in with a printout of one of the vouchers.

'I got this, this afternoon,' he tells us.

We smile at the customer and tell them that there's no problem, we'll match any offer. We manage to save his booking.

'It'll just be a temporary promotion,' I say to the others when the customer has left. 'He thought his shop would be open by now so he bought an email list and sent out an offer. All the supermarkets give you vouchers when a new competitor opens up but they only last a few days then it settles down. He'll probably feel really stupid having sent them out when he wasn't even open.'

'I hope you're right,' Charlie says.

So do I. I always go and try the new store when it opens but then go back to what I know, so perhaps that's what will happen here.

'I feel quite sorry for him in a way,' I continue, trying to lift the mood to where it'd been before this news. 'He obviously doesn't really know what he's doing — sending out offers before he's even open, underestimating the building work. Let's just get on with the job — what do we need to sell next?'

Josie nods and puts her determined face on. 'Niagara Falls still has loads of capacity,' she tells me, 'but on such a rainy day, I'm not sure I'd want to book a holiday near a raging flood.'

'Have we committed volume on it?' asks Charlie, and Josie nods that we have. We all know there is a chance we'll lose money on this if we don't sell the spaces.

'Right then, team,' I say, 'let's show this guy what we can do and if anyone asks about that discount then we honour it — OK?'

Charlie nods. 'Great — so what angle shall we take?'

'Have we said things like "majestic", "wonder of the world", "bucket-list destination"?' I ask. Charlie and Josie both nod as they've done all of that. We pull up the website for some inspiration.

'This looks terrifying,' says Charlie pointing to a jet boat that seems to be heading straight into the rush of the falls while a zip-wire soars over the top.

'You could do a helicopter ride too. Although that looks as if it gets a bit close to the cliff edge for me,' I add. 'In James Bond films, the baddies would probably catch the blade just slightly against the falls and the chopper would go plummeting into the water.'

'So the marketing campaign reads, "*Come see Niagara then die a horrible death*"?' Josie asks. 'You two are a real inspiration.'

'You do better then,' we tell her, and a contemplative silence falls over the shop.

'Boo!'

We don't need to turn around as we all know who'll be standing in the doorway.

'I thought you should know about these,' says Patty handing us a Launch voucher. 'But from the look of you all, I'm guessing you already know.'

I'm not sure a visit from Patty is quite what we need right now but she's here and she offers to help.

'We're stuck,' Josie tells her. 'We're trying to find a new way to sell Niagara Falls.'

Patty looks through all the pictures. They're full of couples embracing against the spectacular backdrop. She picks up some of the pictures and starts creating a collage of daredevil stunts alongside romantic couples.

'How about this,' she says: 'Film poster-style advert using the man in the tuxedo like James Bond, and the helicopter over the falls. You use the headline: "*View To a Thrill* starring you".'

'I like it,' says Josie. 'We focus on the extreme activities you can do but also there's a casino we can take customers to as part of the trip so if zip-wires and speedboats aren't your thing, you can go for the whole glamour experience. You're not just a pretty face, are you?'

'Obviously,' Patty graciously replies.

With the campaign theme agreed, we work until the early hours of the evening getting our marketing message out to customers. Patty keeps us supplied with coffee until we've done all we can and then as our spirit is starting to fade with exhaustion, we agree to lock up the shop and be in early tomorrow to continue the good fight.

I take a slow walk home, letting the stresses of the day dissolve into the cool evening air. The rain has stopped, leaving a pale blue sky and a dying orange streak where the sun is setting. The town looks washed clean as the street lights start to flicker on and reflect in puddles below. After the ups and downs of the day, I need some fresh air and I'm in no rush, so I take my time.

The day had started so well. Josie knew me well enough to be in the shop early on a rainy day and we'd had fabulous banter with the customers. Michael was lovely and thoughtful even if he did have to be chivvied out of the shop, but then Lorenzo and his vouchers took us by surprise. Charlie and I dealt with it. We didn't argue or panic, we just got on with the job. Then Patty came up trumps, too. I have some good people in my life but there may be a snake in the grass now. I wonder how long it'll take before Launch opens. He said a few weeks but he might be lying. Zoe knows about refits but I can hardly just pop round and ask her advice. I usually Skype her on a Sunday night but my mum joins in those sessions and I don't want her putting her penny's worth in. I'll make an extra call to Zoe tonight and ask her.

By the time I get home, have a bath to unwind, and microwave some supper, it's quite late. I decide to wait until midnight so as not to disturb Zoe at work and so she'll have time to get home. I'm trying to be considerate but she's worked out the time here and this unscheduled call from me has her worrying.

'Mum — it must be after twelve there. Nothing's happened has it? Is Gran OK?'

'She's still in the peak of health,' I reassure her, 'which when you consider the amount of cakes and biscuits she eats is quite surprising.'

For a brief second I picture Mum donating her body to medical science when she's gone. They're trying to understand how she lived to be one hundred and fifty on a diet of pure sugar. Of course, Mum being Mum, she's still awake on the operating table and telling them to be careful with their scalpel things.

'Mum — are you still there?' Zoe is sounding panicked again.

I shake myself back to reality and tell her about the new travel agents. I ask whether it would genuinely take as long as a month to finish refitting a shop.

'It depends on what they're doing in there,' she says. 'For a simple layout, I wouldn't have thought it'd take that long. Maybe he's had to apply for a change-of-use permit. What was it before?'

I tell her it was a florist.

'Then I really don't know, maybe they've found damp or something. You're not worried are you? You don't really have any competition at the moment and I know how much you love Mercury.'

I reassure her that I'm not worried, not at all. Although having Zoe ask whether I am has the doubts I've been trying to suppress resurfacing. We say our goodnights and I go to bed but can't relax. I prop up my pillow and open up a search engine. I type in *How to deal with a competitor*, and having scrolled through the words of several business gurus I've never heard of, I'm delighted to see that my all-time hero, Mr Richard Branson, has advice for me in an online business magazine. Eagerly I open the page and his words fly off the screen, striking a real chord.

It's all about needing to welcome your competition with open arms — not letting them walk all over you. Striking the right balance between respecting your rivals and focusing on how you can beat them. You must remain focused on your own team, and on your own products and services.

Focus and respect. Yes — I can do that.

He says you must show ambition, put some effort into creativity and focus on developing the next big thing so your company will emerge as the one that others want to copy.

'Focus, respect and the next big thing,' I murmur.

Yes, Richard, that makes complete sense. That's what I'll do: be respectful but focus on our strengths then develop the next big thing. I knew he'd have the answer.

I switch off the tablet and lie down to sleep, repeating my mantra as I drift off.

Focus, Respect and the Next Big Thing.

CHAPTER FIVE: WITH A LITTLE HELP
FROM MY FRIENDS

Saturday proves very hard work. Word has got round that there will be a new travel agent in town, so it takes all our persuasive powers to convince customers that they should nevertheless book their holiday now — with us. We do fill the Niagara Falls trip but my jaw is positively aching from smiling and pretending all is well. I am certainly ready for a party.

That night, I pick up Michael then Patty and Jack on the way to dinner. We'll get a cab back because I most definitely need a glass of wine. The boys have been assigned the back seat. They are obviously keen to impress our hosts and have come armed with copious amounts of flowers, chocolates and wine. Patty, on the other hand, intends to impress through her sheer presence. She's taken the 'glam and gorgeous' dress code to mean 'use as much perfume as you can' and the car smells like backstage at a beauty pageant. She is also wrapped in an enormous feather boa that she has to keep flicking round her neck as it gets blown away by the car heater fan which she's turned on full whack.

'Turn the heater down,' I tell her, spitting bits of fluff and feather.

'Are you kidding? It's like the Arctic in here. Stop the car. I'm getting in the back for some bodily warmth.'

I have to do as I'm told or I know she'll try and climb over the seat. Michael gets out and offers her his space but Patty settles herself in the middle, then drags him back in.

'You two are keeping me warm,' she says snuggling down between them.

I smile at Michael in the rear-view mirror and he gives me a look of mock horror in return. At least he's getting to know my friends rather well.

We pull up outside our hosts' door and my passengers pile out of the back seat. I, on the other hand, step elegantly out. Charlie and Peter greet everyone with big kisses.

'I'm not even going to ask what you were all up to back there,' says Peter to Patty. Charlie accepts all the gifts and adds, 'Come in, beautiful people and have some champagne.'

We head into their gorgeous home and our perfect hosts hand us a perfectly chilled flute.

'This is already better than Angie's cooking,' says Michael, accepting some bite-size tapas with his spare hand.

'I'll have you know, I can order a mean takeaway,' I counter. 'I even dial the number myself.'

'I give her that,' agrees Michael, grinning at me.

We all sit down and Patty nestles onto the sofa between Michael and Jack.

'A man sandwich,' she declares.

'With a tasty filling,' says Michael, getting an appreciative nod from her.

It is so good to be back with my best friends and I'm happy that Michael seems to fit right in.

'So you don't fancy being a lady of leisure?' he asks Patty.

The room goes quiet as everyone else looks up horrified. The idea of Patty with time on her hands doesn't bear thinking about. Jack chimes in, expressing our collective thoughts.

'I can't think of anything worse. This woman, no matter how much I love her, should never be left to her own devices.

Heaven knows what I'd come home to. Please, everyone, find her a job.'

'Which suits my many and varied talents obviously,' adds Patty.

'They're certainly varied,' I murmur and get a cross-eyed tongue poke from my friend, demonstrating at least two of the aforementioned talents.

Peter calls us to the table and serves a starter of stuffed roast peppers.

'This is truly gorgeous,' says Michael. 'If you offered it on *Dinner Date* you'd definitely win.'

That's our guilty pleasure. In the absence of my girly best friend, I've subjected Michael to a few of mine and Patty's old favourite TV programmes. We have a giggle guessing the compatibility of couples trying to find love by cooking for each other. Honestly, the producers of this show must be in stitches as they pair up vegans and butchers to see if things 'heat up in the kitchen'. Michael gets especially heated up if it's a woman cooking some fabulous cordon bleu dish and the oik about to visit is armed with petrol station flowers and a bottle of Blue Nun. The fact that he believes a man should know how to treat a lady bodes well, I always think.

Back at the table, Charlie is quizzing Jack about his new role.

Jack tells him that he'll be helping children with severe allergies and skin conditions. 'Getting back to what I did before — having spent years applying aftersun to ladies who cruise,' he adds.

'Don't knock it,' says Patty. 'All that practice has made those hands pure magic.'

Jack shakes his head. 'What do I do with her?' he asks.

'Ignore her. It's always worked for me,' I reply.

'Doctor, great hands, working with children. If you ever come over to the other side I'd have no problem fixing you up,' says Charlie and gets a rap on the knuckles from Patty.

'Step away from my man,' she warns him.

The evening is simply glorious. Peter follows the starter with an incredible platter of seafood and the wine continues to flow. Jack is the only one who gets the theme.

'Been inspired by somewhere?' he asks.

Charlie blushes a little and I work it out for myself. Since they got back, the couple have never stopped raving about the tiny island resort in Formentera that they visited earlier this year: the food, the wine, the sun. You'd think they had shares in it. Peter, however, looks horrified to think his hosting skills may have slipped.

'I never thought,' he says to Jack. 'You're probably sick of all this. You were probably looking forward to good old fish and chips or a steak and kidney pud.'

'There's never any shortage of British food aboard the cruise liner,' Jack reassures. 'And of course I come home to a tasty British bird every day.' He raises his glass to Patty.

'Ker-ching.' Charlie toasts the bad pun and Patty gets up to curtsy.

'I couldn't have put it better,' she concedes graciously. 'Come on then, why don't you show us the pictures of this island that's inspired you so much.'

Charlie leaps up and joins Peter to upload their honeymoon photographs to the TV. I've seen them before but it's probably impossible to tire of those turquoise seas. Formentera is a tiny island in the Balearics but a world away from the packaged tour scene. It's where the old hippies used to convene but now it's the A-listers who go there to get away from it all and, now, Charlie too. The setting is so picture perfect. If the couple we know weren't standing in the middle, you'd think they'd been Photoshopped.

'It's hard to believe that places like this really do exist,' I say. 'It's just so romantic and not that far away.'

Michael subtly takes my hand but Patty notices and gives me a sly wink.

'You two look like catalogue models,' she says of Charlie and Peter, 'selling pristine linen or maybe denture fixative. If you bite through a prawn in the next shot it's the latter.'

'Gee thanks, I'm not that decrepit,' says Charlie. Then he sighs and freezes the picture, zooming in on a small white building in the background.

'This is where we stayed and there's our personal hideaway. We went there every evening,' he says. 'It's just paradise on earth.'

'The thing is,' he continues, 'I've heard they're looking for investors now to help grow the business. What if the new investors change it? I'd hate that. It feels like our special place and ours alone.'

'I'm sure they won't change it that much,' I try to reassure him.

'I hope not,' he says. 'It feels like an intrusion already.'

Some might say that I'm giddy on the wine or simply high on friendship, but I hear the words of my hero echoing through my head: *Focus, Respect and the Next Big Thing.* This is it. Fate is calling, it has to be. This is — The Next Big Thing.

'Charlie,' I declare, 'we should invest in it and keep it just as it is.'

Everyone stares at me but Charlie's facial expressions move from shock, to questioning, to delight.

'Do you think we could?' he asks.

'Yes, it's just perfect. It's a beautiful place with a good climate all year round so we could do winter getaways too. And the timing, well, it's karma, it has to be. Richard said to deal with a competitor, we have to stick to what we're good at and look for the next big thing. This is it.'

'Richard?' asks Michael.

'Didn't you realize your girlfriend has Mr Branson on speed-dial?' Patty has confused him even further and gets a scowl from me.

As I'm making this up as I go along, I honestly have no idea what it would entail but fortunately Peter steps in.

'Well, you're not buying a resort, you're simply investing in it to get the exclusive rights. It'd be sort of like owning a share of a very fancy holiday villa and being the only people allowed to let it out.'

'But aren't things OK with Mercury as they are?' asks Michael. 'How would you manage something like this?'

'It would be quite ambitious I suppose but there is a really competent team on site who run everything already,' says Charlie, starting to consider the possibility. 'And it would mean we'd have something really very special to offer our customers. What are your thoughts, Angie?'

My mind is running at a million miles per hour. Richard's advice seemed to make sense, but now that they're taking my idea seriously, I can see this is a big move. I trust Charlie and he knows Mercury better than anyone, so yes, it would be a fantastic offer for our customers. Yes, it would be unique and it could be our next big thing. But, back to Michael's question — how would it work? How much would it cost? I need to work this out for myself. Richard Branson wouldn't invest on a whim. My heart is thumping so loudly, I'm sure the room must be able to hear it.

'I love the whole idea but why don't we start with a sensible move,' I say to calm myself down and get my business head back on. 'Let's find out how much it is and who's staying on in the management team, then get some ideas for the holidays themselves. That way we can create some projections and make sober decisions.'

'Drunken ones are far more fun,' hiccoughs Patty as she gets up to head to the kitchen, no doubt for another bottle of cava.

Charlie hugs me and the mood in the room lightens. It feels like we're going from having a reunion dinner to an all-out party. Charlie grabs the flutes and leads a toast.

'To Mercury and Angie — the Island Queen,' he says and everyone follows.

Michael gets up. 'All these bubbles are going to my head,' he says. 'Mind if I have a look at your garden?'

Peter gets up to show him the way and Michael holds out his hand for me to join him.

'Please feel free to pull out any weeds,' shouts Peter as he leaves us alone.

Outside, the clear night air is instantly refreshing. Michael links arms with me and leads me to sit in the love seat at the end of the garden. He lights the storm lantern on the little table and sitting silently we watch the silhouettes of our friends getting more and more animated as the bubbly flows.

'Tell me if I'm wrong,' says Michael, 'but I think you made that suggestion to cheer Charlie up.'

'Maybe to begin with.' I shrug, not really sure myself.

'It's a big move,' he continues. 'If you didn't mean it, I'll help you find an excuse to get out of it.'

I'm slightly taken aback.

'Don't you think I can do it?'

'Of course I do.'

He takes my hand and gives it a squeeze. I know he means well but he has to understand how much Mercury means to me.

'We have to do something,' I tell him. 'There's a new guy on the block now and even if he makes mistakes at the beginning, he'll soon learn and he'll have new ideas. We can't just stand still. Charlie loves this place and a beach bar has been his dream life ever since I've known him. He didn't *have* to give me the chance to become a partner in Mercury — he could have kept me on as his assistant but he didn't, he took a chance on me when I needed it most. Now if I have the chance to help him live his dream and help Mercury at the same time, I should. If we find that the numbers do stack up, how could I refuse?'

Michael kisses me on the forehead. 'If you're sure you want to, I will be with you all the way.'

I relax and smile at this lovely man. 'Thank you.'

Over his shoulder I can see Patty at the window watching us. She forms a love heart with her hands and beats it against her chest. I try to shoo her away without attracting Michael's attention. It doesn't work and he turns to see what I'm doing. Luckily she stops just before he sees her.

'I guess they want us back in,' he says, so arm in arm we head back into the house.

'You could run *Top Gun* holidays complete with a volleyball tournament,' Jack is saying as we rejoin our friends. 'Patty knows all the songs.'

'This is a beautiful premium location,' protests Peter. 'Not an episode of *Love Island* with a bit of *Danger Zone* thrown in.'

'We could host weddings,' Charlie adds, 'maybe specialize in the LGBT market.'

'Oh and have those beautiful yurts opening up onto the beach,' Michael adds. 'I could build them for you.'

'What a gorgeous idea,' exclaims Peter. 'Big safari tents would be fabulous there.'

'A sort of a Camp-Glamp then,' I add.

'And I could sing "Wind Beneath My Wings" as they walk down that sandy aisle,' declares Patty, determined to have a role. 'Come on everyone, this deserves a conga!'

She lassos Peter with her boa, pulling him up from the sofa then grabs his waist, pushing him around the room. Jack bellows with laughter. I'm beginning to think Patty has found herself a one-man audience who seems to love every anecdote she tells and every song she sings. Patty never really stops doing either, so this is quite a match. Jack soon joins in and Michael looks at me. I release him, so he submits to the inevitable. Only Charlie and I are immune to Patty's magnetism and we watch her lure the others Pied-Piper style around the room.

It's a funny old conga. Patty like a tall blonde nautical figurehead, clenching the eternally young-looking Peter with his dark hair and twinkly green Irish eyes. If any of us have a portrait in the attic, it's Peter. Behind her is Jack, a salt-and-pepper Captain Birdseye, then Michael, who is taller than everyone and has the slim muscular frame and light tan of someone who works outside most of the time. His fine sandy hair is turning grey at the edges but it makes him look like the proverbial gentle giant. I remember him showing me a picture from 1977 when he was eighteen and going through his punk rock phase. Poor lamb, his hair was so soft it just wouldn't stick up, so he had these little tufty spikes which he told me took a whole can of hairspray to achieve. To add insult to injury, he's always had a kind, squashy face and pale blue eyes that could do no wrong — hardly the make-up of a rebellious punk rocker. He must have been glad when that era ended.

'It's a nice dream,' says Charlie, bringing me back to the topic of conversation while we have some privacy, 'but it would be huge.'

'We don't know yet,' I tell him, now determined I'm going to consider this seriously. 'We need to see the numbers and the plans and we can't make this decision at a party, no matter Patty having already chosen the soundtrack.'

He squeezes my hand. 'That's why I need you by my side. I'm far too emotional about that place. You need to keep me grounded.'

I nod and, putting my hand over his, we seal a silent pact to keep each other safe. A little shiver tingles through me.

'It's exciting and scary at the same time isn't it?' I confess. 'But people say you should do the things that scare you.'

'It's not always the best advice,' says Charlie. 'I wouldn't swim through a crocodile pit or get up to a Patty-led conga. Just think, this might make us eligible for *International Business of the Year.*' Charlie lights up the words with his hands.

I was utterly obsessed with Mercury winning a business award last year. I'd been through so much with the divorce that I desperately needed to win, just to prove things were finally on the right track. We eventually won the People's Champion category and the memory of getting up onstage to collect it still sends an overwhelming wave of joy through my body. I have the cut-glass trophy boxed up in bubble wrap, ready and waiting to take pride of place on the mantelpiece of my new home. We also each got a very fancy fountain pen with 'Entrepreneur of the Year Winner' engraved on it. Mine lies in my top drawer and I take it out every morning, sitting it on my desk so customers can see it and I can relive the joy of that night.

'Now, now, no getting carried away. We're taking this one step at a time,' I remind him.

'Obviously . . .' Charlie shoves me excitedly. 'But can you believe we're even considering this? We'll be mixing with the celebs — we could even invite your hero over for inspiring us.'

That seals it.

'Richard,' I'm saying as I show my hero around our fabulous resort. 'As you can see we've followed your advice on the Next Big Thing. It's not quite Necker but I hope you enjoy it here. Come and meet Charlie, he insists on running the cocktail bar himself.'

We sit down to sunset-coloured cocktails Charlie has specially created for the visit. I'm wearing expensive white chiffon and am barefoot, enjoying the feel of the warm sand on my feet. Obviously, after several hours of hardcore pumicing, my tootsies are beautiful . . .

I'm wondering what happened to all the little fishes that used to nibble peoples' feet . . . ? Would they have been released into the ocean? But they'd have a taste for human flesh — that's a B-movie eco-disaster just waiting to happen . . .

'Yoo hoo,' calls Charlie and I shake myself back to reality but I'm still concerned about those fish. I'm going to have to google that.

'You get the prospectus,' I say, shaking myself from my gorgeous dream, 'and then maybe we could take some time to think it through without the help of our enlightened friends.'

I nod at the scene in front of us. Patty has started teaching the boys her Gangnam-style moves and it's not attractive. There isn't an ounce of rhythm between them and I'm not sure what dance Jack is doing but it bears no resemblance to anything else going on.

'Yep, I don't think we're going to get a sensible suggestion from this lot now,' acknowledges Charlie.

'Err, serious bunch over there,' Patty yells from the dance floor/lounge rug. 'If you're not joining in then we seem to have run out of bubbly over here.'

'Dear Lord.' I leap up to get another bottle and avert this major crisis affecting my friends.

CHAPTER SIX: PRETTY VACANT

Patty opens the door with only a small grunt of a greeting.

'The cava-fuelled conga fighting back?' I laugh as she groans remembering it.

Despite both feeling slightly worse for wear, we're off for Sunday lunch and a catch-up. Taking no chances, we're walking to our local pub and as we set off from Jack's house, I have to drag her away. They're blowing kisses to each other until we're thankfully out of sight.

'Blimey you have got it bad.'

'I have.' She sighs. 'But he's funny, clever and totally devoted to me. I mean, what more could a girl want?'

'Not much. Maybe a wine tap in the kitchen.'

'His subscription to the Wine Club comes pretty damn close — there'll be a case on the doorstep every month.'

'Sold to the lady with the drink problem. Marry this man straight away.'

'Well . . .' says Patty, and links arms with me as we walk along. 'I do have some news on that front. He wants us to get a house together and I've said yes. I know we haven't been together long but it feels right, so I'll put my place up for sale as soon as you're ready and then we're going to find something we both love.'

I don't know what to say. The past few days have been quite bizarre and it all started with Patty coming home. At the time, I thought her return would mean things going back to the way they were.

'Wow, that's fabulous,' I murmur. 'Things are really changing aren't they?'

'But the changes are good, aren't they? The new resort sounds fabulous. If you get it, you'll be rushed off your feet with new customers. At least you're going to be busy. I have absolutely no idea what I'm going to do now.'

'I know we joked about it at the party, but don't you just want to spend more time with Jack?' I ask.

She shakes her head. 'I'd love to but he's really excited about the new post and even though he doesn't start for another week, he's always having impromptu meetings with his new boss. We've been back three days and I think I've seen you more than I've seen him.'

'You could have stayed at home with him today, I wouldn't have minded.'

'No chance — he's off again later today for some orientation session before he starts. He really cannot wait to get going,' Patty says, shaking her head. 'Nope, I have to find a new mission in life. You saw the panic in his eyes when he thought I might be at home moping all day.'

I'd like to bet she wouldn't stay at home moping. If I know Patty she'll be getting up to all sorts and begging me to join in. As much as I love her, I do have a business to run.

'Then we'd better find you something quickly.' I hope she sees my comments as the generous concern of a true friend rather than an act of self-preservation. 'Any idea of what you'd like to do?'

Our walk takes us through the park where the candyfloss cherry blossom is in full bloom making this little suburban patch of green simply beautiful.

'I could become a dog walker,' she says on seeing someone handling four cockapoos.

'You hate the cold,' I remind her, nodding at her current ensemble.

She pulls her big coat tightly around her and snuggles into her scarf.

'I'd only work summer.'

'So precisely when people are prepared to walk their own dogs? Anyway, I can't imagine you want to give up the world of entertainment completely. The hounds wouldn't provide much of an audience unless you can teach them to howl in harmony.'

'You could be right there.'

Leaving the park, we continue down a road of small businesses. Patty studies every shop sign we pass, searching for the solution to her unemployment.

'A funeral home,' she suddenly declares. 'I'd never be out of work there.'

'What on earth would you do?'

'Well, people are having themed funerals now, aren't they? Like an Elvis one — I could sing "Crying in the Chapel" or "Can't Help Falling in Love". I tell you there wouldn't be a dry eye in the house.'

She has a spring in her step now and I can see she's on a roll.

'In fact there are loads of songs I could do. There's the really weepy one, "Wasn't Expecting That". I can't watch the video anymore as it has me in floods.

'Plus all the classics — "Knockin' On Heaven's Door", "(Don't Fear) the Reaper", oh, and "Seasons in the Sun". That was so sad and everyone would know the words. The funeral parlour would need to order in extra tissues.'

She starts humming the chorus to the Terry Jacks classic.

'I doubt there'd be applause at a funeral when you've finished,' I remind her — 'just a kind of awkward silence. Could you cope with that?'

'Maybe not and with all that crying, my mascara would be all over the place. I can hardly come home to Jack every night looking like Alice Cooper. I'm not even sure I want to keep singing but what else can I do?' There's a brief pause

34

before she adds, 'I think I'll phone Frankie to see if he has any ideas.' Frankie is the talent manager who got Patty the gig on the cruise ship.

'I thought he only did tribute acts.'

'Oh no, he has fingers in more pies than little Jack Horner. There'll be something for me.'

At that moment, the gastro pub we're looking for appears, so I manage to avoid speculating on what that something might be. Patty, collar up against the relatively mild May weather today, rushes into the building. The pub has several stars to recommend it online and I'm struck by what makes a pub 'gastro'. There is definitely a look. You have to have bare floorboards, a dullish paint colour and witty slogans on the wall. You also have to put herbs in vases and flowers in the salad. Somehow all of this reassures people that the rest of the meal will be good. I wonder if there's an equivalent look for travel agents. Gastro-travel?

'Are you going to gawp at the blackboard all day or can we sit down?' she asks, reminding me that there's also always a blackboard at these places.

I join her at the table and peruse the menu — while checking for the flowers, and sure enough they're there. Not that either of us will be sampling them. Today is not a day for salad. Competitors were never conquered nor new vocations found through salad. We order two Sunday roasts (locally sourced, obviously) and a couple of glasses of pinot noir. Hair of the dog — it would be rude not to.

'So,' starts Patty wasting no time at all — her hands are folded in front of her as if she's interviewing me. 'Tell me what's really going on with you and Michael. He seems really nice and from what I saw he's completely smitten. Is it really all about the two houses having too many ghosts in the closets or is something else going on?'

I hesitate. I wasn't sure whether I'd tell her any of this, but now that I'm here, I can't help but think it would be good to talk this through with someone, someone who's also just started a new relationship. I go for it.

'It's not that I don't want to and you're right, it's not all about the houses or fearing you'll jump out of the wardrobe.'

Patty says nothing but nods, encouraging me on. I take a deep breath and continue.

'My body doesn't look like it did when I was thirty or even forty,' I spill out. 'And it doesn't look like any of those fifty-year-old celebrity bodies either.'

'Neither will his,' Patty says gently. 'I think we all look better with our clothes on at any age.'

'I certainly do,' I say. 'And my body doesn't feel the same either — I just don't get fired up the way I used to. So I just thought if I wait and create the perfect moment then, well, there'd be a distraction from what I look like and I'd find it easier.'

'I understand. So what does perfect look like then? White linen, candles — that kind of thing?'

I shrug, slightly embarrassed by that clichéd vision but it is what I have in mind — definitely the low lighting.

'And have you booked in your vajazzler?'

'My what?'

'You must have read about it, everyone's doing it these days. It might have started with a few celebrities but that's what any man would be expecting in the sack. You can't roll up with your grey wire wool when he's expecting rhinestone.'

I'm horrified and for the very, very briefest of moments believe her. However, she can't keep a straight face to save her life and the rocking shoulders are giving it away. I thump her, then take a big glug of wine.

'I'm terrified enough without worrying about that grey wire wool,' I say, plucking up the courage to ask. 'Seriously though, are we supposed to do something about it? Like dye it?'

'What with?' Patty says. 'L'Oreal's *Just For Pubes*?'

Of course our young waiter picks that exact moment to arrive at the table. The poor blushing lamb serves our meals and makes his escape as quickly as he can.

'Because I have to ask you,' continues Patty, 'is he worth it?'

She swooshes her hair à la shampoo commercial and I have to laugh along. We try to change the subject while we tuck into our food and agree that, if we could only take one food to a desert island, it would be roast potatoes. Meal over, it's back to business.

'You know, there's a danger of overthinking this,' says Patty when the dishes are cleared away. 'He's smitten and you're gorgeous as you are. If you wait for that "perfect moment", it'll never happen. Next time these sparks fly,' she continues, 'just go with it. See where it leads.'

'I don't know. There still might be new things he's expecting that I don't know about.'

'Then you're an extremely lucky woman and he is one lucky man. As I have lots of spare time at the moment, I will school you in the act of twenty-first century lurve . . .'

I don't know what she says next. Patty is drowned out by my internal voices yelling, 'Please *nooooooo*!'

I sincerely hope Frankie has a job for her, as this woman would be dangerous if left with time on her hands.

After the meal, I manage to wave Patty off before any further 'help' is offered, then head home. Climbing out of my day clothes into my slouchies, I take a quick look in the mirror at what Michael would have in store if we ever got that far. I breathe in and hold my boobs up. I do take care of myself so I suppose it's not that bad if we manage to get undercover quickly.

As it's Sunday night, Mum and I have our official Skype session with Zoe who has promised not to mention Friday night's call in my mother's presence. At seven o'clock on the dot, the doorbell rings and I let Mum in flustered and yelling, 'I'm not late, am I?' as she does every week.

'No, as I keep telling you, we ring Zoe and I don't do it until you get here, so you can't be late.'

'You say that but I've seen it on the news. There was this reporter in America hanging on in the background and the newsreader here was just carrying on their conversation not even knowing they had someone there.'

It's sometimes, well, always, best not to argue with Mum. There is no logic to any debate she has. I simply fire up the tablet and place it in front of us then dial Zoe's number.

'Wait, my hair.'

Mum brushes her hair and quickly applies some lipstick. She looks at me. 'Are you staying like that? Zoe's always really smart.'

'It's Sunday night, I'm relaxing,' I protest. 'It's two o'clock in the afternoon over there.'

'You could still make an effort,' she whispers. 'No wonder she's emigrated.'

'Who's emigrating?' asks Zoe from the other side of the Atlantic.

My heart always skips a beat when I see my beautiful daughter's face light up the screen.

'No one, don't worry. How are you, sweetheart?'

Zoe tells us she's fine, and she certainly looks it with her lovely tan and beaming smile. This adventure in New York seems to be suiting her down to the ground. I couldn't be more proud.

'Zoe!' yells Mum as if she has to cross the Atlantic with her projection. 'Are my lips moving at the same time as I'm talking?' She asks this at every session.

'Yes, Gran—' my daughter laughs — 'and that lipstick colour looks lovely on you.'

'Some of us care about our appearance,' comes the murmured response and pointed glare. 'Now how's your James? And that hotel he's building?'

'Awesome, Gran,' Zoe states and with one word expressed so enthusiastically, I can tell that they're both really living the dream and getting cosy with the culture over there.

'I have to admit I don't see much of him. He's like, so into his work, but I don't mind at the moment because everyone wants a piece of him and it's just brilliant.'

I nod sagely but leap in, glad to have at least one opportunity to dispense motherly advice.

'That's great and I'm glad you're doing well too but you do have to find time for each other or the weeks will turn into months and you'll have drifted apart.'

'And your mother knows about things drifting apart,' interrupts Mum as tactlessly as ever.

I glare at her. She is, after all, talking to my daughter about her parents' break-up.

'Make sure you have your date nights, put them in your phone to remind you,' she continues. Mum is delighted when Zoe approves of the plan.

'That's not a bad idea, Gran. I'll suggest it to him. He'll be glad of an evening free of schmooze. So, anyway, what's new with you?'

'Patty's back,' I tell her. 'And we're thinking about expanding Mercury.'

'Wow, Mum, that's amazing. What kind of expansion? Would it be another shop? And what about . . .'

She stops just short of mentioning our conversation about the new competitor.

'It's more of an exclusive resort. I'll say more in a few weeks,' I add quickly. 'It's just an idea.'

'One she hasn't had the courtesy to run past me,' huffs Mum while Zoe and I give each other a sneaky glance.

'That's obviously why I don't want to say too much at this stage,' I say.

'Obviously,' says Zoe, nodding. 'Because when it comes to business expansion, Gran is as knowledgeable about that as she is about dating.'

'Don't you mock, young lady. Those dates will work.'

Zoe and I smile at each other. As soon as we get the prospectus I'll call her without Mum in attendance. As a hotel manager, and now an international one at that, she'll have some ideas about running a resort. Right now, she has to leave to get back to work, so we say goodbye and blow each other several kisses as usual. Of course I'm glad she's doing well but I do miss my little girl.

CHAPTER SEVEN: ISLAND IN THE SUN

Charlie sent off for the island prospectus immediately after the party and since then we've been focusing on business as usual while waiting for it to arrive or for something to happen over the road. For a week now there's been no further sign of Lorenzo and the vouchers have finally stopped making their way to us. I wish I could say that meant we'd stopped thinking about him but every now and then one of us will be caught gazing over at the boarded-up shop, watching the comings and goings. This is exactly what I'm doing now.

I remember an article I once read that said if you chant affirmations every morning, the universe hears and gives you what you want. I've been doing this with Richard's advice, *'Focus, Respect and the Next Big Thing'*, but today I find myself asking the universe to supply endless bacon sandwiches to the builders working over the road. This is because I've noticed that when someone does the sarnie run, they down tools and get nothing done. It seems a very passive way of me delaying the opening and lies more comfortably than my other idea of asking the universe to curse the new shop. I so nearly asked — OK I *did* ask — but have felt guilty ever since. It kind of jars with Richard's *'Respect'* instruction.

When we first started Mercury, I went to a small business event at the Town Hall. Mingling with the other business owners, I was at first terrified, but the chair of the local business chamber encouraged us to help each other. As soon as I offered a small amount of help I felt better and found that the other business owners were more than happy to offer something. Since then we've had lots of help from other small businesses — things like printing our leaflets at a slight discount or using us to book their corporate travel — and it feels good being part of this community.

I do wonder why Lorenzo isn't here overseeing all the work. I'm sure that if I were refitting my new business, I'd be on site every day.

Perhaps, despite his bluster, he could be quite new to all this after all, he did send out vouchers before his shop was even open. I'm torn between not wanting him to succeed but also not wanting to see a fellow small enterprise fail. Perhaps we should extend the hand of business friendship and maybe support him in some way when he opens up. I know Charlie will think I'm absolutely insane but it doesn't have to be a big gesture — just something that shows we're confident and approachable, that we are the elder statesmen in this town and if he settles in behind us, all will be fine.

I imagine myself heading over there on Lorenzo's opening day and maybe bringing him a coffee to welcome him to the high street. I can see him telling the business community how my guiding hand encouraged him. In turn, I'd get Business Angel of the Year and I'd humbly tell people that we're all in this together. Maybe it'll all be absolutely fine. After all, every restaurant, shop and taxi firm has a competitor here — why should it be different for us?

Towards the end of the day, Charlie calls out to me and tells me that the investment prospectus for Formentera has arrived and Peter is heading into the office to talk it through with us. I give Michael a call and ask if he can pop round on his way from work. Not only will he take my side if I need him to but as he runs a property maintenance company and is a very practical man, he'll spot any issues from a mile off. Charlie opens up the prospectus on the screen and then presses print.

We wait and wait and wait while our printer tortures us spewing out one page at a time. When it's all done and our fingernails are completely gone, Charlie picks up a bundle of pages and hands them to me. My nerves start short-circuiting through my body and I'm almost too scared to even hold them. It's one thing making such a huge suggestion at a dinner party surrounded by friends and quite another to make it with only a sober Charlie to prop me up.

'I feel like an actor at the Oscars,' says Charlie. 'I've got an envelope in my hand and in a short while, I'm going to open it and we'll either be delighted or disappointed. The thing is, right now, I truly don't know which way I'm going to feel.'

'I know exactly what you mean.' I take a deep breath.

Peter and Michael arrive just as we're locking up and we all head into the back room without saying a word to each other. Boy this is nerve-wracking and we don't even know what's in the prospectus. We sit down at the dining table and I put my glasses on, trying to look serious and confident before I start flicking through the pages. It's a beautifully presented document as you'd expect, with pictures of the resort to pull at your heartstrings and tempt you into investment. While Charlie starts cooing over the glorious pictures of perfect white beaches I skip past this temptation straight to the summary of the assets.

'So there's a guesthouse as well as a bar?' I ask looking over my glasses at him.

'Guesthouse, small private beach and of course the beach bar,' Michael reads from the brochure. 'And they all look in very good condition.'

'It seems to be a pretty self-contained pitch,' adds Peter. 'They're looking for people to work with this infrastructure rather than suggest any major works. The events Mercury is famous for would really suit this and the wedding idea is pretty spot on.'

I nod intelligently. I'm struggling to hold onto this calm demeanour as the excitement bubbles up. This really does look right up our street. I nod at the boys and together we open the page that outlines the investment requirements.

'Oh, Angie, it's not completely unaffordable,' says Charlie, squeaking gleefully as I try not to giggle along at his enthusiasm. He's reading my mind.

'No,' continues Peter who seems to automatically put his Business Investment Adviser hat on at the sight of numbers. 'I've taken an educated guess at the likely outlay but you two need to assess the potential bookings. The resort itself is already a very profitable enterprise and it would definitely boost the core business. It needs a bit of a refresh but it doesn't currently do weddings, so if you were to add them, you'd probably increase both yield per customer and capacity with a respectable outlay.'

This is what I need to hear. As lovely as it is fantasising about a beach bar where Patty organizes the dancing and Charlie mixes a Tropical Sunset cocktail, Peter seems to know what to say. I can't help thinking that this has come at exactly the right time. It's the extra string to our bow that we need and something any competitor couldn't possibly compete with. We'd be in a different league.

'How would we fund this?' I ask.

'If trading levels stay as they are, you could take some capital out of Mercury quite safely,' Peter says. 'Or you could look for an investor or even borrow the money and keep the businesses entirely separate.'

Throughout this, Charlie is trying not to burst with excitement. Then he can't stop himself and grabs both my hands, clutching them to his chest.

'Think about it, Angie. The Mercury Travel Island Retreat. I mean to say, how utterly fabulous is that?'

It happens again — I'm picturing myself in that exclusive resort, waving politely at the celebs staying with us. I'm tanned, confidently negotiating with the locals and signing important documents. I have world-renowned business

43

dinners overlooking the sea and an agent keeps pestering me to write a business autobiography. Oh no, Mum has just appeared. She's telling them, *'This heat plays havoc with my ankles. Just look at the size of them.'*

She's showing her swollen legs off to my esteemed guests. What on earth is she doing in my fantasy world? I shake myself from my ruined dream and see that I have two pairs of eyes on stalks waiting for me to speak. I so want to do this but questions keep racing through my head: how do you run a business that you don't sit in every day? Who makes the beds in the guesthouse? How do I stop my mum getting a visa to travel? I try to shake them off, hoping that I'm not in charge of bed-making in this future world. I try to think of a sensible question, one that an international businesswoman would ask.

'Is this really feasible?' I say eventually. 'Peter — you have to tell us honestly, are we kidding ourselves? I mean most businesses don't expand this much do they?'

'No most fail before they get here,' says Peter. 'And it's a risk but a manageable one.'

'It would be incredible,' says Charlie. 'Our own exclusive resort. We're not mad, the numbers really stack up too, don't they, Peter?'

'They do and you can see that. You already have a loyal customer base looking for new ideas from you but it would be hard work, keeping Mercury at its current levels and starting something like this.' He has his independent advisor voice on.

'Hard work, *schmard* work,' dismisses Charlie. 'Not a problem for this team.'

I tidy up the prospectus newsreader-style and lay it in front of me. The guys say nothing, but watch me and I leave a dramatic pause before announcing, 'OK. Let's do it, let's take it to the next stage.'

Charlie leaps up and hugs me, then Michael joins in. Once untangled from the hug, Peter shakes my hand as if we've already won the bid. I'm excited, scared but excited. I have to stay focused.

'What do we need to do first?' I ask.

'Well, there's a deadline for all interested parties, so you'd have to get your proposal in by the end of May,' Peter replies. 'They'll favour ideas that can get up and running quickly — which yours can, but before you even start drafting that proposal, you have to be completely sure that you want to do this. I'd advise you both to take some time and discuss it quietly. Go in with one good idea well executed, like the weddings, and then develop the proposal. I'm happy to help with that. Remember, you may not get this however good your ideas are   the owners might prefer someone else's bid.'

'But at least we'll have tried,' Charlie gushes. 'And our idea will be the best, I just know it.'

If Charlie's enthusiasm could win the bid, then we'll probably walk this, but for now we have to get back to the day job. I clear up the coffee and tidy up the prospectus telling everyone that I'll get copies sent through to them.

'Let's each take a week to look through the details on our own. Charlie and I will assess the potential for sales, Michael if you look for any infrastructure and maintenance issues and we'll get our numbers to Peter to stress test the business plan. If we're still as enthusiastic when we've really interrogated this, we should start the proposal and get an appointment with the bank manager.' I receive nods all round.

'And just in case you need additional inspiration . . .' From his man-bag, Charlie hauls out a pile of style magazines and brochures with colour schemes and accessories for the yurts.

'Numbers before cushions please, Charlie.' I shake my head in mock-despair but nevertheless take them and have a quick flick through.

The brochures are stunning and I can imagine any bride looking at this resort and wanting to be married there. Somehow, the beachside setting and the horizon beyond look so full of hope. As if the wedding is the start of a huge adventure, a voyage to be taken together. You almost have to look to the future when you're standing in front of an infinite ocean. *'You can do anything, you can go anywhere,'* it seems to call out.

I think back to my wedding with my ex-husband Alan. It was a very traditional church affair as was the fashion at the time. It was post-Charles and Di, so big dresses and conspicuous consumption were all the rage. Mum insisted on inviting every relative twice removed as well as friends and neighbours. I barely knew some of the congregation but small weddings were just not done. My side of the church was crammed so Mum could sleep easy knowing that she'd shown everyone we were a popular family. I dread to think what she'd have said if I'd asked for one of the modern weddings people have these days. Mind you, I doubt I'd have asked for one. I can understand wanting a small registry office or something very personal like Charlie and Peter had but I can't imagine copying those couples who choose to get married dressed as Batman and Robin or in deep-sea-diving costumes. Do they really look back to the day with fondness? I wonder how many look at their wedding photos and cringe? My wedding dress with its puff-ball sleeves looked a bit OTT by today's standards but at least I can say it was in fashion at the time.

However, to me Formentera looks timeless and I believe that anyone looking back at a wedding on this island will remember it lovingly. The more I think about it, the more I want to do this despite my nerves. I love Mercury Travel and I get so much joy from making sure every holidaymaker has an absolutely marvellous time, one that will be talked about and reminisced over for many years. Charlie and I do take the time to make every event special and we would do the same if we ran these weddings. If I put myself in the shoes of our future brides, I know that every sense would be running wild when they got to this island. They'd be mesmerized by the stunning beauty but also the sound of the ocean, the sensation of the light breeze and the aroma of . . .

'Oleander — they're native to the Island, add a splash of colour and have a beautiful perfume. They're perfect for a romantic evening stroll.'

I'm pulled back to the moment by Michael who is holding up his phone with a picture of a bright pink flower.

'I started reading up on the island for today and spotted all the stunning flowers you'd be able to use for the weddings,' he adds swiping through pictures.

'Thank you,' I say. 'They really are gorgeous.'

Out of the corner of my eye I spot Charlie and Peter folding their arms knowingly.

'I think we might have our first customers,' murmurs Charlie.

He gets my very best look of scorn for that comment but inside I'm smiling.

CHAPTER EIGHT: MOVING ON UP

Charlie and I turned out to be pretty useless when it came to reviewing the prospectus separately, so agreed to work on it together and have met up every evening this week to develop the proposal. The requirements of the bid are that the new investment partner brings in new ideas, more tourism to the island, and with that more employment. The wedding idea seems to fit the bill perfectly. We've already worked out the cost of buying the yurts and safari tents, of investing in a makeover and of marketing our new service. It's a significant investment but the business plan is definitely achievable. We've also researched the weddings market and we're both completely gobsmacked by the amount people are spending these days. Traditional nuptials in this country make a quick jaunt to our island look like an absolute bargain, and reduces the need to invite those relatives not liked. We decide we're best mentioning that little nugget in our conversations with the happy couples rather than in our brochures.

So far, it's all looking extremely promising and we're sure any bank or investor will be chomping at the bit to get on board. We're having no problem with the first draft of our proposal the ideas are flowing. We've asked Peter to double-check everything, to challenge our thoughts and put together a number of cash-flow spreadsheets for us. We want to know the worst-case scenario and the best case. By the end of the week we're convinced that this is not only a good idea it's one we're truly excited about. It fits Mercury perfectly. Now we just have to convince the bank manager that it does, and we have an appointment to see him next week.

So after all that, come Sunday morning, I feel quite flat. This house suddenly feels big and empty. Patty is coming round later with the estate agent to value it but after that, it'll be very quiet. I wonder if Michael is free today? I text him.

R u working today?
Till 6 — could meet you later
Fab — will make dinner
Looking forward to it x

I exchange contracts on my new apartment next week and they've said I should be completing very soon, so Patty needs to start selling this place ready for her new life with Jack. She arrives minutes before the estate agent and then we dutifully follow him around the house answering pretty obvious questions.

'Centrally heated, is it?'

We nod, resisting the urge to say, 'No — those radiators on the wall are makeshift xylophones in case we get the urge to play a little tune actually.' We all trail upstairs as he measures each bedroom and checks the wardrobes. Fortunately, I've had enough time to give a quick hoover round and dust the surfaces with an old sock. I look like the ideal house guest.

'Is there loft space?' he asks. 'People like to know that there's potential to add value to a property.'

I blame TV despite the fact that I'm as addicted to these programmes as the next person. Once upon a time we lived in houses but now we own 'properties' and they never stop blethering on about 'potential' in these shows. And you know full well that most people won't get any further than putting up fancy wallpaper to create their feature walls, never mind knocking a great big hole in the dining room.

'Yes, let me show you the ladder,' says Patty, unaware of my internal ranting.

The estate agent goes up into the loft while we stand on the landing.

'Wow,' he yells down, 'this is enormous. So much scope up here. Did you never think of having it converted?'

Patty ignores him and I remember back to when she and Nigel were going to do just that. He was always starting new hobbies and one year, having watched far too much *Sky at Night*, he decided to get into star-gazing. He even bought himself a very expensive telescope but then had nowhere to use it. Outside in the garden was always too cold and peering out from the bedroom made him feel like a peeping Tom, so they decided to convert the loft and turn it into his observatory.

'Anything to keep him quiet,' Patty had said.

The plans were drawn up, Nigel bought huge posters of the constellations and planets but then the cancer struck. Hopeful that they'd beat it, they went ahead, getting planning permission and even hiring a project manager. Then one day Patty came home from hospital and rang me. I asked how Nigel was and will never forget her words: 'I've cancelled the loft conversion.' That's all she said.

So no, that room doesn't say potential to us and if I'm recalling that moment, Patty certainly must be.

The estate agent looks positively buoyant as he leaves the house and promises to get back to Patty with a valuation. She gazes absently around the living room as if taking stock for the final time. I remember how I felt when my family home was sold after the divorce. It was one of the saddest days of the entire break-up.

'Are you OK?' I ask her and she nods.

'More than OK. I never thought I'd see the day I was ready to move on. I never thought anyone could make me laugh as much as Nigel did.'

She picks up her wedding picture from the mantelpiece. I remember that day so clearly: when the vicar announced he could kiss the bride, Nigel grabbed Patty and threw her back in a Richard Gere *Pretty-Woman*-style hold and yelled,

'Kiss me, you fool'. Patty is obviously remembering the same moment. 'He got his movies a bit mixed up.'

'It was a great day,' I tell her gently, holding her arm.

'It was and he was a great husband,' says Patty. 'I think he'd get on with Jack.'

'I think you're right.' I let the room fall silent for a moment.

'I had some brilliant times in this house. But . . .' Patty perks up after a few moments and stands tall. 'I'm ready for my new life and I'm going to start by clearing out that loft.'

She takes the stairs two at a time and then the ladder. I'm out of breath when I stand next to her in a loft that hasn't been touched for at least five years.

'Jeez,' I say looking at all the boxes. 'You two were hoarders.'

Patty heads over to a particularly dusty old suitcase.

'It isn't just our old stuff. I have some of Joy's here from ages ago.'

Now I'm excited. Joy was Patty's mother and a legend of her own making. I've heard so many tales about her, how she hated being called Mum as this made her sound too old. She was an actress and in all of the photos I've seen, was simply glamour personified. Even though I never met her, I was in awe of the very idea of her. She died young at the age of thirty-six, in a car crash, exactly as beautiful people are supposed to. Patty opens the suitcase and starts rummaging through some black-and-white photographs. I kneel down beside her and she passes them to me one by one.

The first one we come to is of a stunning teenager in her black capris and skin-tight sweater. She has the most amazing figure and looks just like the classic 1960s bad girl. Joy used to tell us that when she was seventeen, she saw The Beatles at the London Palladium. They'd just released 'She Loves You' and it was number one in the charts but you couldn't actually hear them singing because of all the screaming girls at the concert. I remember being so envious that she was around to witness the beautiful young John Lennon and all that sexual energy exploding onto the music scene for the first time.

'Is this Ritchie?' I ask pointing to the Jimmy Dean lookalike posing alongside her and knowing the answer.

'That's him,' sighs Patty. 'Mr Julian Richard Egerton. The name didn't suit his freestyling image. Nor did a daughter apparently.'

Patty's mum fell pregnant after running away with Ritchie to try and get into the *Top of the Pops* audience. They succeeded and were pushed to the front of the stage because they looked so young and fashionable. Of course, I've heard this story many times over the years and I've been shown the back of their heads on several television reruns. Being conceived like this is part of Patty's personal myth and apparently explains her destiny in music. Ritchie and Joy split up when Patty was just seven because Joy wanted to be free to embrace the sexual revolution of the era. Patty never really saw her father again.

'He sent me some birthday cards for a while but Joy moved around so much he had no chance of keeping up with us, even if he'd wanted to. I never knew him but it didn't stop me missing him.'

There are always two sides to every decade and while Joy was doing the Free Love thing in hippie camps, my mum was thinking that Stepford looked like a nice clean place to live. Being an unmarried mother would have been an unspeakable blot on our family. Patty hands me another photo where this time there's an explosion of gaudy colour, miniskirts and mascara. Joy is smiling and Patty stands at her side like a sort of mini-me.

'We were doing the festivals then,' says Patty. 'We slept in a van wrapped in Joy's Afghan coat. It was freezing and the van leaked. We stunk of wet goat by the morning. It put me off cashmere for life.'

The next pictures are of the peace rallies that you sometimes see in history programmes. But Joy lived them.

'This is where she met the crowd who persuaded her to try drama school,' says Patty. 'She was a natural apparently. After that I spent five years being dragged around the country to various repertory theatres, lodging with other luvved-up actors in the worst B&Bs you've ever seen.'

'It's hardly surprising you ended up touring the world as cabin crew, is it?'

'Not really,' replies Patty. 'I was only eighteen when Mum died and throughout our lives, I hardly stayed in one place for any length of time. My schooling would have been non-existent if the theatre crowd she hung out with hadn't been so well educated and bohemian. I knew every classic text and could order drinks in four languages by the time I was seventeen. So airlines seemed a natural fit after she went. I just kept roaming the world until I met Nigel. He was my home, my rock. I stopped feeling lonely when I found him.'

Patty drops the pictures back into the case and opens another box. We both squeal with laughter at the sight of our younger selves in our air-stewardess uniforms.

'Oh my God, that must be 1985 when we first met and I joined your cabin crew,' I say to Patty. 'How on earth did I get that little stewardess hat on top of that enormous perm?'

'Oh Lord,' Patty continues, 'do you remember this uniform?'

She hands me the picture. We're both proudly modelling the latest update to our navy suit — a red pussy-bow scarf.

'We thought we were the bees' knees.'

'Especially when we rocked it with red shoes and plastic earrings.' I cringe.

'And look at your eye-shadow — you've co-ordinated with the jacket and scarf!'

'Well, you've matched the lipstick to the shoes,' I reply.

'God, we look like Boy George—' Patty shakes her head — 'with less style.'

As well as the photographs, there are naff souvenirs and postcards, piles and piles of postcards from our travels.

'You forget these things even existed,' I say, picking them up. 'They're a casualty of picture texts now.'

We used to send ourselves cards from every stopover even if we had to send it from the airport hotel. Sometimes we would even send them to each other. Reading the daft comments we wrote to one another takes us back in time. The one I find next is of St Basil's in Moscow. It's from me and I've scrawled 'Patty arrested by KGB for draining country of vodka' on the back.

We'd had to take a tour bus around the city but leapt off to have our photos taken at the Kremlin wearing our big furry Cossack hats. We'd watched as the citizens solemnly paraded past Lenin's tomb, some still wearing the peasant-style clothes we'd associate with *Doctor Zhivago*. Patty starts humming 'Lara's Theme', so I know she's thinking the same thing.

'I really liked Moscow,' she says. 'It felt so daring just being there.'

I nod, remembering the moment when, as a young twenty-year-old I told Mum I was going to Russia. It was the era of Reagan and Gorbachev and she was horrified. She lectured me about being brainwashed into communism or kidnapped and tortured as a Western spy.

'Don't go smuggling any arms,' I remember her saying.

'Most mothers tell their daughters to be careful on the underground,' I'd replied. 'I'm hardly likely to get a Kalashnikov in my vanity case.'

'I don't know what one of them is but you just be careful on the underground too,' came her final warning.

If she'd seen the underground in Moscow she wouldn't have worried. They were truly magnificent halls built to honour the ordinary people and display their craftsmanship. Patty is holding up a postcard of Stockholm.

'But this was my favourite city.'

I remember. As a tall blonde party animal she felt right at home and we went there several times, including 1992. Sweden had just won the Eurovision Song Contest and although it was being hosted in Malmo, its capital city was definitely up for a party.

'What are you going to do with all of this?' I ask putting a pile of cards down.

'I don't know. It seems wrong to throw it all out but then I shouldn't keep living in the past.'

'Why don't you have the photos digitized?' I suggest. 'And maybe just keep a couple of postcards.'

She nods but packs everything up just as it was.

'We had some really great times, didn't we?' She smiles.

'We'll still have them.'

'But it'll be different from now on won't it? As much as I love Jack, girls always have a little more fun on their own. Maybe we should have one last fling,' Patty suggests.

'I know just the thing,' I say as I wave her goodbye.

* * *

A quick call to Charlie and it's all sorted. Patty and I will be escorting Mercury Travel customers on their next trip to Amsterdam. This Sunday has been much livelier than I'd thought it would be and I still have Michael . . . oops — I'd forgotten about that. I still have Michael coming round expecting dinner. The doorbell rings, signalling his arrival. I let him in and he walks in sniffing the air.

'I know I promised dinner and I could pretend that I'd planned a cold platter,' I say, 'but Patty's been round and I lost track of time.'

I head into the kitchen and bring out a bottle of red.

'So I can offer you this as the starter. And for the main course, I have lovingly prepared *le fromage et les oatcakes*?'

'Just perfect,' he says and I join him taking a glug and devouring a chunk of wonderful smoked Cheddar.

'To us,' he toasts.

I snuggle into Michael with my feet tucked under me. Our glasses seem to have miraculously emptied themselves, so Michael tops them up. As he leans over me, his lovely outdoorsy smell sets my heart racing. I kiss him on the shoulder. He leans back and kisses me on the lips.

'I could stay if you'd like me to.'

I return the kiss and the loins start stirring. I hear Patty's voice echoing in my head, *'You are beautiful as you are, don't wait for perfection, relax and just go with the flow.'* This could be it.

Houston, I think we are ready for lift-off.

I put my glass down and run my hands down his chest. My heart is pounding and my mouth is dry, this could really be it.

But then a horrible image starts to appear in my mind. I try to block it out but it's like that thing when you're *not* supposed to think about pink elephants and all of a sudden that's all you can think about.

Houston, we have a problem. Stand by for details.

No, not now. Please not now.

But it's too late, she's there. My pink elephant.

Or rather a huge pink Stetson sitting on top of Patty's head. The most vivid image of her ever is playing through my mind, drowning out any romantic thoughts. And she's doing that song, drawled in her best country and western singalong voice. The one she uses for 'Jolene'.

'Heee's a rrrh-i-ne-st-oone caw-buoy . . .'

She's winking at me in a howdy-doody way. It's no good Michael and I can't possibly compete with that.

Houston, abort mission. I repeat, abort mission.

I try to pull myself away from that kiss as demurely as I can without completely destroying the moment. It's no good. I have to escape Patty, her Stetson, Michael and the kiss. I leap up from the sofa and send my glass flying. I'm covered in red wine and I think we can safely say the moment has passed.

'I'm really sorry,' I blurt clumsily, 'but it's been a tough day and I'm probably more tired than I realized. I should just go and tidy myself up then get a good night's sleep.'

'I'm sorry . . . I didn't mean to . . .' Michael stutters as he gets up. He tries to help me blot up the wine with a napkin but I just grab it from him and push him away.

'I'll let you get some sleep,' he says before leaving. At the door he leans in to give me a peck on the cheek and then decides against it.

I slump back down. What on earth have I done? How must he be feeling? I can probably guess the answer to that. Exactly the way I felt when I tried to show my feelings for someone — rejected and humiliated. I have to do something about this. I know Patty was joking about the vajazzling and stuff but there might be things I need to know. I don't want to lose this man.

CHAPTER NINE: MONEY, MONEY, MONEY

Michael hasn't called since Sunday and if it weren't for the impending appointment with the bank manager later today, I think I'd be in pieces. I'm pacing the house before heading into work, forcing myself to focus on this and this alone. I've read and re-read our investment proposal and it still looks good. I shouldn't be nervous but I am. It's a bit like attending a parent's evening. I always knew that my daughter was no trouble at all, but still always had a niggling doubt that someone might know more than me and was about to spring it on me. The other thing making me nervous is that Lorenzo has been out and about a great deal this week, so I think the shop must be very nearly finished. Maybe the bank knows more about the new travel agency than we do. They might be bidding for the same resort — although heaven knows how they would have found out about it.

Peter also suggested that rather than borrow the money we could try and find an investor to help with the resort, arguing that we might be about to have our hands full. Looking for a third musketeer didn't really feel right for either of us but we agreed to give it a go. Peter asked around his networks and quickly found a couple of people he knew were looking for an opportunity.

Charlie and I were rather shocked when, a couple of days ago, he turned up at the shop and said, 'Guys, I know it's short notice but can you meet someone for a coffee tonight? Just a chemistry meeting for now. He's looking for a quick investment and might be right for you.'

We agreed to meet up and at the end of the day we were shaking hands with a very handsome young guy (unfortunately he'd be competition for Charlie being the most handsome man in the office, as he frequently likes to tell us. And on that note, I'm the most beautiful woman over forty here — we have very fragile egos at Mercury).

'I've just sold my internet business,' the investor told us over his flat white, 'and looking to reinvest quickly with a bricks and mortar I could add value to.'

I nodded, assuming we were the bricks and mortar.

'Your business is perfect for me,' he continued. 'You've got physical sales but no online presence. Your SEO is pretty non-existent and your social media feeds aren't truly optimized. If I work on these and maximize their potential, I think we could clean up.'

'And what travel experience do you have?' asked Charlie.

'The industry doesn't really matter, the techniques are the same,' he answered with froth over his upper lip. I resisted the urge to get out my hankie and wipe it for him.

'I spent the whole evening flummoxed,' I told Peter later when he asked us how it went. 'I know we should do more on the internet but I think I want someone who talks beaches not bytes.'

Charlie agreed but Peter wouldn't give up and sure enough, a couple of days later we were in the same coffee bar with a man whose perma-tan told us he either travelled extensively or lay on sunbeds. He caught Charlie looking him up and down in contemplation.

'Golf in Portugal,' he explained. 'I'm just back from a week out there. The golf market is pretty lucrative, you know.'

I do know from one of my other failed attempts at a relationship early this year. The potential investor invited us to sit down and then called one of the assistants over to take our order. It's a self-service café and they looked a bit confused by his request but did as they were asked anyway. He definitely had a presence but I quickly felt more like his underling than his partner and I could see Charlie bristling.

'I agree,' I croaked, referring to the golf. 'We looked into golf trips earlier this year because ideas have really driven our growth, so we're looking for someone who can create new markets.'

'Music to my ears,' he said. 'I have so many ideas I could use to turbo-charge this business.'

He went on to tell us our growth was hindered by having only one outlet and a centralized business model (whatever that is), that we were missing out on the hipster market and sports tours. We could franchise the club idea and allow people across the country to start their own version of Mercury, then we could lay back and just watch the money roll in.

'But we enjoy what we do. We travel with our customers and that's part of the fun,' said Charlie.

Our potential investor waved away his comment. 'If I invest,' he said, 'I'll take charge of these expansion ideas so you don't need to worry about them. I'll hire people who know the markets and I'll double our turnover within the year. It might take a little extra capital from all of us to begin with but it'll be worth it, we'll rake it in.'

'Sounds good,' I pretended badly when he eventually let me get a word in.

So we didn't like him either and increasingly we didn't like the idea of someone else joining us. Peter did try telling us there was still plenty of time to find someone and perhaps the next one would bowl us over, but we both shook our heads.

We're happy together and like an old married couple, we're not looking for a threesome to spice things up. Hence today's appointment to beg the bank for money instead.

I glance at my watch and know it's time to head off rather than be late on today of all days. I imagine I will be on tenterhooks all day so to get myself in the mood for the day ahead, I look in the mirror and pull a really mean look. I don't feel invincible and I need to, so I belt out the chorus of 'Eye of the Tiger', put my mitts up and start jabbing away to get me in the mood. I can't help but imagine Patty's boxing ring routine as I do.

'No one messes with Angie Rocky Shepherd,' I say, doing a karate kick at my reflection and nearly losing my balance.

'Stop it now,' the sensible angel on my shoulder tells me. 'Get there looking respectable for goodness' sake. No scabs on knees or black eyes.'

I know banks don't lend money easily these days, but Mercury has a good track record and even if it hadn't, this is about the Formentera investment and our projections for that look very healthy. Weddings and all the hen and stag parties are huge business now, so they have to be able to see the potential there. The more Charlie and I talked through the opportunities we could develop, the more we truly believed that we simply could not give this chance of a lifetime up. It excites us in the same way launching Mercury did and we're dying to have something to announce the second that Lorenzo opens up.

We're both in the shop this morning. I'm too nervous to do very much but the team are keeping me calmer than I would be if I'd stayed at home. Charlie is practising our pitch to Josie: 'So as well as weddings we could do vow renewals and maybe even picture-perfect engagements,' he tells her, 'with that private stretch of beach and those gorgeous safari tents we could make it the most romantic place on earth.'

'I'd give you the money,' says Josie. 'But if I were the bank manager I'd also try and wangle a free visit, so be ready to offer some bribery.'

I'd already thought we could suggest that if we needed to, although I doubted the bank would be as blatant as our little Aussie friend. Her lack of subtlety makes her the perfect sounding board. She's brutally honest with us and if we ever present an idea that she thinks won't work she'll tell us it's a 'massive no-hoper'. She doesn't mince her words, so I know she believes in this, too.

'You've tidied those brochures three times,' says Charlie watching me pace the shop. 'Shall I make us a coffee before we go?'

I shake my head. 'Knowing my luck, I'll spill it all over this blouse.' I tidy things once more.

Three o'clock ticks round slowly but as soon as that big hand announces the hour, I exhale loudly: time to go. I nip to the bathroom to refresh my make-up and when I emerge, Charlie has put on a suit jacket and tie. He looks awfully serious.

'We built this business, girl,' he says and I'm not sure whether he's trying to convince himself or me, 'and we did it together. Now we've come up with another absolute cracker of an opportunity. They'd be mad not to back us, completely barmy.'

He gives me a kiss on the cheek before Josie pulls us apart, tutting.

'Enough of that, we need a quick check,' she says to me. 'OK, no lipstick on teeth, skirt isn't tucked into knickers and there are no ladders in the tights. Perfect, you're ready.'

Then it's Charlie's turn. 'Shoes polished, fly up, no "kick-me" Post-its on your back — you're good, too.'

'Go get 'em,' she adds as she pushes us towards the door, 'and don't come back with less than a million.'

I smile, but butterflies and other less pleasant insects have already started swarming around my stomach. Charlie picks up the spiral-bound business plan and we're on our way.

The bank is in the city centre — we could have gone to the branch across the road but we decided we'd rather not risk bumping into Lorenzo on the way. He would have asked what we were up to and unfortunately it's in my nature to be polite, so I would probably have told him and kicked myself later.

The bank is in St Ann's Square where there has obviously been a food market going on. It's quiet now and the stalls are packing up. If mum were here she'd be going round each one asking for end of day bargains. I used to look at market stalls as just a place to buy things, but now I think about the entrepreneur behind them. Especially if it's a really small stall, because they've probably just started up and it's all they can afford. When we come out, I'll buy something from one of them, but for now, it's time to look after our own business.

This branch is extremely modern with high ceilings and bright décor. As we stride past the main reception through to the business lounge, I'm boosted with a little sense of pride. We're here legitimately — we're local business people — award-winning at that. I'm desperate to catch a glimpse of myself to see whether I look the part but the office is all etched glass and inspirational slogans. One of them reads: *The only thing between you and your dreams is BELIEF.*

'Yeah, right,' says Charlie, spotting it, too. 'Turn us down and we'll remind you of that.'

We sit down in the reception and this time I graciously accept the coffee I'm offered. As a real-life businesswoman, I must demonstrate the ability to drink coffee without spilling it. I take tiny sips and have a light-bulb moment: tiny sips and nibbles must be how celebrities stay thin and clean — you never see anyone at the Oscars with a red-wine stain down their Chanel.

Someone comes out of the manager's office and I take a discreet glance at the customer leaving and try to decide whether he looks more worthy of a loan than us. He's wearing hiking shoes and a baggy jumper, so either he runs a gardening business or an internet company, or he hasn't made as much effort as we have. I guess you can't tell who the successful business people are these days. I've never seen any pictures of Zuckerberg, the Facebook guy, in a suit and I doubt he'll have any problems getting a loan if his billions ever run out.

'Ms Shepherd and Mr Hagan?'

Oops, our turn. I get up and shake the manager's hand, trying to work out whether he has kind eyes or not. I think he does.

'Really pleased to meet you,' he says. 'My mum loves your trips.'

At least he knows who we are. We enter the office and close the door.

'You've had an impressive growth record,' says the bank manager, reading our accounts. 'You've done extremely well considering the many potential issues in travel.'

'I think it shows the diversity in our offer and our experience in spotting a great opportunity,' I say, getting my rehearsed argument out early in the conversation.

'Our strategy is never to go head to head with family operators but to focus on our niches. Initially that meant baby-boomers and now we're looking at weddings,' adds Charlie in his rehearsed serious voice.

'I know.' The manager smiles. 'As I said, my parents already travel with you — and who wouldn't want to get married here?' He flicks through the prospectus, obviously awed by the beauty of the place.

This seems to be going extremely well. He's either going to give me the money or, as he's not wearing a wedding ring, try and haggle for a discount for his own nuptials as Josie suggested. I'm distracted again trying to work out how much discount we should offer and whether that would constitute a bribe. When I get back to the real world, the tone of the conversation has changed.

'But an impressive past doesn't guarantee a future,' he is saying, closing our proposal. 'Times have changed.

'Not only do we still have all traditional internet players — and they're growing like fungus — I lose count of them — but companies like Groupon are now taking the weekend-break market and I have seen a full wedding package in one of their emails at an incredible price. So it's even tougher out there right now and that's if we manage a year without infectious diseases, terrorism or erupting volcanoes to disrupt travel.'

'There is never a year without an obstacle,' Charlie tells him, 'but each time we've faced one, we've found a way around it. The core business is strong and people still want to go on holiday. We just have to continue to be inventive.'

'And you have done to date,' he replies. 'I just think you'll find it tougher, especially as you'll soon have a new competitor right opposite to distract you from the very thing that's made you successful.'

So he knows about Lorenzo.

'In fairness to us,' says Charlie, 'we've faced challenges before, and anyway, this is about a completely bespoke venture.'

The manager nods but adds, 'True, but you can only make a success of it if the core business is running well.'

'We know the travel market and we're both absolutely committed to this enterprise,' I assert. 'Whoever comes along, we know we can make it work. Charlie recently honeymooned on this island and has first-hand experience of the true potential, but beyond that the numbers and the forward bookings make this a sound investment. We wouldn't be sitting here if we weren't completely confident that as a team we have both the resourcefulness and tenacity to optimize this opportunity no matter what the competitive circumstances.'

I spot Charlie just managing to stop himself giving me a round of applause. My heart pounds. Bloody hell — where did I get that speech from? I'll use it again.

Forty minutes later and the discussion is over. We're back out in the fading sunshine and the city centre has started filling with people having post-work drinks. We find a small café with outside tables and get some coffees. I'm not hungry but I order cake just to help their sales. I exhale and we sit quietly for a moment taking in the decision we have to make.

The bank manager had said he could see the potential in the wedding business, that the proposal was robust if not cautious, and that as directors, we'd proven we had staying power. We'd both perked up at that point. Then he added that he couldn't ignore the issues with the travel industry or the new competition, so he needed some security. The nuts and bolts were that should we win the second-stage bid, we could have the loan (I think my little heart leapt at that point), but only if secured on the Mercury Travel Club (it sank very quickly) or some other collateral.

When I think about it now, it's as if the bank manager were a magician. He led us into a room with a long table covered in smooth white linen. He asked us to place the things we value most — our business and our pride — on top. If we put a single foot wrong, he was going to whip away the cloth and might leave us with nothing. And somehow he made us feel grateful for all of it too. I guess that's banking for you.

'What are you thinking?' asks Charlie.

I picture Richard Branson, now wearing wings and a white suit like Frenchy's guardian angel in *Grease*. '*The Next Big Thing*,' he's whispering to me.

I pull myself up and face Charlie. The bank will write to us to confirm the terms of the loan within the week but given what we know, we could decide it's just too much of a risk. I can't face going back to the shop and telling Josie that we were too cowardly and that we've given up already. If we truly believe in this, and I know that we do, it will be a success.

'We can do this,' I tell him. 'We can do anything.'

CHAPTER TEN: STARRY STARRY NIGHT

'Can I take you out to dinner this Saturday?' Michael asks. 'We haven't seen each other since last week.'

I have to confess that when I saw Michael's name appear on my phone, I was quite nervous. I wanted to make the first move but didn't know what I'd say. Typical Michael, he's chosen his words perfectly: 'last week' to let me know he remembers what happened and 'out to dinner' to reassure me it'll be on safe territory. He's holding his hand out to me and all I have to do is take it. I want to but not yet. Fortunately, I have a genuine excuse.

'That sounds really lovely,' I say hoping he reads as much into my words. 'But I have to work. I'm hosting one of the Around the World in 20 Artists weekends in Amsterdam.'

'I thought you were doing the Barcelona one.'

'Ah no, I've swapped with Charlie. He's doing Barcelona and I'm doing Amsterdam. Van Gogh etc.'

This is the trip I thought would be perfect to do with Patty. I've swapped with Charlie because Barcelona is months away and I wanted us to have some quality girls' time soon.

'I could do tonight but it would be late. We've loads to do before we set off.'

'I'm really sorry,' says Michael, 'I can't. I've agreed to go to a business dinner with some guys from the team — to celebrate a building we've just helped re-open.'

I'm relieved that we've both had the chance to turn each other down. We've spoken, we're good and we've agreed to get together when we're less rushed. Result. I'm sure Patty is wrong about going with the flow. Things do have to happen in the right order to be perfect: Charlie and I finalize this proposal and send it off. We win the bid and take out the loan. Lorenzo turns out to be a damp squib and moves on quickly. The wedding business is a tremendous success and the loan is paid off in double-quick time. I move into my fabulous new home and then, when I'm sure everything is just as it should be, we make mad passionate love and live happily ever after. I've visualized it all happening just like this, so obviously it's going to. We can't just squeeze in a random night on the sofa and expect sparks to fly.

I've no time to think about that now. Charlie and I continue to work on our bid all afternoon. The first draft proposal that we took to the bank was pretty spot on so all we need to do is tweak some of the wording, adjust the numbers to give us a little leeway when it comes to negotiating, and ensure that our vision is as magical as it can be.

'We should add a personal statement from you and Peter about your time there,' I say.

'Oh my God, yes,' agrees Josie. 'I could do a compilation of your honeymoon photos and you add a voiceover saying how much you love the place. It would probably mean so much to them knowing that one of the bidders really cares about what happens to the resort.'

Josie and Charlie head off to put this together and I check everything is in place for the weekend. The five-minute video they come back with has me practically in tears. Against a backdrop of beautiful scenes from his stay on the island, Charlie simply says that the place means everything to him and Peter and that he wants to keep this paradise as perfect as it is so that other people can have the same fairy-tale memories.

'I did it in one take.' Charlie beams.

I could tell. His words are so heartfelt, it couldn't be a script. With this alongside the ideas and the numbers, we have to be in with a chance.

'Are we ready to send this?' I ask and Charlie nods.

I compile all the pieces and we each check them one final time. Then, standing over the PC, the three of us count down, 3-2-1, and press the button. It's done. I imagine our papers sprouting wings and flying across the ocean like they would in a Disney film. They flutter down and land neatly on a whitewashed desk in an office by the ocean. It sounds far more romantic than they get printed out in a grubby city centre admin cubicle and plonked into someone's overcrowded in-tray.

* * *

The next day, our short journey to Amsterdam goes without a hitch and before long we're leaving Schiphol and heading for the city centre. With all the travel club members safely unpacked and happy with the hotel, the first place we take them to is the Van Gogh Museum. After all, it is an art tour. While our clients go off with a proper art guide, Patty and I take a meander through the galleries on our own.

'Do you think when he was painting this pair of shoes he ever in his wildest dreams imagined people queuing up to see them?' Patty asks, contemplating one of the lesser-known works. 'And why? I mean, you all have these blossoms and landscapes and flowers and then you have a pair of tatty black shoes — he could have at least picked a pair of nice ones.'

'He's an artist. He's supposed to be unfathomable.'

'He succeeded.' We potter for a couple more hours and then meet our group back at the entrance. From their lively discussion I can tell they've enjoyed the tour and I have to call for some quiet before I can tell them where we're going next.

I've always held that most couples like different things, so an art weekend has to have more than art to it or at least half my guests would be bored.

'Next up we have a cycle tour of the canals and flower markets,' I tell them, consulting my varied itinerary.

'On a bike?' asks Patty looking horrified.

'Obviously — you can ride one, can't you?'

'I suppose so — haven't done it for years but I guess it's like — well, riding a bike.'

We walk to the start of the tour and we're all fitted out with bikes and helmets. Although all of the Mercurians knew we'd be including a bike ride on the tour, many of them haven't ridden a bike for years and there's much laughing and squealing as we all start wobbling around the square. The bike-hire attendant watches Patty as she puzzles over the vehicle in front of her.

'So how do I get on this?' she asks.

'You just need to put your leg over . . .' starts the guide and I count to ten. One . . . two . . .

'If I'm lucky,' Patty guffaws, looking at the guests for some kind of applause. There is lots of giggling but I ignore her — I've heard it's the best way to train naughty puppies too.

We negotiate the crowds of expert cyclists swooping in all directions. Everyone looks so confident and fast over here. I'm terrified to take my hands off the handlebars, so I can't signal where I'm going. To compensate, I stick close behind the guide — but this means having to cycle quickly to keep up. By the time the tour is over, I'm gasping for breath and my heart rate probably matches that of an Olympic athlete doing a 100m sprint. I'm glad we chose to do it as I think we saw more of the city, but I'm equally glad when we get back to the beginning and dismount, giving back our trusty steeds.

'Ooh — my second-best feature is glad to get off that thing,' says Patty rubbing her butt in a very unseemly way. I don't ask her what her best feature is.

'Please tell me it's something alcoholic next,' she asks.

'They probably serve alcohol on the canal boat,' I tell the guests. 'At least we'll all get to sit down.'

'I'm not sure I can,' says Patty as we walk bandy-leg-ged along the canal to the mooring of the glass-topped boat which will show us the rest of the city at a more sedate pace. We're served a glass of chilled wine and we sit back watching the gabled buildings go by, only vaguely listening to the commentary being narrated over the tannoy. My customers are relaxing, taking in the views and chatting to each other, so Patty and I head for a quiet spot at the back of the boat.

'I'd forgotten how beautiful this place was. Why have we never been back here?' I ask as we clink glasses.

Patty shrugs. 'Lots of other places to visit I guess, but I'd come again. We could bring the guys — maybe when the canals have frozen over and it's all romantic. We'd be all wrapped up wearing those big muffs and we'd get glasses of warm schnapps.'

I think she's seen too much art this morning, as her fantasy is straight from a Hendrick Avercamp painting. It sounds wonderful, though.

'Things will be really different soon. We'll be doing all those things that couples do. Having dinner as foursomes and inviting each other to barbecues . . . Do you think he'll move in with you?'

I think about it, and although I'd love to be opening the door to someone when I come home at night, I've a few fears to conquer before then.

'I'd quite like it to be all mine before I even think about it being ours,' I say cautiously. 'But I don't see myself moving again so who knows. Maybe if things go well?'

'On your perfect night you mean?' She smiles, mocking me only slightly. 'Well, we'll have to get you some underwear while we're out here to make sure it is perfect. There are probably a few places that could fit you out with a sexy little number.'

'My vision doesn't involve looking like I stepped out of the red-light district, if it's OK with you.'

We sit quietly but she's put the thought in my head — what should I wear? In my dream I'm in a silk negligee like they had in 1950s films but:

1. Where the hell do you buy 1950s negligees?

71

2. Given the number of candles in my perfect seduction scene, I'd have to be bloody sure silk isn't flammable.

But what do people wear in bed together these days? Before they get to the comfy PJ stage? By the time my ex left me, we were both wearing big woolly socks to bed. I'm sure there has to be a stage before you get to that. Patty had been on her own even longer than me when she met Jack, and despite not wanting her advice I am curious as to how she coped with the first time after all those years.

'Did you get all dressed up for the first time with Jack?' I venture. 'You know, go for the sexy look.'

She laughs. 'Err — I suppose you could say that.'

She takes a gulp of wine. 'I was that nervous. After all, he's a doctor, sees hundreds of women and some of them on the cruise are pretty damned gorgeous. I didn't know what he'd think of me. I mean I wanted to make an effort but I didn't want to look like a reject from *Bouncy Babes II*. We stopped off at a port with a gorgeous market and I found this little lacy number. It was very tasteful and covered up the wobbly bits but still looked quite sexy in a demure kind of way.'

'Don't raise your eyebrows like that — I can do demure. I planned it all for our night off. We'd have dinner, then a romantic evening stroll and then back to my cabin. I'd disappear into the bathroom to change into something more comfortable and he'd pour the champagne. I imagined myself opening the door to reveal a vision of beauty and him being unable to resist. So I had this perfect night planned just like you.'

'I'm guessing that's not what happened.'

'Too right it didn't. The night before, I was hosting a Spice Girls tribute. You remember what I used to do — tell the audience I was auditioning for some new members as they'd all gone off and done their own thing? It was bloody hilarious — I had about twenty Baby Spices and no Sporties. I was in my Ginger get-up and the one who won the Posh competition turned out to be a bloke. He was the worst dancer you have ever seen but the crowd loved him.

'Jack couldn't stop laughing when I told him about it. We were sort of on a high because of it and then one thing led to another and before long we'd both broken our leave of absence, so to speak.'

'So for your first time in several years you were wearing a Union Jack Ginger Spice outfit?'

She nods matter-of-factly. 'And he could certainly tell what I wanted, what I really, really wanted.'

It could only happen to Patty but it's a relief to hear she was nervous, too.

'That's why I think the lesson is not to take it all too seriously,' she concludes. 'You'll be fine. I'll lend you a ginger wig if you like.'

I laugh and picture Michael's puzzled face as he turns up to my new place and finds me in that get-up. Somehow I don't think that'll do the trick twice.

The boat trip comes to a stop, so I gather up my customers and we head into one of the canal-side restaurants for dinner.

'So will you be singing for us tonight?' one of the customers asks Patty.

She shakes her head. 'Alas, I've given my farewell performance,' she replies to the dismayed crowd.

The dinner is very jovial, with Patty recounting her days on the cruise. Then, as we're getting ready to leave and the plates are cleared away, it starts pouring with rain outside.

'Stay for a schnapps,' says the waiter. 'It's just a cloudburst, it'll soon pass.'

The customers are happy to stay inside, so we take up the offer but inevitably one schnapps leads to another. If you had your wits about you, you'd know the moment you'd had too many glasses of schnapps: it's the moment when it starts tasting OK. Your first always burns the back of your throat and you vow to have no more. The second feels strangely warming and by the third you're finding out the name on the bottle and planning to buy some when you hit duty free. If you do this, it'll lie gathering dust in your drinks cabinet until one very dark day when you have absolutely nothing left to drink and the world is about to end, then you'll get it out.

We have to get out of here before any more is consumed, so I tell the waiter we'll just have to brave the weather. I pay our bill and when he brings me the receipt, our lovely waiter also supplies us with several cheap, plastic pac-a-macs. They're the thinnest pale pink plastic ponchos you have ever seen, but we all pull them over our heads and step out into the rain. Patty looks across at me and bursts into laughter. 'You look like a giant condom!'

We all turn and catch a glimpse of ourselves in the windows — yep, that just about describes it. The Mercury Travel Club stands giggling at its glamorous reflection. I take a picture for our end-of-year calendar. Thunder roars above our heads and the downpour gets heavier.

'Come on,' I yell through the din, 'we have to get into a bar or something.'

We peek from under our hoods and spot a Heineken sign hanging above a pub-like door. Heads down we hold hands, and screaming through the puddles make a dash for it. Pushing the door open, we get inside and, panting, pull our hoods down.

'Have we died and come to heaven?' says Patty looking round at the wall-to-wall room of gorgeous Dutchmen.

We walk to the bar.

I've read the Dutch are the tallest people in the world and it certainly seems that way. In our sensible city-walking pumps — now soaking wet and squelching with every step — my middle-aged customers and I are at eye level with a room full of broad muscular chests and solid pecs. It would be so tempting to just check they're as firm as they look. Patty is obviously thinking the same, as I see her tentatively lifting her hand in that direction. I grab it, preventing an international incident. I may have been out of circulation for a few years but these guys are gorgeous and I can still appreciate a work of art when I see it. Isn't that what this weekend is about?

As we get to the bar, the entertainment starts and a drag artist gets up on stage singing 'What's Love Got to Do With It?' and I imagine Poppy O'Cherry would have something scathing to say about how out of tune they are. Patty sips the frothy beer we've ordered and I can see she's just chomping at the bit to sing it properly.

One of the customers nudges her: 'You should show them how it's done.'

I have to be ready to grab her if any song she knows is played but I'm too slow and it's too late. The opening bars of the next song have everyone dancing and Patty, thrusting her beer at me, leaps onto the stage, pulling up the hood of her plastic mac. Sensibly the drag artist steps to one side and lets her get on with it. The Mercury Travel Club push through the crowd to get to the front of the stage for this: Patty's European comeback.

The locals are in stitches as the fifty-something-year-old English woman in the bad plastic cape does the robotic moves made famous by the one and only Kylie Minogue. She blasts out the words of the song, 'Can't Get You Out of My Head'.

I don't think anyone ever will.

CHAPTER ELEVEN: SECRET FEAR

Happy that our first day has definitely provided some unforgettable moments for the guests, we head to bed at around midnight. Patty and I are sharing a room and she's as gleeful after her performance as my mum in a cake shop.

'I've still got it, haven't I?' she yells from the bathroom.

'The need to show off?' I reply.

'Star quality and that certain je ne sais quoi that keeps the crowds entertained.'

She emerges with her hands outstretched, ready to receive bouquets if anyone's throwing. I throw a hairbrush, which she catches before bowing.

'Well,' I say, 'I certainly ne sais quoi what you've got but it was a good laugh. It reminds people why Mercury is so unique. They won't get that anywhere else.'

'Are you going to hire me for every trip, then?'

'That's not what I meant. I was talking about the whole day: the art, the bike ride, the canal trip, the schnapps and then you of course. I mean it has been pouring with rain for most of the day but that's not the bit you remember, is it?'

'It certainly isn't. What time are we on duty tomorrow?'

'I need to be up for first breakfasts at seven but you can lie in if you like. I have to set an alarm though.'

I pick up my phone, which is completely dead and needs recharging. That explains why Charlie hasn't called. He usually checks in at the end of the first day. I plug it into the charger and as soon as I have some juice, messages start to beep in. A voice message from Charlie checking everything is doodle-dandy (his words). I send him a text saying that in fact it's all *yankee-doodle-dandy à la mode*. He'll understand.

Then I spot Michael has sent me a picture message. It's from the welcome dinner he mentioned. Everyone is dressed to the nines and he's standing there beside a gorgeous Indian lady being given an envelope.

'What is it?' asks Patty and I show her the picture.

'That's a good-looking threesome,' she says and I grab the phone back in despair. I check the time and as we're an hour ahead, and he's been out at this do tonight, he's probably still up. The phone rings for a while and just as I'm getting my message ready, he picks up.

'Hi there,' he yells. 'You rang! Are you having a good time?'

'We are,' I tell him, 'and by the sounds of it so are you. Are you still at the dinner at this time of night?'

'It's kind of turned into a party now. I've just come out onto their balcony so I can hear you. Did you see the picture?'

'I did, what happened?'

'They gave us a little bonus for completing everything on time — the team were really chuffed.'

I can hear the smile still in his voice.

'Who was the lady in the photo?' I ask, trying to sound casual.

'That's Nimmi. She's gorgeous isn't she? And such a nice person. I wouldn't be surprised if a couple of my team have the hots for her.'

'Neither would I.' I laugh. Well, I do that laugh thing which sounds and is completely fake, hoping Michael doesn't feel that way.

'Tell Patty that I have a treat in store for Jack,' he continues. 'The bonus was an all-expenses trip to Lords   he'll love it. It's a fabulous ground.'

Before he'd mentioned the cricket ground bit, I'd envisaged us all trooping off to Lourdes and couldn't imagine why Jack would be thrilled to go there unless he needed a miracle and wanted Patty to be blessed with some modesty. No chance.

'I'll tell her,' I say as we say our goodbyes and I hear someone dragging Michael back to the dinner.

'What will you tell me?' asks Patty.

'We're going to see some men playing with their balls.'

'So what's new?'

And with that we both turn out the lights and snuggle down.

But I don't sleep.

Or at least I don't seem to.

I'm picturing Nimmi looking beautiful. She's handing a cheque to some schoolchildren. Maybe that's what she does all the time, hand things to people. She's stunning and Michael's whole team obviously thought so. I imagine that even in jeans and a jumper she looks effortlessly stylish. I then wonder what she wears to bed. I bet she doesn't freeze at the crucial moment and I bet she doesn't wear jammies.

2.40 a.m. Jeez, have I just spent all that time wondering what a woman I've never met wears to bed? When I have to be up in four hours looking fabulous for my own job? I flick back to Michael's message and look at their smiling faces. I wonder if I should explain what I'm really scared of. I wonder if he'll understand or just despair. I wonder if he'll wait much longer. I never thought he might be surrounded by gorgeous women in his line of work. Would I wait if he told me he was afraid he couldn't actually do it anymore? That's stupid, it's not the same thing at all . . .

I must doze off for a while because after seeing in 4.30 a.m., the next thing I know, the 6.30 alarm is going off. I reach out and switch it off, then get straight up in case I fall back to sleep. That was no way to prepare for a day of more art.

Today, it's the Rijksmuseum for Rembrandt and then the Stedelijk for some modern art. I can't bear the thought of being inside all day, especially not in a place that encourages contemplation. I get to breakfast before any of the guests and fill a mug of mind-blowingly strong coffee. I think this strength was meant for an espresso cup but it does the job. I smile and make polite conversation with everyone. Patty gets a round of applause when she enters the breakfast room. Well, she stands in the doorway until people start to notice that she's there and then they take the hint. Boy, am I going to need her today.

'Let's get this over with then,' she says. 'The sooner we've appreciated the art, the sooner we can get back on the schnapps.'

I reassure my guests that today will be a calm and cultured day. I can see some very tired people and I can't imagine more than a few of them spending a night dancing in a drag club before this trip. Anyway, we have one of Amsterdam's top restaurants booked for our final meal together. I just have to stay awake that long.

Vermeer must have been a funny old soul. He certainly wasn't one of those artists you struggled to understand. He didn't paint huge blocks of purple and call them something obscure like *Passing the Salt*. His paintings — *The Milkmaid*, *Woman Reading a Letter*, *View of Houses in Delft* — yep, they pretty much do what they say on the tin. The only one I know (*Girl with a Pearl Earring*, obviously) isn't here, but even if you hadn't known what it was about, you could have guessed from the name. It's almost as if he just kept painting and at some point, someone told him that he had to name them. Being an artist he found this a ludicrous idea, so he just pointed at the pictures lying around his studio. 'Right then,' he probably said, 'that one's "girl in a red hat", that's "girl in a blue dress" and that one's "woman with a jug".' In my imagination he has a very broad Yorkshire accent.

Anyway, the classics done, we head to be dazed and confused at the Stedelijk. Actually, I quite like some modern art, especially sculpture. I always visit the Tate Modern if I'm in London, although in fairness that's because of the cocktail bar on the top floor. It has one of the best views of the

Thames ever. I've read that this Dutch gallery has an extension that looks like a bathtub and as we approach it, that's certainly what it looks like from one angle. From another it looks like a spaceship hovering above the ground.

'This is probably what they call bold architecture,' says one of the guests and we all nod in quiet agreement.

I send the guests off with a guide and take a seat with Patty in the huge atrium.

'Please tell me that's not modern art,' she says, nudging me. I look up and laugh.

'No, I think that's genuinely a mop and bucket.'

A cleaner comes and takes them both, much to our relief.

'I had to get you smiling somehow,' says Patty. 'What's up?'

'Just tired. I didn't sleep much.'

'I wasn't snoring, was I?'

I let out a little snort. 'Yes but it wasn't that. I was just thinking about Michael.' I cannot confess my imaginings even to Patty.

'Bless, love's young dream. He sounded like he was having a good enough time without you though.' She laughs. 'Fancy him winning a trip to a cricket ground and still seeming delighted with it. He's not hard to keep happy, is he? Still, it'll be nice for us all to get away for a weekend together . . .'

I smile, bury my head in the guidebook and try to ignore Patty's musing. A weekend away, for all four of us, where Patty and Jack will be all loved-up and we'll be in double rooms no doubt. We'll leave them after dinner and they'll be snogging like kids in the lift while I panic that it's all going to go horribly wrong again.

'Are you listening to a word I've said?'

I'm not. I'm thinking that Michael is a wonderful guy who doesn't seem to want to give up on me, not like my ex. He gave up pretty damn quickly.

'Come on, girl. What's up? Tell Aunty Pats.'

I inhale and go for it: 'I did what you suggested before we came away. You know, I tried to go for it.'

'Go on.'

'It's like, I can't wait to get my hands on him but then when it gets to the moment, my body seems to seize and put up a "Do Not Pass Go" sign. The more I try to get things flowing, the worse it gets. I know you laugh but I really think I've forgotten how to.'

Patty nods. 'Juicy Lucy has left the building.'

'What do you mean?'

'Hormones,' she says. 'They play havoc at this stage in our lives.'

'Did this happen to you?'

Patty nods. 'Oh, yes, and I'd had a five-year leave of absence before Jack. Imagine that. It was like rolling a stone from a long disused cavern. It was like stoking an old boiler. Mind you, it's roaring now.'

I don't laugh at her attempt to humour me. She gives me a hug then rummages in her bag and hands me a card.

'There are things you can do. When you're ready, take a look at this.'

CHAPTER TWELVE: GET THE PARTY STARTED

Charlie called me the moment our flight home from Amsterdam landed.

'He's having a launch party,' he said with a note of panic in his voice.

'Who?' I ask, wondering what I'll wear to this mysterious invitation. Then it dawns on me. 'Oh, you mean Lorenzo don't you?'

'Yes, do you think we have to go?'

'If we've been invited,' I reply. 'And aren't you curious to see the place?'

Charlie mutters something non-committal.

After we've ended the call, I realise that, somehow, I hadn't actually expected the opening to ever happen.

I get through the baggage reclaim and customs in a bit of a fog then say goodbye to our customers adding that I hope I'll see them on another trip soon. Suddenly saying things like that doesn't seem like a simple adios — it feels more like a heartfelt plea.

* * *

When the day arrives, Charlie isn't at all keen on going to Lorenzo's launch party but I remind him of my '*Respect*' mantra and tell him we should be happy to help out fellow entrepreneurs. He sticks his tongue out at me but agrees to be an absolute saint when we are at the event itself.

I'm very curious to see what Lorenzo has done with the shop and how he plans to differentiate himself. After all, he's opening up in the same street as a successful competitor and that's either very foolish or equally foolhardy. His shop windows have been covered up throughout the refit and even today, the day of launch there's still a big poster around them simply advertising the night's event.

He's gone for a rocket theme, which is a bit predictable given the name of the shop, but in my humble opinion, over-promising a little — unless he genuinely has found a way of getting customers into space. If he has then he's definitely going for a different target market. He won't get my mum up there.

'Will there be food?' Patty asked when I told her about the event.

Strictly speaking the evening is for the local business community but Patty would certainly provide an independent viewpoint, so I assure her there will be and she agrees to come with us. I know Caroline will be there as the owner of the book store as will many of the restaurateurs who've supported Mercury over this past year.

Charlie and I are proud of the offers or free gifts for our customers we've negotiated with local commerce — such as a bottle of prosecco with any booking to northern Italy, or a 'cooking with spices' book when they return from India. It's been one of our selling points and shows how much we value our customers — and local businesses who supply us. I hope Lorenzo isn't going to start making similar offers. It might not just be our customers who have their heads turned. The local business community might also prefer working with him.

Charlie paces the floor all day and constantly checks through the window to see if anyone is going into Lorenzo's shop.

'Act like it's not happening,' Josie tells him. 'As you keep saying, there's more than one pub on the high street and they survive. We'll be fine.'

I agree with her but still, a fleeting image crosses my mind . . . a pub where the only remaining customer is the toothless old geezer who's forgotten where he lives. I hope that won't be us tomorrow.

'Even the most loyal can easily have their head turned by the new and shiny kid on the block,' says Charlie.

I give him a punch and say Josie is right, although it should be us reassuring Josie not the other way around. 'No chance,' I say. 'Where else could people get the special blend of fun and chaos that we bring? We already have some fab reviews for Amsterdam.'

I take the details of some new offers that have come through to us and call several customers, just to show my colleagues that my mind is still on the job and, of course, to follow Richard's advice — *Focus*.

Soon, the hour arrives for us to close Mercury and get ready for the party.

None of us go home first, so there's a queue for the loo and for the mirror in our cloakroom. Josie has a quick squirt of deodorant then changes her top and freshens up her make-up. I hide in the loo and change into a bought-especially-for-the-occasion wraparound dress that exudes professionalism. I see myself as the more experienced business woman, confidently off to support a fellow small business. A woman ready to give advice on what he's doing wrong. I would love to do something with my hair but Charlie is hogging the mirror. He's brought what Josie calls his 'pulling shirt' — an expensive pale blue number that shows off his eyes perfectly.

'Wow,' she says when she sees what he's wearing. 'What are you trying to do — seduce him into shutting down?'

He ignores her and finishes applying his hair wax.

'Peter's going too,' he tells us. 'I can't have his head turned by the interloper.'

'That would never happen,' I say.

Patty arrives as we're all ready to go. She's brought four cans of gin and tonic with her and pours them into the mugs lying on the draining board.

'Classy,' says Josie. 'I'm glad some Aussie has rubbed off on you all.'

The three of them toast 'defeat to the enemy' and take a big gulp for courage. I don't join in but instead scold their lack of business camaraderie. After all, Richard advises respecting your competitor before crushing them. Nevertheless, I take a drink at the same time. The bubbles fizz up my nose and I end up choking and coughing. Not exactly the elder-states-woman image I'm going for.

Crossing the road, David Bowie's 'Space Oddity' flows out of the new store and the doors are open. I wonder whether he's managed to find more than one launch-themed song. I can't think of many more — 'Fly Me to the Moon' — but that probably isn't trendy enough.

We walk into the shop and at first I'm confused it looks nothing like a travel agency. Rustic wooden tables and benches run the length of the shop, making it look like some Nordic mountain hut. Along the centre of the benches are iPads for customers to use. There are no brochures anywhere. The fabulous aroma of freshly ground coffee is all pervading and at the far end of the room there are hessian bags of coffee beans and copper scoops. As if to demonstrate what we're supposed to do, Lorenzo scoops up some beans, grinds them and puts them into an individual cafetière. He hands this to one of the guests who looks as overawed as we probably do. The walls have been completely stripped back and keep up the rustic-techno theme with old storm lanterns hanging beside huge plasma screens, displaying high-definition images of dream locations from Instagram. A blackboard lists *Hot Destinations*.

'Oh no,' I whisper to myself with a sudden realisation of what I am seeing. 'It's Gastro-Travel.'

I wish I wasn't standing open-mouthed when Lorenzo makes his way to us and asks, 'So what do you think?'

I genuinely don't know what to say so go with the safe. 'It's very different.'

Fortunately Peter, who has now joined us, has his wits about him. 'So tell me how you see this all working?'

Lorenzo is only too pleased to explain his vision. 'Well, travel has become really commoditized with people looking for the lowest price and forgetting it's about adventure,' he starts. 'That's why you guys have done well — you keep adventure alive. But what you haven't done is keep up with technology. You're still showing people websites they could be viewing at home and using the old brochures — definitely not cool.'

We've just been told off.

'We use the technology that suits our customers,' defends Josie, 'and our emails are definitely cool — I write them.'

Lorenzo suddenly looks impressed and shakes her hand vigorously. 'You're the one! I wondered who was writing all that mad stuff — they're great.'

Peter asks about the screens and iPads.

'The screens can show any destination at any time,' explains Lorenzo. 'You pick a picture and we take you there. It's all visual — you choose with your heart. And if it's raining I can fill this place with sunshine, or if there's an ace programme on the Northern Lights, I can stream the catch-up channel and inspire people. The whole place can change mood with one remote control.'

'Then the iPads,' he continues, 'they're for making the bookings and transferring payment. Plus we'll tell people they're welcome to search for a cheaper price but chances are they won't. I want the whole vibe of this place to say "take-off".'

'I want it to say bugger off,' mutters Josie, and I elbow her discreetly.

'And who do you think you'll attract?' asks Charlie.

'Gen Z,' says Lorenzo confidently. 'So with you looking after boomers we should be friends. By the way, you have amazing eyes — I'm sure everyone tells you that.'

I swear Charlie blushes and Peter winks over at him as he does, while Josie chokes on her drink. There's a bit of an awkward silence, so I decide to channel my inner Richard and extend the hand of business camaraderie, no matter how I'm feeling.

I make my big elder-stateswoman gesture. 'I'm sure we can be friends,' I tell him. 'We're both small businesses trying to compete with the big guys and we are targeting different people. I want to give you this — for luck.'

I hand him the boxed pen I got for winning the People's Champion award.

'This means a great deal to me,' I tell him, 'so keep it safe and you can return it to me when you win your own.'

He thanks me, puts the pen in his inside pocket and taps it to show it is safe. I tell myself it's only a loan and I'll get it back. Lorenzo then excuses himself to go and talk to the local press and we huddle.

'I can't believe you gave him that,' says Charlie. 'Has it ever left your sight before?'

In truth, even now, I can't believe I gave it to him either. I was trying to show that I wasn't scared of him and when I was thinking of a gift that would demonstrate this, my prized pen was the thing that kept springing to mind. I hope Lorenzo realizes how much it means to me and takes care of it.

'It was an act of respect and camaraderie. I'm sure I'll get it back,' I lie.

'Maybe,' says Charlie unconvinced. 'Anyway, what do we think of the place?'

'I don't like it myself and I don't think it'll attract any of our customers.' I lie again and wonder how many fibs I'll be allowed to tell before my nose starts growing.

'I don't know,' says Peter. 'Tablet sales are colossal among baby boomers and Gen X. I bet most of the Mercury Clubbers have one.'

I certainly do and I'm never off it. Patty joins us from her mission to mingle and eavesdrop on people.

'So,' I ask, 'what are people saying?'

'They like it and so do I,' she says, 'especially the free coffee.'

I picture our traditional-looking shop alongside this and know his is far too new and exciting to ignore.

'We have to do something,' Josie says to Charlie. 'Not this but something to show we're not past it.'

'I agree. I wish we had Formentera sewn up,' he replies. 'But for now let's see how far a little bribery will go — let's advertise some special offers.'

He goes off to find a local journalist to see if we can get a feature. I spot Lorenzo talking to Caroline and wait until they're finished before heading her way.

'How was he?' I ask as nonchalantly as possible.

'Ambitious. He asked me to develop him a book tour themed around self-actualisation for Gen Z and Y.'

'What the hell does that mean?'

'Places of mindfulness and self-discovery, that kind of thing,' she says. 'Maybe reading the Dalai Lama's book in Nepal while on a yoga retreat.'

'And are you going to do it?' I ask cautiously. I have no right to ask her not to.

'I don't know if I can turn down the business,' she tells me. 'But it's strange he's copying your book trips idea.'

I imagine anyone could have thought of it. Books bring places to life, so it's understandable people would want to visit those places. I sigh, accepting that we really shouldn't underestimate this guy. I know I have to get back out there, touring local clubs and groups to sell the benefits of Mercury. I spot the president of the local WI and head towards her. When I addressed that group last year, we were beseeched with bookings.

'Hello there,' I say cheerfully, 'this place is amazing isn't it?'

I'm relieved to hear her say it's a little overwhelming.

'Is there any chance of me coming along to talk about the gorgeous new destinations people are heading for?' I ask. 'We have some wonderful offers at the moment.'

She tells me she'd be delighted to hear me speak again and knows the WI members enjoyed my last talk. I start to breathe a sigh of relief but am stopped mid-exhale as she gets out a schedule and offers me a date in three months' time.

'Lorenzo has just offered us a series of workshops on travel photography and is giving everyone free access to airport lounges so we can start our travel in style,' she tells me. 'We've never been in so much demand.'

Her joy is my pain. So he's trying to link up with Caroline and copying my talk-tour idea? Hardly the Gen Z audience he mentioned. What else is he up to? I sidle up to Charlie who looks every bit as miserable as I'm starting to feel.

'No joy on the local press,' he tells me. 'Lorenzo has booked space for the whole of the summer with the condition that he's the only travel agent in there.'

'Can he do that?' I ask.

'If he pays enough,' says Peter rejoining the circle. 'I hate to say it but this guy means business. It wouldn't surprise me if he sent those vouchers out before he opened on purpose. They forced you to start giving discounts didn't they? You honoured those vouchers, thereby taking less money and potentially damaging the business.'

We look over at him holding court among a group of women, Patty included. They are hanging on his every word as he illustrates the story he's telling by flicking up some images on the screens. Pictures of the Great Wall of China have the whole room engrossed and I can see how you could be tempted to book up there and then. Knowing we need a strategy but feeling defeated in the here and now, we decide to call it a day. We shake hands with Lorenzo, wish him luck and say goodbye.

Logically, it makes sense for him to copy us to begin with, after all we've done really well. But I hadn't imagined he'd bother us as soon as he was up and going. The Mercury Travel Club isn't just a business to me. I dreamt it up, invested everything I had in it and have loved every minute since. It's more like a member of the family and right then, I feel as if my beloved child is about to be bullied by the new boy at school. I am already regretting handing over my pen and my maternal shackles are well and truly up.

Josie and I pick up our coats and are heading out of the door when Lorenzo leaves his groupies and darts towards us.

'Can I have a word?' he asks Josie, pulling her to one side.

I step out onto the street and wait, inhaling the fresh air. He can't be trying to sell Josie a holiday surely. I try to stay calm and remember all of Richard's advice. I've shown respect but I also have to learn from this competitor. I think through everything he's said and shown us.

Our customers do like the personal service we provide but if he's going to copy that, advertise everywhere and give fabulous discounts then they'd be mad not to take the cheapest price. No travel agent can afford to give much away, so hopefully, I think, he'll stop that soon — but we have to do something until that happens. Thank the Lord that the one thing Lorenzo doesn't have is a team like ours. We'll think of something, we always have in the past and we will again. Josie re-appears, slamming the door behind her.

'So did he try and sell you a holiday?' I ask.

'Not exactly.' She turns to face me. 'Sneaky swine thinks he's God's gift. He offered me a job.'

CHAPTER THIRTEEN: WHEN THE GOING GETS TOUGH . . .

The tough, start selling holidays as if their lives depend on it. I know it's not as catchy as the original song, so I should probably leave lyrics to other people in future.

The job offer backfired on Lorenzo — far from feeling flattered, Josie feels threatened. Like a frill-necked lizard her hackles are up and she's on the attack. We acted quickly after the launch party and all week we've been working round the clock to contact all our business accounts to try and tie up their corporate travel for the year, and we offered each and every one a discount they could pass on to their employees. It's quite a big discount but it's for a very limited period to try and stop people going to try out Launch. We retained most of them, but some businesses had already been tempted away by our nemesis. Unfortunately, we're not making much profit on any of the sales but we've decided that getting some revenue in is better than nothing at all.

Josie has taken a leaf out of Lorenzo's book about being current: she's trying to capitalize on a documentary about the Outback that was on TV. She sent out an email with a link to the video trailer and urging customers to get in touch for special offers. She's offered to give them her personal native advice based on what they want to see — we're still waiting for customers to start calling but we're sure they will.

In between selling holidays, Josie and Charlie keep dreaming up plans to bring Lorenzo down a few pegs. I can't join in. Not because I don't want to but because despite Mr Branson's calm advice, I'm starting to bubble with anger. I've concluded that he's the third most horrible person I've ever met (the first being my old PE teacher and the second the ex-husband, obviously) and I'm angry that he's had the nerve to open up opposite us. I'm angry that he's using our ideas, that he's stopping us advertising and that he blatantly tried to poach Josie AFTER the thieving hound had casually accepted my precious pen as a goodwill gift. What sort of low life does that? You would never catch me or mine stooping that low.

'I think this one belongs to you,' says a voice at the doorway, jolting me from my indignation. 'She was wrecking my technology — nice try.'

I look up and see Lorenzo frogmarching my mother into the shop. I get up and take her from him, muttering a quiet 'thank you' as he leaves.

'Go on then, Mum. What have you done?' Whatever it is, she's just handed our competitor the moral high ground I was proudly occupying.

'I just went in to see what all the fuss was about,' she huffs. 'They've got free coffee in there you know.'

I should have warned Lorenzo about giving out freebies this woman can sniff them out from miles away. Then again, maybe that's our backup plan: letting Mum and her cronies bankrupt him without us lifting a finger.

'Mind you,' Mum continues, 'no biscuits. Cereal, that's what they're giving away — bowls of cereal. I mean to say, we've all had breakfast before we leave the house, haven't we? We don't want a bowl of bran flakes for our mid-morning snack. Someone should tell him.'

'It's very trendy now,' I explain. 'There's a café in the city centre selling just cereal for a fiver a bowl.'

She waves her hand at me incredulously. 'Don't be daft. I'm not falling for that one.'

I won't even mention all those cat cafés that have sprung up, then.

'So, anyway, he threw you out for eating all his cereal, did he?'

'I wouldn't touch that stuff. No, he said I was going to break his little eye-patch things.'

I roll my eyes, as I can see she's just playing to the room now. In her late seventies, my mother sees absolutely no point in accepting social norms any more. After a lifetime of being utterly respectable, she has decided that now is the time to do whatever she pleases. If there was an award called 'Pensioner Behaving Badly' — she'd probably win. Nevertheless, Josie is loving it.

'Eye-patch? Oh my God, you mean the iPads? Hilarious, go on, what did you do with them?' She's dying to know the details and is giving Mum the audience she wants.

'Well, I didn't like the picture on the screen and wanted to change it,' she explains. 'So I just picked it up and shook it.' She demonstrates her actions, shaking an imaginary tablet violently.

'Mother, dear,' I say, shaking my head, 'it's not an Etch A Sketch and you know it, you're not daft.'

Josie and Charlie are doubled up with laughter.

'Oh I can just picture it,' cries Charlie through his tears. 'Good job she didn't think you had to write on the screens.'

'Well done, Mrs Shepherd.' Josie laughs. 'You've made my day.'

Despite myself, I can't help but join in the giggling. Just the thought of Lorenzo and his cool cat customers being disturbed by a septuagenarian blunderbuss.

'Was it busy?' Charlie eventually asks when he's calmed down.

Mum nods ferociously. 'Oh yes, and people were tapping their watches on them screens to book their holidays. It looked dead easy.'

'Just so you know, your old Sekonda wouldn't work,' I tell her just in case she tries to give that a go too. Mum looks round at our shop.

'It makes this place look a bit shabby really. Have you been this quiet all morning?'

And there it is — the thing none of us are actually saying to each other. We've been quiet all week, but rather than confront it we've pretended to be pleased to be able to finish up the admin or clear emails while we wait for our marketing efforts to start working. Well, the emails are clear now and not many more are coming in. Mum senses she's dropped a clanger, so leaves us to 'get on with things'. The three of us sit looking at the floor until Charlie breaks the ice.

'So what are we going to do?' he asks.

The silence continues for a moment and I imagine, like me, the others are running through options in their heads. I don't want to turn Mercury into a lightweight version of Launch — I genuinely don't think that's what customers want. Then again, our shop is empty, so perhaps I've got it wrong. We only decorated a year ago but perhaps I was too traditional back then. The wine bars and restaurants that have opened in the past year have looked so different with their mish-mashed furniture and retro crockery. I wonder if you only like retro things when you don't remember them the first time around. I couldn't wait to get rid of all those garish seventies tea sets and now I can't find a coffee shop that doesn't use them. My mind is wandering again and the guys are staring at me, waiting for a response.

'Before I do anything, I want to ask some Mercurians what they think,' I say. 'I'm too biased and I just don't know what we could be doing differently.'

'Well, I'm going to step up the marketing even more,' says Josie. 'More emails, reviews, social media — you won't be able to move for hearing about the great times people have had with Mercury.'

'And I'm going to tidy the shop up,' adds Charlie. 'I'll go in a completely different direction to Lorenzo — a bit less clutter but a bit more luxury, maybe some velvet . . .'

We let him ponder his interior design while we get on with our tasks.

Josie is on a mission and she unpleasantly cracks her knuckles before she starts. She pulls up all the compliments we've been sent over the year, all the customer photographs and the publicity. She drafts a very funny text reminding people where they were last year and showing where they could be this year. She creates a video of customers saying they've simply had the best time ever and loads it onto Facebook, then edits a clip of the award ceremony when we were voted the People's Champion for our customer service. Finally she emails everyone on our database, the Mercury Travel Club calendar, telling them that anyone who books next week will be entered into a draw to win a fabulous prize.

The next day, Charlie gets to work. Instead of velvet, he's decided to emulate our (hopefully) future island beach bar, replacing our wooden window blinds with floaty voile curtains, creating a brochure-reading area with some white rattan furniture, and deciding on a uniform of turquoise shirts over linen trousers. They're going to look pretty creased by the end of the day but this is not a time to criticize any effort whatsoever. Instead of a coffee bar, Charlie has stuck to his theme and has a range of ready-made cocktails chilling in a little fridge, non-alcoholic ones of course — we have to ensure Patty doesn't take up permanent residence, after all.

Charlie's interior design is definitely noticed but the marketing seems to be getting nowhere. The very few customers who cross our threshold are lingering a little longer, meaning we have more time to tell them about the trip, but by the end of the week we've charmed the espadrilles off as many people as we can and the bookings are nowhere near last year's levels. What is happening? It's time for me to go out and do my job — to ask people what we're doing wrong.

Josie, Charlie and I invite some of our customers to talk to us about Mercury and we meet in a private room of the local pub, getting everyone a free drink for coming along. Although Mum would have come along anyway, I still have to get her one, and seeing as someone else is paying, she has the bloody cheek to ask for a bottle of 'that sparkly stuff you all go mad over' for her and her friends. She'd better book a holiday after this.

Josie starts the conversation in a relaxed way. If she hadn't, I'd be at risk of falling to my knees pleading, 'Why, oh why have you deserted us?' which probably wouldn't inspire them.

'It's so good to see you all,' she says. 'I remember you two from the karaoke in New York.' She points at a couple who had led the singing on that trip and they take a bow.

'What's been your favourite Mercury trip?' she asks and the room becomes animated.

'Oh, when Angie got propositioned by that man in Monaco,' says one and Mum feigns shame at the memory.

'Oh, dancing the waltz in Vienna,' says another.

'When Patty was part of the Granny-okies,' comes a cry from the back.

They're all such fond memories of our first year as the Mercury Travel Club but nostalgia can't keep a business going. I keep my voice calm and start to ask about now.

'So what do you think about the new trips we're advertising?'

There are lots of positive murmurs in the room.

'And do you like all the emails and messages?'

Again lots of positivity rises from the group.

'Oh, they're so funny,' says one.

'They make you feel like booking up straight away even if you weren't thinking of a holiday,' says another. So I decide to ask the key question.

'So are you going to book up?'

Our customers look at each other fairly puzzled.

'I did book,' one of them starts to say. 'I clicked on the link you sent in that second email and put my card number in, it was so easy.'

Other people in the group nod to say they did the same. I start to have what seems like a near-death experience. I'm floating outside myself again and what must be less than a minute of silence seems to last for hours. I don't know what has happened but none of these people are booked up with us and I don't want to cause a panic. Charlie picks up the thread.

'Has anyone still got the link by any chance?'

One of the customers gets out their phone and shows Charlie the email they're all talking about. Josie takes the phone from his hand, her eyes nearly bursting out of her head. She signals me to take a look.

'What's happened?' I ask.

'It's Lorenzo,' she says quietly. 'He must be on our mailing list and when I've sent out our email, he's just pressed "reply all" offering something very similar and a discount if they click the link and book up immediately. He's stolen our ideas.'

'Is our holiday safe?' asks one of the group who sensed our unease and has been trying to listen in. We reassure her it is. It's just been booked through Launch rather than Mercury. They assume the agency is just another branch of ours as we both have intergalactic names. We smile and let them think that for now.

I can see Josie getting angrier but I'm more concerned for our customers. I hope he's going to take care of them. If they do believe Launch is a new Mercury Travel branch, then everything he does will reflect on us. We need to stay calm and agree a strategy. For now, I lead the group back to talking about the great times we've had together and then we end the discussion earlier than planned. We now know what has happened and we have to work out what to do about it.

As the last customer leaves the room, Charlie, Josie and I sit stunned.

'Is what he's done legal?' I ask.

'Don't bloody care,' says Josie. 'I'm gonna chop his balls off.'

'As much as I'd like to do the same, I think we should start by talking to him,' says Charlie. 'He can't behave like this.'

'Coward,' replies Josie, finishing her drink in one combative gulp.

* * *

We get some advice before confronting Lorenzo and asking him to start playing fair. His response, like the legal advice, is that he hasn't done anything strictly illegal. He received an email alongside lots of other people and he'd simply replied to them all with an offer of his own. If anything, we'd been at fault for not protecting our customers' details. As he says this I realize that it's true — we should never have included email addresses that could be replied to and if we kick up a fuss then we might just find ourselves worse off. I can't believe he's bluffing and the last thing we need right now is a data protection scandal.

The next day we close up slightly early and catch him as he's locking up. A high-street brawl isn't going to enhance our reputation but Josie goes for him before I can get hold of her.

'You're still a scabby old snake,' Josie tells him. 'Why don't you get some ideas of your own?'

'I couldn't help myself. I just loved what you'd done,' he tells her. 'Honestly, Josie — your emails are brilliant. I hope Mercury knows how lucky they are to have you. I'd double your salary if you worked for me.'

'In your dreams,' spits Josie. 'You even give slugs a bad name.'

'Although it wouldn't surprise me if they sacked you now,' he baits her further. 'I'm presuming it was you who sent out the unprotected email? Directors can be prosecuted for giving out customer details you know.'

I have to stop her hurling her rucksack at him. There's no point in arguing and I think he's enjoying it far too much. I could kick myself right now. He's right. It was our mistake and we did just hand him our customers on a plate.

I round Charlie and Josie up then take them to the pub for a conciliatory glass of wine to help us calm down before we get home.

'I'm so sorry,' sighs Josie. 'This is all my fault.'

She really does look as if she's been punched in the stomach.

'It's not,' Charlie tells her and I give her a hug to show I feel the same. 'Lorenzo seems the type to cause trouble whatever we do and at least we know what we're up against.'

'So now we can beat him at his own game,' says Josie. 'We can sneak into his backroom and cut off his electricity so none of his damn flat screens work.'

'What, in a Catwoman outfit?' I say, picturing Josie all dressed in black, doing fancy gymnastic moves over infra-red beams. I watch too many movies, I know.

Charlie grabs Josie in a friendly headlock.

'OK, missy,' he says, tapping her on the head. 'Let's knock some reason into you. We are NOT going to stoop to his level — OK?'

She barely mutters, 'OK', so he grabs her more tightly.

'Louder,' he insists. 'I want to hear you say it like you mean it.'

'OK!' she yells and he releases her before he gives her a kiss on the cheek.

'Come on, guys, what can we do?' I ask. 'We need to show him we're no pushover.'

'Well, I'm going to search the email file and take his name out for a start,' says Josie.

'We need to win the Formentera bid more than ever,' adds Charlie. 'It would be easy to back out with all of this going on but I think if we had such an exclusive offer, it would take the wind out of his sails. We need to change league.'

I nod my agreement. Now is not the time to back down and I'm glad Charlie has said it first.

'But until that happens, we need another big holiday idea,' he continues. 'One that he'd never think of and couldn't possibly copy.'

* * *

As I walk home, I try to think of something that fits the bill. A big idea that can't be copied. What can't be copied? My phone beeps with a text message, cutting through my fuddled state.

Hello stranger — fancy dinner?

I sigh. I haven't seen Michael since before Amsterdam. Fortunately for me, he has also been really busy and hasn't had the time, so it's been easy for me to put things off. I know I need to think about Patty's suggestion before I see him next, but with Lorenzo pretty much exhausting all my time and my mental capacity, I haven't had time to do that either.

When we do meet up next, I don't want him to feel rejected again. I do want to get things back on track but when I'm in a better frame of mind.

Raincheck? Work insane

Let me help

Part of me thinks it would be good if we did meet in the neutral territory of the shop, talk about work and then perhaps go on to eat and talk afterwards. What would I say? Patty understood but you can't exactly have the conversations you have with your girlfriends with the man in your life, especially when it's still a fairly new relationship. If someone were to ask me for advice, I'd probably tell them to be open and honest but let's face it, no one ever takes their own advice. Even if I weren't in this dilemma, it isn't exactly a happy-go-lucky time right now so I'd rather delay any extra pressure to get things back on track. I'd rather not feel such a failure in every area of my life. Unable to think of a text that might explain all of this I write: *Maybe later*

OK is the only reply I get all night, without even a kiss at the end.

I'm disappointed but also very slightly relieved.

CHAPTER FOURTEEN: HEIGH-HO

I lay awake for much of last night wondering whether I should have called Michael. The answer is probably yes. A text can't, and obviously didn't, express the angst I'm feeling now. I'm sure it sounded like a brush-off and I didn't mean it to but I feel a bit overwhelmed. I feel as if I'm on a shore watching two boats drifting away. One contains Michael, and the other, Mercury Travel. Except the Mercury boat isn't drifting — it's being stolen. I can't let this happen. I have to perk myself up.

'Because that cocky upstart is not ruining my precious Mercury,' I tell my reflection as I get dressed for the day ahead.

I look at what I'm wearing and notice that subconsciously I've dressed down. I look like a 1930s austerity woman in dull browns and greens. I take it all off and throw it on the bed. Rifling through my wardrobe, I pick the brightest dress I can find, a purple number because I've heard this is the feng shui colour of prosperity and wealth. The colour of travel and people at the moment is unfortunately grey and I don't think that would help us today. Despite the fact that I know I'll be crippled by the end of the day, I add killer heels and make a mental note to pack some fold-up slippers in my bag for when I'm behind the desk. Make-up and earrings finish off the look and once again I am Angie Shepherd, entrepreneur. Victor not victim.

Despite my superhero outfit, the shop is quiet again. The customers who do cross our threshold are finalising bookings rather than making new ones. Still, I'm glad I dressed up. When someone tells me I'm looking lovely, I'm able to bluff: 'Well, it's a lovely day and things are going nicely. Who wouldn't want to get dressed up for today?'

Charlie smiles every time I say it. He nodded at my outfit when I came in, so I can tell he knows what I'm doing. I manage to keep the smile going for the whole day but come closing I'm delighted to let it drop.

'Why don't we hang on for an hour or so and have a bit of a brainstorm,' says Charlie as we lock up. 'I can't imagine you're ready to walk home yet — those shoes must be killing you.'

I'm more than happy to be able to kick them off for a while, so take a seat and rub my poor tootsies. Josie pulls a flipchart into the shop and writes 'Attack Plan' at the top.

'This isn't just about Lorenzo, it's about getting back our focus,' I say. 'We shouldn't forget that we're bloody good at this. Our customers have come back from our trips completely happy. He hasn't achieved that yet. This is about Mercury showing people that we're still doing what we do best.'

Charlie gives me a round of applause and hollers, 'Here, here.'

'And on that note,' adds Josie, 'I've designed a tapas and wine tour and I've got a discount on beginners' Spanish for anyone going.'

I give the round of applause this time as Josie jots it down.

'The "Around the World with 20 Artists" tour seems to still be working well. Is there anything similar to that we can do?' asks Charlie.

'What about "Around the World in 20 Beers"?' says Josie.

'Beer? Why would anyone want to do a beer tour?' I answer and instantly regret questioning the idea, as Charlie looks rather impressed.

'It's just like wine tasting,' says Charlie.

'Oh yeah,' Josie tells me, 'and it's huge now. Craft brewing is just massive in this country and abroad. It's the same as craft gin distilleries   they're all the rage. You could pretty much go anywhere and the breweries usually give free tours too, so it could be brilliant value.'

'And there are some gorgeous ones along the Romantische Strasse in Germany,' says Charlie.

'So there'd be something to keep everyone happy,' I say, starting to understand the potential. 'It's a stunning route such a chocolate box type of place — it would be a beautiful place to visit even if you're not interested in beer.'

'Sounds good,' says Charlie, 'and I really think northern Europe is going to make a comeback for holidays. There was that TV show filmed there in spring and I think it opened people's eyes. Some places are truly beautiful and it's only a short flight. When's the best time to go? I mean could it help us now?'

'Definitely, October would be nice, lovely autumnal colours and not too cold,' Josie says and we all agree. 'It doesn't need to be just Europe, either. We could take people to Boston. It's really big on craft distilleries and they'd get the New England leaf-peeper experience too.'

Josie marks it up on the attack plan just as there's a loud banging on the door. We all jump, never knowing what to expect these days, but it's only Patty (again).

'I thought you had a job interview,' I say.

'Brilliant, doing what?' asks Charlie.

'Working as a waitress in a cocktail bar.' Patty grins, happy to be able to trot out the line she's been rehearsing for days.

'You do know Phil Oakey won't be coming in to sweep you off your feet, don't you,' Charlie says. 'How did you get on?'

'They told me they'd let me know,' says Patty. 'In the sort of way that you know they're going to say "no" as soon as they don't have to do it face-to-face. Honestly, you'd think the world didn't want gorgeous women in the prime of their lives.'

'Never mind them, come and help us,' says Charlie.

Patty looks at our flip chart and grimaces.

'A beer tour? Doesn't sound like my kind of trip. I'm more of a Kir Royale kind of girl.'

'Then you're missing out,' Josie says. 'You should try some of the fruity beers.'

Patty is not convinced, grimacing as if we've just force-fed her cod liver oil.

'I get wine tasting,' she says. 'They're all different but beer just tastes of beer.'

I knew there was a reason we were the best of friends. I don't feel as daft questioning the idea now.

'Rubbish, come out with us this weekend and my Matt'll show you the difference between a Dizzy Blonde and a Nutty Brewnette,' says Josie. 'And they're beers, not you and your best mate,' she clarifies, seeing our puzzled expressions.

Patty makes herself at home and we're restarting the brainstorm when Peter knocks on the door, far more politely than Patty did, it has to be said.

'Got your message about the brainstorm,' he says to Charlie. 'Need any help?'

'We could always do with a bit of extra brain power.' Charlie leaps up to kiss him on the cheek.

I hadn't known this session would turn into a free-for-all. I could have accepted Michael's help if I'd known. 'How do we tell people about all of this?' I get us back on track. 'We've got a brilliant idea but he's bought all the advertising space and we can't really trust our email for a while. He might use a fake address next.'

The silence that follows is broken only by the sound of cogs whirring in our heads. Well obviously it isn't really but I imagine it happening as we all search fervently for a way to market our holidays.

'You could use Facebook,' Peter suggests, 'but he's bound to be following you.'

'Even if he isn't, we'd still only be reaching customers who've already travelled with us,' says Charlie. 'We need to be telling new people about these ideas to grow the business.'

'How about creating a news story rather than trying to advertise in the local paper?' I ask. 'It's worked before.'

'Hmmm,' replies Charlie. 'The thing is that we're not the news anymore — he is.'

I sigh, knowing that he's right.

'What about asking your customers to recommend a friend?' suggests Patty lifting the low mood that threatened to settle. 'They get a discount if they bring in a new customer? They like you so they'd probably do it.'

'Not bad. Get customers we know to tell other people,' I repeat nodding my head.

'And we could do it on a much bigger scale than just our customers,' adds Josie suddenly very excited. 'I could link up with the bloggers and get them to talk about the trips.'

Charlie and I look at each other and then at Josie. Obviously we've heard of bloggers and some of them are rather famous but they usually have cookery programmes.

Seeing the confusion written across our faces, Josie explains, 'There are blogs about everything including some really brilliant craft beer and CAMRA blogs. They're followed by people who want to hear new ideas. I'm sure they'd love this. I'll see if any bloggers would help. They're looking for ways to make the blogs pay, so if we can maybe offer some sort of commission or discount for their members?'

Charlie and I nod. I'm sure we can do something and it would probably cost less than we're giving away to match Lorenzo right now.

'And Lorenzo will never be able to keep tabs on everyone who's recommending us,' Josie adds, showing that he's never very far from any of our thoughts.

At least she looks fired up again. It's the first time I've seen her smile, truly smile, in days. With a plan to defeat her archenemy, Josie's eyes shine and she cracks her fingers again — the signal she's ready for business. I hope it works, not just for us but for her. She's been completely gutted since the email debacle despite our reassurances that it wasn't her fault. It's been a good start, but we still need more.

'An idea that'll knock our customers' socks off and have them queuing to get through the Mercury doors — that's what we need,' asserts Charlie. 'Something that his nibs over the road can't possibly copy.'

'I know, what about a mystery trip?' Patty declares with gusto. 'Lorenzo can't copy it if no one knows where they're going in the first place.'

Having already been slightly dismissive about the craft brewery idea that Josie and Charlie loved, I don't want to rain on this one but I'm beginning to wonder whether my friend had a few of her marbles washed overboard on that cruise ship.

'Would we know where it was going?' I ask — just to check.

'Of course we would,' Patty answers, looking at me as if I'm the insane one. 'But customers would sign up with just the promise of an adventure.'

'It's exciting in principle,' says Charlie, 'but people can get cheap mystery trips online, and anyway, our Mercurians like to know it's not "mystery" as in "dodgy".'

'So what if you call it a Luxury Treasure Trail then?' suggests Peter. 'That sounds more indulgent.'

'It certainly does — how would it work?' I ask.

'OK then, how about this. You start by gathering every-one in a fabulous hotel for the night.' Patty has taken up the reins and is making it up as she goes along. 'It's a dressy affair full of mystery and intrigue — think *Da Vinci Code* meets *The Great Gatsby* — then in the morning, they get a clue for where they'll be staying the next night.'

'I think the competitive element would really work in corporate travel,' adds Peter. 'It could be great team building.'

I start to see the potential of this and am suddenly buzzing.

'I'm getting it. We start our Mercurians in a wonderful hotel, we have a luxurious dinner and at the end, give them the clue for their next destination.'

'That's just what I've said.' Patty twirls her finger at the side of her head. I ignore her.

'They can bring their own cars or we can hire them something really special like a Jag or Porsche,' I continue, picturing the scene. 'I think people would love it. They can work alone, in pairs, in teams. It's entirely up to them. They can't set off before breakfast but then the race begins. We award points for anyone reaching the next destination and bonus points if you're first there. You have to send us a selfie at the location to prove you got there. That would mean the holiday would actually promote itself and we'd keep changing the destinations for the next trip.'

'Would there be a prize for the most points?' asks Charlie, and I nod enthusiastically.

'I do like it,' he adds hesitantly, 'but it's a helluva lot of work. How do we make up all the clues?'

'My dad,' I exclaim. 'He'd love to develop this. After all, it's a giant quiz and he'd be in his element.'

Dad has been running the caravan club quiz teams for years and has notebook after notebook filled with trivia about every subject you can think of. He's the only person I know who actually reads the credits at the end of movies. He jots down the name of the producer, director, musical score and even the stuntmen. They rarely come up unless the film wins a BAFTA, so he could save a lot of time waiting until the award ceremonies, but he likes to tell me he's a purist. He must have a book about geography. He could pick a country and invent a tour for us based upon the most obscure facts he has.

'Let me just ask him,' I suggest, 'and if we like what he develops then we can put it out there and if not, we get back to the drawing board.'

'What do you think, Josie?' asks Charlie and we all turn to look at her. She's suddenly looking a little deflated.

'It's fab but so much work for everyone,' she says. 'I'm really sorry — if it hadn't been for me and the email, none of this would be needed.'

'That's rubbish.' Charlie gives her a hug. 'He'd have found another way to make things difficult, that type always does. And anyway, look at the silver lining: if you hadn't sent that email we wouldn't have this fabulous new idea.'

'Will it be enough though?' she replies gloomily, looking around at the empty shop.

'Of course it will, grumpy-drawers.' Charlie gives her a friendly punch. 'Thousands of customers will want to take part, celebs will find out about it and it'll be the new Gumball Rally. We'll become famous, make millions and then bathe in champagne. You'll have bubbles up your bits before you can say "Death to Lorenzo".' He manages to get Josie smiling.

'I'm sorry,' she says. 'I promise to pick myself up and get selling the hell out of these. I'm not really the advert for a happy holiday right now.'

'If we had more goth customers you'd be perfect,' I tell her and she pokes her tongue out at me, order restored.

'Come on,' calls Charlie, 'group hug.'

The four of us gather for a squeeze. When I come up for air, I catch a glimpse of someone turning his back on us through the window. Michael walks away hurriedly. My shoulders drop, weighed down with guilt. Me, standing here hugging my friends and accepting their help must look awful after I've told him I'm too busy to see him. I try to untangle myself from the hug but he's gone before I get to the door. I give him a call but it goes straight to voicemail. I try to sound cheery and explain I didn't know either Peter or Patty would be coming tonight. I promise to call him tomorrow but tell him that he can call me at any time. I hear nothing all night.

CHAPTER FIFTEEN: LESSONS IN LOVE

'Are you sitting down?' Charlie asks me at 6 a.m.

'No, I'm lying down and still in bed,' I tell him. 'Why are you calling me at this hour? Nothing's happened to Peter has it?'

'Well, he's passed out with excitement but you will too when I tell you the news.'

Dramatic pause from Charlie. I sit up and stretch my face awake and can hear Peter performing a drum-roll in the background.

'We've been shortlisted,' he eventually exclaims.

It takes me a while. I'm thinking, for what? Then it dawns. They've had our proposal for a month. It has to be.

'We're down to the last three bids for the island partnership,' Charlie confirms.

That weird shiver you feel when something unbelievable happens starts to flood through me. When something you really want looks as if it may just come true, you don't feel euphoric the way they do in films. At least I don't anyway. An eerie calm spreads through my body and I'm not really sure what it is. Realisation? Relief? Fear? Probably all three.

'Are you still there?'

I tell Charlie that I am. 'I'm just taking it in.'

Before I became a partner in Mercury, I used to help my ex-husband with his business, so in the logical half of my brain I know I'm no dumbo. I know that if I work things through in my mind then I can usually do them, but I think somewhere in me I have that imposter syndrome. The one where you think you're going to be ousted as a great big fraud no matter what you achieve. I've read that even the most successful businessmen and women get it, so I haven't just made it up and I'm feeling it right now. This whole thing doesn't seem real but it actually is. Charlie and I wrote a business plan then someone miles away, who doesn't even know us, looked at it and said, 'That one looks fabby-dabby.' Well, they probably said something more businesslike, but in essence . . .

'Have you fainted or something?'

'Sorry, Charlie. It's brilliant. Huge and brilliant. I can't quite believe it, can you?'

'Not really. When I saw that we had an email from them, I sort of expected it to be a rejection. I was all geared up for that and when I opened it, I had to read it twice.'

'So what happens now? How do they decide between the final three?'

'They've said they love the weddings idea but want us to create something unique to help spread the word.'

That helps to settle my nerves a little. They're not just having us on. Charlie and I can easily build on the plan and make our original thoughts more gorgeous. We can do this.

'And we should also take stock of the investment requirement now we know what we're up against with Lorenzo,' adds Charlie.

He didn't need to say that. We both know that since Launch opening, things have been tougher than we'd anticipated and although we're fired up about the new ideas, we have to sell them and get customers through the door. We've a lot to think about before we move into the second stage of the bid. We agree to meet up this evening and having hung up the phone, I jump out of bed, my head spinning with ideas and obstacles in equal measure.

I check the phone before I get into the shower. There still hasn't been a call from Michael since the group hug in the shop — no messages or emails either. I've left lots of voicemails but I need to find time to go round to see him. Why is everything coming to a head at once? It's going to be such a big day. Before I go into Mercury I have to head to my parents' house to explain the treasure trail concept to my dad.

I've chosen the early hour of my visit carefully to coincide with sampling hour at our mum's favourite supermarket. She'll be gone for ages, eating her way around the store.

* * *

Dad greets me at the door and we grab cups of coffee before heading into his snug. It's a distinctly Dad kind of room. None of Mum's cushions or flower arrangements   instead models of vintage cars and rows upon rows of books. There's a layer of dust here that wouldn't be permitted anywhere else in the house but Mum is not allowed to touch anything in this room. Apparently she once threw out some old paper, which turned out to be 'important' quiz notes hence, her banishment. It must drive her nuts and I imagine that's part of the reason he does it.

Dad is excited by the trip idea as soon as I start talking about it. I knew he would be as it combines his love of cars and questions. His only beef is that if he develops the trail, he won't be able to take part in it. I promise to find another quizmaster to challenge him if this one takes off.

'So I can pick any country?' he asks.

'As long as people would want to go there,' I reply. 'You may have millions of quiz questions about Afghanistan but I think I might have trouble selling a holiday there.'

Dad starts pulling out quiz books and atlases. I love that he's going to develop this with old-school technology.

'If I take questions from Google,' he explains, practically salivating as he leafs through the pages, 'they'll be easy for others to find. Just one mobile search and they'll be there.'

He's now so engrossed that I feel like a spare part in the room, so say goodbye and head towards the door. I don't get out in time. Mum turns the key in the lock and jumps when she sees me.

'I thought you were a burglar,' she tells me.

'With a handbag?'

'You might just be after the building society books or something to steal my identity. It's a real thing you know, someone could be out there pretending to be me.'

Oh Lord, I hope *no one ever* steals Mum's identity. What would they do? Pound the reduced aisles together? The thought of two of her on the rampage is just too much to imagine.

'Anyway,' she continues, 'shouldn't you be at work?'

I explain that I've asked Dad for some help with a treasure trail.

'You could have asked me,' she huffs. 'I used to watch that TV programme with Anneka Rice. Will you need someone to go up in a helicopter?'

I very quickly tell her I won't.

Mum heads through to stand at the door of Dad's study and I follow.

'I thought today was sample day,' I say.

'It's supposed to be.' Mum holds her hands up in despair. 'But Moira's daughter has gone and had a baby, so she's giving up the sampling to look after her. Who's going to look after me and the other regulars? The new girl might be a bit mean with the giveaways.'

Moira is the woman who hosts the sampling table. Over the years, she has become one of Mum's best friends, probably because she is in charge of giving out free cake. It's highly inconsiderate of her to choose to look after her first grandchild rather than my mother. What was she thinking?

'You know Patty needs a job,' I tell her, lighting a bulb in my mum's brain. I can see it through her ears. 'She might enjoy doing Moira's old job.'

'That's a brilliant idea,' she says. 'Patty knows what a proper slice of cake looks like. She wouldn't be doing all those thin pieces you can barely taste. I'll tell Moira about her.'

112

I may have just netted a double-whammy: Patty and my mother fully occupied in one fell swoop. What a day this is turning out to be.

'How's my own granddaughter doing?' Dad asks. As we're lurking, he's given up trying to concentrate on his books.

'Really well,' I tell him. 'She's working very hard, maybe too hard though. She told us she's hardly seeing James at the moment. I do worry about them.'

'Well, you know what they say. The apple doesn't fall very far from the tree,' says Mum.

I frown at her. 'What do you mean?'

'Have you told her?' Mum directs the question at Dad. He sighs and gives her a 'don't interfere' look. I hold my arms out to indicate that someone needs to tell me.

'Michael came round late last night,' he says gently. 'He brought some tools back.'

I could guess at the significance of this but Mum spells it out. 'Because he thinks it could be a while before he sees us again.'

'Did he say that?'

'He didn't have to. Why else would he bring them back? Have you two split up?' Mum wags her finger at me and I shake my head.

In my mind we haven't, but I can see that my schizophrenic behaviour really might look that way. Running for my life at any attempt to get intimate, taking Patty on the weekend away, communicating only by text, the group hug last night and then leaving millions of voicemails. If it had been the other way round, I'd have given the tools back even earlier. Damn it, I hate it when Mum is bang on the money.

'You need to book one of those date nights, too,' Mum continues to lecture.

'What do you think, Dad?'

He stands up and gives me a hug. 'I'm the last person to ask about relationships. But I do think that you obviously have a lot on and you probably don't need to do all of this alone. He's a nice guy you know and would love to be helping you. It's in his nature.'

113

I nod, knowing that he's right and leave the house before Mum can offer advice, too. I walk slowly, trying to straighten things out in my mind. When I think about the future, he's in it and despite everything that's worrying me right now, I don't want to lose him. I really don't. Suddenly I'm back on that shoreline and I notice that Michael's boat still has a tow rope attached to a mooring. Just one tug and he'll start drifting back to me. I need to see Michael today and I can't accept no for an answer.

I call him repeatedly and on the fourth time he answers.

'Hi there, it's the invisible woman,' I say laughing. 'Michael, I'm really sorry that I've been all tied up in the business. I've been a complete pain in the backside.'

He mutters an '*it's okay.*'

'Please forgive me,' I continue. 'After all we went through just getting together, I don't want to lose you but I'm out of my depth with all of this. I was trying to keep the tougher parts of my life out of our relationship so that when we're together we don't have to worry about Mercury or Lorenzo or anything else for that matter. But I realize now that's not going to work. Please let me try again.'

'You don't have to try and protect me,' Michael says softly. 'Relationships are about dealing with the tough times too.'

'I know and I'm sorry.'

'Shall we meet up tonight?' he asks.

I'll be reviewing the proposal feedback with Charlie and although my instinct is still to keep work and pleasure separate, I have to let Michael in if I'm serious about this.

'That would be perfect,' I say tentatively, 'but there's something I have to do tonight. We got through to the final three bids, so we have to go over the island proposal but it would be absolutely brilliant to have you there. Do you mind? Please say you'll come.'

Fortunately he's happy to come along.

* * *

114

After working hours, Michael appears at the shop door and I let him in. We're both fairly sheepish but pretending all is well. Charlie senses the slight awkwardness and does what he always does — he makes Michael feel at home.

'Thank goodness you're here,' he gushes. 'We need the man behind the yurt inspiration. Come on, sit beside me.'

Michael dutifully sits down at the table between Charlie and Josie. I join them opposite with Peter. Each of us has a copy of the proposal and the feedback given to us. We look through the questions we now have to answer. There are some health and safety issues, some legal requirements and some clarifications on the timescales. Michael studies them and tells us that he can tackle anything to do with the grounds themselves. Charlie gives him a pat on the back and I'm relieved that he's involved so quickly.

'I can review the legislation,' adds Peter. 'The questions look quite straightforward, so I'll get a lawyer friend of mine onto them.'

'So we need to get creative,' I say to Charlie and Josie. 'How do we make the resort famous yet still keep it exclusive?'

Silence.

'It'll always be exclusive because it's quite a small resort,' begins Charlie. 'You couldn't host a cast of thousands there.'

'Is there anything else the bride and groom can do there?' I ask thinking of those snorkelling weddings but really not wanting to suggest it.

'There's a stunning catamaran cruise at sunset,' says Peter. 'You could make that part of the package on the day before the wedding and show that you're boosting other local businesses.'

'Everything you've said and shown us, just conjures up the most beautiful images,' adds Michael. 'Do you need any more than that? Isn't it enough to capture the couple's imagination?'

He's right in a way, we shouldn't aim for gimmicks. The resort sells itself when people see it. When Peter and Charlie showed us their pictures on the big screen . . .

'Can we do something on TV?' I suddenly ask, then work through my thoughts. 'It's a small island, so not everyone will be able to go even if the couple want them there. They'll have a video of their wedding and people will be posting up pictures but what if we go one step further? What if we stream the wedding somehow and you can join it live? Is that kind of thing possible, Josie?'

'Totally,' says Josie. 'I can look into that if you like?'

'You could check with Patty,' I suggest. 'Her friend Frankie might know people.'

She heads off to call our leading lady.

'I have some other ideas about making the experience truly unique,' Charlie says. 'I was thinking about the bride's jewellery and wondering whether it could be made locally. The rings can be bought nowhere but on the island. They'd be a constant reminder of the beach.'

'That sounds wonderful.'

'And how about a free seventeenth-wedding-anniversary trip?'

'Why seventeen? It seems a long time to wait,' I say.

'Seventeen is the shell anniversary. It's perfect,' Charlie gushes.

It's lovely and I can picture the couple strolling along the beach on their return to the island and choosing each other a gorgeous mother-of-pearl shell that means everything to them.

'I adore this idea,' I tell him. 'It really celebrates love and togetherness. We just have to do it.'

It also says future to me. It says Mercury will be around to celebrate the shell weddings of our first guests even if Charlie and I are long retired. That would be glorious.

'It's nice to think about a future when all of this is a huge worldwide success and Lorenzo just a speck on our dim and distant past,' I say.

Looking through the numbers, it is going to be tough and we definitely can't finance it from Mercury reserves. That option is well and truly gone thanks to all the heavy discounts we've had to give.

116

'We can still pull out of this now if you're not sure,' says Charlie. 'We've proven that we had a good idea, but if the timing isn't right, we can say no and we should have the courage to do it.'

This is the second time he's given me the chance to back out. I'm not sure whether he's nervous or he thinks I am. Surely he wouldn't have been thinking of all the new ideas if he wanted to give up on this dream. I remember him telling me that he was too emotional about the resort and he needed me to be the practical one. I have to give him a practical reason for continuing. I really want Charlie to have this.

'It wouldn't be sensible to back out,' I tell him. 'Look at the revenue forecasts for the wedding idea compared to what we're achieving now with Mercury. If Lorenzo keeps up this game for any length of time, we'll need the island to prop up the travel club. It's a really sound investment, Charlie, and one that we're going to be really good at. Let's take that bank loan and make a real go of this.'

Charlie leans over the table and practically strangles me with his hug.

'Have I ever told you just how much I love you?' he declares, planting a big kiss on my cheek. 'After me, you are the luckiest man in the world,' he tells Michael.

I look quickly at Michael to try and read his thoughts. He's just nodding. And blushing.

CHAPTER SIXTEEN: SWEET DREAMS
(ARE MADE OF THIS)

I think I read that three of the top ten most stressful things you can do are: start a business, start a relationship and move house. Well, expanding a business, defeating a competitor and rescuing a relationship while trying to move house must also count. Death is also on that list and there is a danger I might murder my mother and best friend right now for reasons I will come to shortly. I get the keys to my new apartment soon and with everything that's been going on, I completely forgot about it until a letter from the solicitors arrived to formalize the completion date. We've also redrafted the second-stage bid with all our new ideas and informed the bank that we're through to the next stage. Having done all I can for Mercury, I'm looking forward to a day focusing on my new house. It's a nice distraction and also a perfect way to show Michael that he's part of my future. We're still slightly tender around each other but I'm really trying.

'I'm going to look for some new furniture,' I tell him. 'Would you like to come and help me pick out a sofa? After all, you'll be sitting on it as much as I will.'

That last bit was so obviously added to make a point, but he laughs and tells me he'd be delighted to.

'Unless you'd rather take Patty,' he adds.

I most definitely would not rather take Patty right now. She's unemployed again after a sampling stand-off with my mum. As if I don't have enough on my plate. In the middle of this week, I found two very unwelcome visitors hammering on the door just as I'd filled the bath and was about to spend the evening relaxing.

'This woman is an absolute nightmare,' said Patty as she barged through my door with my mother hot on her heels. 'She got me fired.'

'I had a right to, you were doing it all wrong and besides, I got you that job in the first place,' replied Mum.

I thought longingly about the hot, scented bubbly water upstairs knowing that I'd be waving it goodbye in a few hours as it flowed down the plughole, flat and cold.

'You didn't get me the job. You just suggested it. I got it for myself by absolutely nailing the interview,' continued Patty. 'They probably recognized my natural ability to engage the public and my love of food.'

'They could hardly miss that,' sniped Mum. I scolded her with a big frown.

'So I started today and there was a brand new summer puddings range. I had to ensure everyone got the chance to taste them,' explained Patty, 'but that was near impossible because SOMEONE went up and down the aisle at least three times until she'd finished the plateful all by herself.'

'There was plenty left,' protested Mum.

'Only because I kept some hidden until you'd gone.'

'I knew you'd done that!' said Mum. 'I watched you from behind the crumpet aisle. I saw you'd got some underneath the counter. I thought you were taking them home.'

'That still didn't give you any right to hijack my trolley and yell out to everyone I had a hidden stash.'

'They had a right to know,' Mum said.

'She caused a riot,' continued Patty. 'Then, no sooner had we got the summer puddings sorted, she starts telling the customers that I'm doing it all wrong.'

'She did soup in the morning,' Mum told me, horrified. 'I mean everyone knows soup is for lunchtimes or evenings when busy professionals are passing through.'

'I can sample things when I like,' replied Patty, 'and at least I knew you wouldn't be stealing all the soup or the beer.'

'You see?' said Mum. 'She's sampling things I don't like just to annoy me.'

I had no idea how on earth I was ever going to arbitrate an amicable settlement here. Patty had entered Mum's sacred domain and I couldn't see it ending well.

'Then there was the Irish Cream,' Patty says. 'Were you aware that for most of the morning your mother props up the sampling trolley, downing little cup after little cup of booze?'

'You can't talk,' said Mum, and I had to agree on that one. 'You're not supposed to drink the samples and I saw you from behind the teacakes.'

'Did you spend your entire day hiding in the bread aisle spying on Patty?' I asked. 'Peering through the Krispy Kreme iced rings like a masked superhero.'

'This is serious.' Mum frowned. 'Mornings are biscuits, cakes and cocktails or drinks for ladies. That's how it should be and demonstrators shouldn't scoff everything.'

'She complained about me,' Patty protested. 'And now, thanks to her, it's not my job anymore. I've been asked not to go in again.'

'Mum,' I sighed.

She struggled to find a look that says triumphant and apologetic at the same time. I told Patty how sorry I was but Mum just left the house murmuring that she was right and Patty was wrong. I felt guilt and despair that this didn't work out for my friend.

'I'm sure she didn't mean it to end this way,' I told Patty. 'She's stubborn but wouldn't do anyone any real harm.'

'Don't worry about it,' she said at the time. 'I've got another interview next week. But I'm free at the weekend if you fancy doing something?'

'I'm busy,' I replied too quickly, 'with Michael.'

So it's a bloody good job he said yes to this, and no, I certainly don't want to go sofa shopping with Patty.

It's Sunday and Michael's picked me up. I'm really looking forward to having somewhere of my own to come back to each evening. I've lived in other people's houses for nearly eighteen months now and whereas I wasn't ready to settle anywhere when my divorce first happened, I now know who I am and how I want to live. I have a vision of the type of furniture I want to buy. When I was married there was always a compromise. I love the overstuffed soft fabric sofas that swallow you up and hug you when you lie on them — my ex liked the more sensible firm-seated stain-proof leather. Of course we always went with his choice as it's hard to argue against practicality. At least I managed to persuade him to go for tan leather rather than the black he wanted. What is it about men and black leather? As we drive along, I drop a few hints that this will definitely not be on my shopping list.

We drive out to a rather fancy furniture emporium on the borders of Cheshire. I am determined that I will not shop anywhere with one of those perpetual half-price sales. The more people protest that I'm getting a bargain, the more I'm sure that I'm definitely not. Michael has washed the car and we've both dressed up a little more than we'd normally do for a shopping trip.

'I thought we could go out to lunch afterwards,' he tells me. 'There's a pub not far away with a good reputation.'

I smile at him — he's taken the hand I offered in apology and lightly embraced it. I positively skip out of the car when we pull up outside the store and, taking Michael's arm, I walk tall ready to design my future home. After all, it will be the place the photographers will come when we win International Business of the Year for our Formentera venture. Perhaps Michael will be in that picture, too.

The store is huge and as much as I love shopping, I can't imagine what it must be like for the assistants in furniture shops. For many years they used hard-sell techniques so we customers avoided their advances like a fox running from the hounds. Nowadays they're keen to tell us that they won't hassle us but they're there when they need us. If no one needs them, they hang around not even allowed to sit down on the sofas. I hate it when people come into our shop and say they're 'just looking'. I can usually tell what type of holiday they need and if they'd just let me help I could have them happy and on the way to their perfect destination. If they don't ask, they'll probably end up arguing and settling for something fairly average. I determine to keep the assistants busy today and ask for lots of help. We make our way through the dining section into living rooms.

'When I was a kid,' says Michael out of nowhere, 'I dreamt of being locked in a big department store overnight — especially at Christmas. I was going to hide in one of the wardrobes until closing time and then I'd come out. I'd get biscuits and chocolates from the food department, build a big Scalextric from the toy department and then fall asleep in a king-sized bed. If we ever walked through the furniture department, I'd be on the lookout for the perfect wardrobe.'

'Sounds like a film script — *Adventures in Macy's* — or something like that. I need a wardrobe. We'll go up after sofas and see if there's one big enough for you.'

'It wouldn't work here — they don't sell Scalextric.'

We reach the sofas and I spot an assistant deciding whether or not to come over and talk to us. I smile at him and approach him directly.

'Could we have some help, please?'

The way his face lights up, I could have just told him he'd won the lottery. I explain the new duplex in the converted mansion house, describing the high ceilings and big windows.

'I want something that makes you sigh with delight every time you sit on it.'

'And it has to be wine proof I'm guessing,' he adds, showing remarkable intuition. After all, he's only just met me.

I protest that I'm as sober as a judge (honestly) then follow him past the leather into the velvet section. I stroke the wonderful fabric, almost purring with delight. This is exactly what I'm looking for. My ex would never have allowed this in the house. The assistant tells me I can have any design in this fabric but suggests a very plush corner unit.

'This needs a large room to do it justice,' he says, 'but by the sounds of it, that's exactly what you have.'

I think I do, but fortunately the ever-practical Michael has brought the room dimensions with him. He checks them and tells me I certainly do have the space for it. I think I've actually started salivating over this sofa imagining Michael lying down one side and me on the other with my head in his lap. As if reading my mind he takes one side and puts his feet up, patting the space beside him. I look at the assistant briefly and he tells me to go for it. I take my side and lie back. I kick off my shoes and let out a relaxed sigh — I guess this is the one then. Still sitting on the sofa we pick up the swatch book and flick through the colours. There are lots of pale colours verging on neutral and although I envisaged a pale minimalist look for the new place, there are some beautiful shades here. Bold colours for a brave new start. There's a gorgeous teal that takes my eye — it would be so different and when the photographers do come round, the teal will complement my chestnut hair perfectly. I can't admit to the guys that I'm choosing a sofa colour to match my hair though, can I?

'That's the one,' Michael suddenly says. 'Opulent, indulgent and rather sexy. Like someone we know.'

He's picked a deep damson which is all of those things. I love it and I'm all a-flutter with the added flattery. I nod in agreement — it is beautiful.

'It would also probably hide the wine stains better than the teal,' adds the assistant.

Sold to the lady with no shoes on.

Having made the first decision rather easily, we have a wander around the rest of the store. We have to find that wardrobe after all. I don't see anything I like but Michael still indulges me by getting into a couple, trying them out for size while pretending to be checking the build quality. He peeks out of one and waves me over.

'You could fit in this one, too,' he whispers. 'They'll never find us.'

I drag him out telling him I want the lunch he's promised me. We walk through the rest of the store arm in arm passing the bed and mattress department. Michael pauses, looking at the signage that tells us that a mattress should be replaced every eight years.

'I should think about doing that,' he says. 'I can't think when mine was last replaced, certainly more than eight years ago. My back's been aching of late.'

'Ugh, then you definitely need to buy a new one,' I tell him, in truth thinking more about him sharing it with his ex-wife than the state of his spinal health. 'I insist.'

He sits on the edge of a few. 'Too soft,' he says, then, 'far too hard.'

Finally, just like Goldilocks, he finds one that's just right. He lies back.

'I like this one. It really supports your back without being rock hard. Come and try.'

I join him bouncing on the edge and then lying down. I say, 'Yep, you'd get a good night's sleep on this but I already have a bed in storage.'

'Michael, how lovely to see you.' A high-pitched voice causes us both to bolt upright like naughty school kids caught having a snog. A glamorous-looking woman — probably older than me but working hard not to show it — is smiling at us, or more likely, him. Her lipstick colour matches her nails and it's a very flattering colour but I imagine she won't be happy when she looks in the mirror and finds it across her teeth too. She looks me up and down.

'And moving on too, I'm so pleased for you.'

She tilts her head sympathetically then moves away, whispering to her friend who throws a look back at us.

'Who and what was that?' I ask, getting up. Michael just shakes his head and promises to tell me when we get to the pub.

The car journey is slightly awkward as I'm wondering whether she was an old flame or maybe even a fairly recent one. As much as I try not to ruin the fabulous morning we've had, I can't think of any other topic of conversation, so sit quietly gazing out of the window. Fortunately, the pub isn't far away and within twenty minutes we're there and seated. Michael nurses his ginger ale while I take a sip of sauvignon blanc and wait for him to start.

'Sarah wasn't the first who thought that a widower would be a good target,' he says without looking up at me. 'She was one of the "casserole crowd" when Jenny died. Neighbours I'd never even met suddenly emerged bringing pots of stew and trays of lasagne telling me I had to eat.'

'I didn't bring you any food.'

'Thank heavens for that.' He laughs and I pretend to be hurt. 'It sounds really ungrateful but I didn't want them there. They all came armed with a bit of homespun advice too — honestly, I couldn't escape from it. There was always someone or other telling me "you have to move on" or "Jenny wouldn't want to see you starving yourself". How the hell did they know what she'd have wanted? Christine there was one of the worst. She also used to do a bit of tidying up and I'm ashamed to say I just let her. It was far easier than arguing.'

He swirls his ginger ale like a whisky and looks up at me for the first time in his confession. 'Then one night, I was just settling down to watch the news and the doorbell goes. It was Christine with a bottle of wine in one hand and a beef casserole in the other. She was looking all made-up and I just presumed she'd been out somewhere.'

'Oh you poor naïve man,' I say, knowing what's coming next.

'I remember feeling obliged to invite her in and the smell of her perfume as she walked past me into the house. It was so strong I think I choked on it.

'I put out some glasses and cutlery then poured us each a glass. She knew where Jenny kept the crockery, so I assumed she would be serving the food and left her to it. To be honest, I just wanted the meal over with as soon as possible. She took a while, so I went into the kitchen to see where the food was and there was something different about her. It took me a while but then I realized she'd let her hair down and was doing all that swishy stuff with it. She walked over to me and took a glass of wine. I didn't know what to do, so I picked up mine and took a huge mouthful. She stroked my hand and told me we'd have the beef afterwards, when I'd worked up an appetite.'

I snort my wine. This is the worst seduction scene I've ever heard and I wasn't even involved.

'A bonk for a bourguignon,' I say, channelling Patty. 'It seems a fair deal to me.'

'It wasn't funny at the time.' Michael laughs. 'I felt this panic rising in me. I couldn't think how I was going to get out of it. I didn't want to hurt her feelings but there was no way at all I was attracted to her. I told her it was too soon, I wasn't ready to move on. After that I became referred to as *"Poor Michael, you know — the one whose wife died"*.'

The food arrives and we both focus our attentions on dividing out the condiments: tartare sauce for his fish cakes and a French dressing for my salad. We sit quietly and I wonder why he's told me all of this now. He could have just said she was a neighbour.

'So I know what it feels like to be rushed into something when you're not completely sure,' he adds quietly, looking directly at me. 'Even if we've taken some time to get where we are, I will wait for you.'

I stop eating and take both his hands across the table. 'Is that what you think — that I'm not sure?'

'I can't tell. I did try to ask if you wanted me to stay the night but even I knew it was a clumsy effort. I knew I'd made a mess of it.'

'No, you didn't,' I tell him. 'I panicked. And this may sound stupid but it's been a while for me. Plus I'm not really that comfortable being at Patty's, or staying at yours with all the memories it holds — especially the bed.'

Michael shakes his head and grips my hands tighter.

'Is that why you want me to get a new mattress?'

I nod, grimacing.

'We're as bad as each other.' He sighs. 'If I have to change every stick of furniture in the house to make you feel comfortable then I will and we'll start today going back to that shop and getting a new bed to go with the new mattress.'

I feel a surge of affection and admiration for this man and the honesty flowing from him.

'Thank you,' I say as he lifts my hands one at a time and kisses them gently. 'I've been really nervous.'

'Well it's been a while for me too,' he says. 'So I might have forgotten how to do it anyway.'

I giggle. 'Well, I suppose we'll find out when I get this new flat, won't we.'

He clinks his glass against mine. 'Roll on removal day.'

CHAPTER SEVENTEEN: PICTURES OF YOU

When Josie called Patty to see if she knew anyone who understood live streaming or digital channels, it set off a chain reaction. Patty called Frankie, her former agent. He was delighted to hear from her and asked if she wanted an audition for a home-shopping channel. The company producing the show would also be able to advise us on the live wedding channel if we won the bid for the island. And so we find ourselves with an appointment to talk about our idea.

After work Charlie, Josie and I take the tram down to MediaCity in Salford Quays and we'll meet Patty there. Like many old industrial areas, it has been transformed of late and now houses internet and TV production companies. Instead of shipyards and canals ferrying goods to all parts of the country we have courtyards selling frappuccinos, and airwaves ferrying news and entertainment. I guess it's our own version of Silicon Valley and it has a real energy and buzz. I live only a couple of miles from this place but it's a different universe. The huge glass-fronted buildings that house the main TV channels are like spaceships compared to the red brick Victoriana of the rest of the city.

The BBC moved here a few years ago and I watch as a group of schoolchildren line up for a tour of the studios.

They enter the building then nervously stop in their tracks — there's a real live Dalek from the kid's show *Doctor Who* in the foyer and he's programmed to say 'Exterminate' whenever anyone walks by. I bet they're going to behave for the tour guide now. It's just a delight to watch.

We check the address we've been given and move away from the docks. The production company we're meeting aren't in one of these glossy glass-fronted buildings looking out onto the river but are in an old warehouse behind all the glitz. The director of the production company comes into the reception to greet us. We're meeting him before Patty does her screen test. Completely at home in this trendy otherworld, he looks just like the guy I saw waiting outside the bank manager's office. I suddenly feel very suburban and yet I did try to dress for the occasion. How come two people can wear black jeans and a T-shirt yet one of them looks trendy and the other looks as if she's just stepped out of M&S? Probably because I have.

Josie looks very at home as we follow his lead into the studio. I have to say I'm curious to see inside this mysterious world and am glad that we go into a proper studio for the conversation and not just an office. It's a tiny area surrounded with thick black curtains and there's a podium (for the presenter presumably) on one side and a kitchen island at the other. A TV camera stands at the front of the space, so presumably it can swivel one way if they're filming a cookery programme and the other way if it's a quiz show. When you watch this you think it's a huge space but it's really no bigger than our shop. We're shown to seats behind the camera — just where a studio audience would be. All around us people busy themselves adjusting lights and cables, each of them knowing their role instinctively.

'So this was one idea,' says the director. 'It's a full show about the wedding. It's a couple of hours showing the journey up to the big day. We'll have a presenter interviewing the couple about how they met, who proposed and how — the whole before thing. Then we'll move on to the preparations, choosing the outfits, cake, rings and what they saw in Formentera. Why they wanted to get married there. We have a bit about the tension leading up to the big day, maybe rings don't fit, bridesmaid gets pregnant or flights delayed — we'll find something. Finally we're there, it's the big day, time to walk down the aisle. We'll show some of the preparation on the island and then the presenter tells everyone to take their seats, we're about to cross live to the ceremony. Cue the love-birds walking down the aisle.'

He stops and we look at each other slightly overwhelmed.

'It's a lot bigger than I'd imagined,' I say.

'It seems that way but the great thing is very little of the filming takes place overseas,' he tells us. 'We get a lot of content before the wedding and do the edits way in advance.'

'And how would we film the Formentera piece?'

'It's really easy and most phones have good video cameras these days. If we needed to I'd find someone local and train them up.'

He seems to think everything is feasible, so we promise to get back to him if we do win the bid. I guess Patty is up next. I wonder whether she's here yet?

'Yoo hoo, everyone!' — and suddenly I can answer my own question.

'Blimey, this is all a lot smaller than it looks on TV isn't it,' I hear her say to someone without a hint of nervousness. Then my dearest friend appears before us.

'What on earth have you done to your face?' I ask.

She looks like a Native American. There are white stripes down her nose, her cheeks and across her forehead.

'Are there cowboys chasing you?' I ask.

'Ooh, I hope so,' she says, not taking offence at all. 'This, my dear ignorant friend is . . .'

'Contouring,' finishes Josie. 'Here let me blend it a bit for you.'

Josie starts to rub the edges of the stripes, giving Patty a slightly more normal appearance. I've obviously heard of contouring, the art of giving yourself cheekbones, but had no idea how it was done. Clearly Patty hasn't either but has been educating herself on the art via YouTube videos.

'As I haven't had the chance to lose the ten pounds this camera is about to put on,' says Patty, 'I thought I'd better create an optical illusion.'

She takes off her coat and gives us a swirl. She's wearing a lovely shift dress with black panels down the side.

'Contouring and bodycon,' admires Josie. 'Girl, you're pulling out all the tricks.'

Patty smiles appreciatively as the studio team come out onto the floor. The director greets Patty very professionally and shows her where she has to stand. Then he attaches a microphone and asks for a camera check. He peers into a little screen beside the camera. Looking over his shoulder I can see the lighting has turned Patty's odd make-up into a more defined face she actually looks good. The director asks for a sound check, so Patty stretches her mouth and starts singing the tongue twisters she always did before a show to loosen her up. She starts with *Peter Piper picked a peck of pickled peppers* then adds one of her very own making, *Red Rioja, white Rioja and a bowl of olives*. She has us giggling but we're given a stern look so we stop. We can't help ourselves, it's all ridiculously exciting. The director seems satisfied with the sound so moves behind the camera with us. He then utters the words I have always wanted to hear in real life, 'Lights, camera and . . . action.'

They've given Patty a bag of flour and she has to pretend it's the home-shopping product of the day. She has to extol the virtues of it but also has to ask an imaginary co-presenter lots of really daft questions.

'How perfect do you think a top-of-the-range juicer would make your mornings?'

To her credit, Patty manages to ask all the questions as if there is someone there and as if they've told her something really interesting. It's a bit wooden but it is her first time.

The director suddenly yells, 'Cut', then gives a round of applause as a studio audience would and we follow his lead.

'Word perfect,' he says, 'but could we inject a bit of you into it? Roll.'

Patty does at least ten takes of this and is getting quite hoarse by the end so the director calls a break, or rather he tells everyone to 'take five', which again I find exciting — they really do say these things then. Patty is offered some water, which she grimaces at.

'Is there any food?' she asks and the slender young production assistant who looks as if he survives on espressos scurries around trying to find something.

'There's a full Farm Kitchen hamper out back,' instructs the director and it appears a few minutes later.

Patty forages through it pulling out a range of gorgeous foods: cheeses, hams, fruitcake and whisky. She finds something she can eat easily and opens a packet of biscuits. While she's distracted the production assistant takes the packet and offers us one, too. Oh my word, they are crumbly, buttery, spicy, lovely, and Patty obviously thinks so, too.

'Oh, these truly are divine,' she declares, her face expressing every crumb of pleasure. 'How on earth do they make them taste this good?'

'You should try the rest,' says the director. 'Can someone make Patty a plate of the other goodies, please?'

The assistant plates up samples from the rest of the hamper and lays them out on the kitchen island. Patty needs no invitation to go over and start tasting each one. My mother will die of envy when I tell her this tale. She'll declare that if Patty got all this free after denying her a couple of morsels in the shops, then there's no justice in the world. I can't wait to taunt her with it.

'Patty, could you tell us what you think of each dish, please,' says the director, 'in your own words. Pretend they're options for the wedding buffet.'

She picks up the cheese and chutney, perfectly arranged on a little oatcake then, taking a mouthful, her eyes roll heavenwards. 'Now I have just come back from a luxury cruise ship,' she says with her mouth only partly free of food. 'And they serve delicacies from all over the world: French Brie, Italian Carboncino — no I'd never heard of it either — but this, well this beats them all. Is it British?'

She holds up the wrapping to read it. 'Yes, it is,' she declares, 'well there you go. The best cheese I've ever tasted right here on our doorstep.' She takes another bite and continues, 'You know that moment when you're in a restaurant and they serve you something so wonderful you don't ever want it to end? Your other half is making conversation and all you can think is *stop talking, I want to concentrate on this gorgeousness in my mouth*? Well, that's how this tastes. I don't want to be talking to you lot, I want to be by myself with a glass of red and plateful of this and I don't want to be disturbed all evening — not even by all of the Hemsworth brothers inviting me to a party.'

'Brilliant,' says the director. 'Now could you try the fruit cake?'

Patty reluctantly pauses in her labour of love and looks at the cake.

'I have to confess,' she says, 'fruit cake is not my thing. Nevertheless, I'll give this a go.' She takes a bite and her eyebrows rise in pleasant surprise. 'Well, that's not what I expected at all. It's really soft and moist. It's absolutely crammed with fruit and they taste as if they've been soaked in brandy. Now that's the way to get your five a day I can tell you.'

'OK — cut,' calls the director. 'That was great, Patty. I think we have what we need. There's a lounge on the top floor of the building over the road. I'll just do a very quick edit and meet you there.'

His assistant shows us to the lift and presses the button. We head to the very trendy building we're directed to and then to the glass-fronted roof terrace, which must have been built simply to watch the sun setting. Outside, the sky seems enormous above the river. An expanse of fading blues and greens reflect in the magnificent mirrored buildings of the docklands.

We all make ourselves comfortable on plush sofas in an eclectically furnished lounge where a waitress takes our order. I love to people watch and could probably grab a tub of pop-corn and settle in for the night in this bar. Beautiful young things earnestly discuss crucial subjects (or so it appears) and studiously try not to stare when a famous newsreader or televi-sion presenter walks in for their after-work drink. In my youth we'd have the cocktails lined up but this generation sip slowly through slender straws, their mobiles lie at the edge of their fin-gertips and they're checked frequently. At first, you think a few of them are smoking but then you realize they're vaping. No wonder they don't drink much they don't have a hand free.

The director joins us within the hour and sits in the middle, putting his tablet on the table.

'I haven't done any enhancements,' he tells us, probably thinking that will mean something to us, 'just put together the clips.'

He plays the video and Patty's first performance as the bag of flour sales pitch begins.

'I don't look too bad,' says Patty, and we agree she doesn't.

'It's not bad for an amateur,' says the director, risking physical violence for using the 'A' word. After all, as Patty frequently reminds me, she has been paid for her entertain-ment services.

'You follow a script, express yourself and stick to your mark,' continues the director.

Patty grins as if she's just done a handstand, forward roll and got her first gymnastics badge.

'But look at this.' The director plays the hamper footage. It is full-on Patty: her facial expressions, her humour, her stories and her obvious love of food.

'Your personality really comes through when you're talking about something you absolutely love, like food.'

Patty looks at me and we both nod acknowledgement of that fact.

'So I think with the right product,' he continues, 'you might be a natural in front of the camera. When you're allowed to move around and be yourself, you hook your audience straight away.'

'I do.' Patty smiles.

'So I'll be letting Frankie know,' adds the director, 'that I could certainly put you in a few casting reels. I can't promise anything, who they pick isn't up to me, but we'll see how it goes.' With that he shakes our hands and leaves.

Patty screams with delight. 'Can you believe it?' she squeals. 'I'm going to be on national TV.'

I can't, but then again there is much about my best friend's life that leaves me completely incredulous.

CHAPTER EIGHTEEN: YANKEE DOODLE DANDY

'You are never going to believe this,' Patty yells down the phone as I'm opening the door to the shop. 'Frankie rang me up and asked me to do a one-off gig.'

'Wow, first TV and now singing, you're in demand.' I shake off my jacket. It's a very warm day already and I've dressed for comfort rather than the season.

'You'll never guess who for. Are you sitting down?'

I tell her that I am and roll my eyes at Charlie, not knowing quite what to expect next.

'OK then, your friend across the road has just tried to hire me to sing at Launch later this week.'

I am so gobsmacked I can't pull together a response. Patty has to check several times that I'm still on the line. I beckon Charlie over and put the phone on speaker.

'Say that again Patty,' I croak and she does so for Charlie's benefit.

'Why?' he manages to ask.

'Because I'm a born entertainer and worth every penny,' Patty says, missing the point a little.

'No, I mean what would you be singing? Why does he want singers in the store?'

'It's for a promotion, a Fourth of July thing. I was asked to do some American songs like "Chicago", "New York, New York" and "I Left My Heart in San Francisco" — that kind of thing.'

'Tell me you said no,' I plead.

'Of course I did,' huffs Patty. 'I'm no traitor but I thought you'd want to know.'

We thank her and ring off.

'Well, at least we know what he's doing next,' Charlie says looking at the calendar.

It is the Fourth of July in a couple of days and it is a good sales idea. We should have thought of it.

'He'll be able to get other singers, so I doubt the lack of Patty will scupper his plans. What should we do?'

'Get the flags out,' says Charlie. 'We know how to throw a party just as much as he does.'

When Josie comes in, we brief her on the plans we've just discovered and over the coming days we start to deck the shop with red, white and blue bunting. We dig out some road-movie themed music and we gather all our US offers to have ready for customers coming in. Across the road we notice some comings and goings but there doesn't seem to be too much action.

By the time the fourth of July arrives, I start wondering whether he did abandon the idea after all. It doesn't matter now — we've started so we have to forget about Lorenzo and get on with selling these trips. Fortunately there's something in the States for everyone, so whether people want cities, mountains or beaches, we have great trips to show them.

We're mentioning some of the ideas we have to the first customers of the day when suddenly there's a huge noise outside. We all rush to the window to see that while we've been working, TV camera crews have set up and are filming a marching band complete with baton-twirling majorettes coming down the road. Everyone has stopped to watch them. Naturally, they come to a halt at Launch and perform some acrobatics before taking a bow and disbanding to a huge round of applause. Then, from out of the store, street vendors stroll out with trays bearing pretzels, which the crowd are more than happy to accept. A couple of people browsing in our shop make embarrassed noises and head over the road.

'He puts on a good show, I'll say that for him,' says Charlie.

'It doesn't mean people will buy a trip,' adds Josie. 'They're not going inside yet.'

It's true, they're not as yet. Lorenzo seems to have created a party on his doorstep but it seems to be staying there at the moment.

'I'm going out there,' says Josie, and she takes some of our offer leaflets and we watch as she walks among the crowds handing out our details and pointing to the shop. She succeeds in getting a few customers into the shop, their hands still full of pretzel.

Of course it doesn't end there. I'm trying to concentrate on our own business but none of us can when we spot Tom Cruise grinning and shaking hands with the good people of Manchester. Of course it's not the real Tom Cruise but a really good lookalike. And he's so good that from here I can hear Charlie's heart beating faster.

'Would it be really bad if I go across and have a selfie with him?' he pleads, both of us knowing it would be awful but that he'll end up doing it anyway. I shrug and he heads out leaving me alone in the shop.

Tom Cruise is joined by Elvis, Lady Gaga and Donald Trump — who seems to be getting the most requests for selfies. Then the Rat Pack turn up and start crooning away. *This was a much better option than Patty*, I think rather disloyally.

'Are you doing these offers to America, too?' asks a customer who's battled her way into the shop.

I tell her that we are, that we can match any offer and we can do it in a more sedate setting.

'That's a relief,' says the customer. 'It's all good fun over there but you can't get through the crowds. It's nice that you're so quiet.'

I smile in that awkward way you do when you get a backhanded compliment. It's the equivalent of the mean girls at school saying 'You're so lucky you're not popular — I just get no time to myself.' Although I know this customer doesn't mean any offence to us at all.

'Sit yourself down and we'll get your trip arranged, calmly and quietly,' I reassure her.

We start to discuss what she's looking for and as I only have one customer in the store I can focus on her needs completely. I feel like Nero fiddling while Rome burns but I can now understand why he just wanted to keep out of the way.

'Are you offering the free insurance?' asks the customer, before explaining that today Lorenzo is giving free travel insurance on all US bookings. I try my best not to sigh with despair.

'Do you need insurance?' I ask her and am relieved when she tells me she doesn't. I promise to try and get her a room upgrade instead and she leaves happy — and we've made our only booking of the day.

I look out at the street party still going on. Charlie has left Tom Cruise and is helping Josie with the leafleting but it seems that although people are taking the flyers from them, they're also putting them in the bin as soon as their backs are turned. Lorenzo is bound to be cutting prices as well as offering this free insurance, so why would they go elsewhere? I wish I knew how he could afford to do all of this. Oh no. My eyes are drawn to a commotion at the edge of the crowd. A circle of people starts to form. They have their phones out and are evidently amused by the scene in front of them. It's a scene which seems to involve Donald Trump and . . . my mother. I have to go and get her. I lock up the shop and rush over to hear her lecturing the orange man in the blond wig.

'You do know you're wrong about this climate thing, don't you?' she's telling him. 'Those poor polar bears have nowhere to rest.'

Mum's knowledge of global warming comes pretty much exclusively from BBC documentaries, so I'm guessing the lecture will focus on animals.

'And you lot eat too many of those burgers. They're very bad for the planet.'

Trump tells her that's nonsense.

'No, it's not,' protests my mum very loudly. 'It's all those cows — belching and trumping like troopers.' She thinks about it and adds, 'Was that named after you? Trumping?'

The Trump actor raises his palms to the sky and says something about 'making trumping great again', which has the crowd in hysterics and my mum indignant. I rush in and pull her away, trying desperately to hide my face.

'I had to tell him,' Mum says as I'm dragging her away.

'He's an actor — you didn't have to tell him anything,' I cry out.

I pull her back towards the shop to see a couple of potential customers pointing at something on our front door, then turning away. Lord knows we can't afford to have people leaving us. When I reach the door I see that someone has put up a huge hand-written notice saying *SHOP CLOSED*. It doesn't take a genius to work out who might have done this, so I take a look across at Launch, and sure enough, Lorenzo is there, pointing an imaginary shotgun in my direction. I rip the notice down as Charlie and Josie return, bringing some of our regulars with them. I can't risk letting Mum out again, so I instruct her to make us some coffees. Once again we settle down to make the most of what's left of our day.

'Keep pedalling, Ange,' I tell myself. 'Keep pedalling.'

CHAPTER NINETEEN: HOME SWEET HOME

On the day that I get the deeds for my new flat, I'm wrapping up my wine glasses (I had to leave them till last, obviously) in pages of the local paper when I spot a photo. Bloody Lorenzo shaking hands with the sales manager of a local football team. He won their fan travel contract this week. We went for that business but he beat us on price, yet again. We offered a fabulous deal that wouldn't have made much money, so I truly don't know how he managed to undercut us. The team did offer us the chance to bid again but we're already losing too much money because of him. I hate losing out to him even when walking away is the best thing to do. At least it's not a premiership team. I'm still annoyed by everything he does but I can't let him get to me today. There has to be at least one thing in my life that Lorenzo can't ruin. The flat will be my sanctuary, the one place he can't get to me. And as there's a video intercom on the door, I can even keep Mum and Patty out should I need to.

Having waited so long for this day, when it finally arrives, it has taken me by surprise. With so much focus on the second-stage island bid and the everyday battles with Launch, the day of the house move managed to sneak up on me and when I read my calendar entry for this week — *NO*

LONGER HOMELESS! — I had to double-check that everything was really in place.

The removals company arrived on time and managed to extradite me from Patty's with ease and so having blown her a final goodbye kiss, I'm actually on my way.

My new place is an apartment in a gorgeous converted mansion house. As I drive through the grounds towards it, the sense of excitement I felt when I first viewed it a few months ago surges through me. I didn't want to have to find a new place to live after the divorce and somehow nothing felt right. I searched so many different types of house, then I found this place and it was perfect. It said 'new start' and was so different from my family home that I knew if I moved here, I'd definitely be starting afresh. Gone are the neat lawns, flowerbeds and hanging baskets that I consistently failed to look after, here I have communal grounds. They're perfect for a deck chair and a Pimm's but they're maintained by a team of professionals, so I don't even need a pair of gloves. Hurrah!

My old family kitchen was a hotchpotch of crockery and cookware collected over the years. The plentiful cupboards were filled with gadgets and recipes I'd never, ever get round to attempting. Nonetheless, I'd held on to them convinced that one day I would become Manchester's answer to Nigella. Of course it was never going happen, so they were one of the first things to be thrown away in the clear-out. The only gadgets in my new kitchen are a built-in wine cooler and the fanciest of microwaves. This kitchen was built for someone who eats not cooks, and I love it.

I'm just dying to show this place off to someone, so I check the time and then Skype Zoe who will just be starting her day. I hold the tablet up and scan the room to show her.

'It's fabulous. Honestly, Mum, that kitchen is so you, absolutely not designed for cooking. Now show me the rest.'

Delighted that she's as excited as I am, I take my tablet into the granite bathroom.

'Wow,' says Zoe, 'a wet room. It's stunning.'

'Your gran is horrified by the idea,' I tell her. 'She kept yelling "but there's no curtain, it's just not right". I had to promise to lock the door every time I'm in.'

We laugh and I walk us into my new huge bedroom, which overlooks the grounds and makes me feel like the lady of the manor.

'Now this room just cries out for a four-poster,' says Zoe.

I've brought my own bed out of storage as I bought it a year ago, but maybe Zoe's right and I should just abandon it and get a four-poster.

I put that idea on my mental to-consider list and move on to the spare room.

'And this would be your room for when you come to stay. Obviously I'll have moved the boxes by then, so there'll be plenty of room for you and James.'

'It looks fabulous, Mum,' says Zoe, 'it really does. You so deserve it and I can't wait to visit.'

It warms me to hear her say that. She was very upset when the family house sold and although she's making her own way now, I want her to feel that she always has a home with me. I haven't told her this yet but I did keep all of her teddy bears from the old house, so when she does come to visit she'll find them lined up on the bed like they always were. She'll probably die with embarrassment.

After we've said goodbye, I sink down into my new sofa — delivered bang on time — and silently scream with excitement. I'm finally here! This move feels like the end of one journey and the beginning of another and I have to mark this occasion appropriately. I head back into the spare room and start digging through the boxes stacked up there. Eventually I find what I'm looking for: the cut-glass trophy Mercury won for the People's Champion Award. I take it out, give it a quick wipe with my sleeve then place it right at the centre of my mantelpiece. I sit back and look at it. Less than six months ago we were at the top of our game — getting rave customer reviews and selling out every trip we created.

I dreamed of winning that award and then bringing it back to a place of my own. I've achieved both now and am newly filled with resolve. That man won't take our customers from us — Charlie and I have worked too hard to let that happen.

Having taken this Friday off, I have the whole day to myself and spend the next two hours unpacking, cleaning and making my new place a home. When I've done as much as I can, I realize my stomach is rumbling. It's nearly eight o'clock and I think I deserve a break. I have a shower in my new fabulous wet room using the gorgeous new toiletries bought especially for tonight. There will be no bargain-bucket shower gels in this place — colour co-ordinated Molton Brown body washes and lotions only. Feeling soft and silky, I put on a new kimono and do a twirl. I look the part. In my mind, I'm the poster girl for go-getting independent women and I start belting out the only words I can remember to 'I'm Every Woman' (which is effectively the chorus). I uncork a bottle of sauvignon blanc and search for a takeaway menu on my phone. Just then the door intercom buzzes and I jump before I realize what it is. My first visitor.

I pick up the receiver and see Michael waiting by the front door. I take a deep breath. At least I look fabulous. I buzz him in and wait nervously as he finds his way up. His hands are full with flowers, champagne and, knowing the route to my heart, a takeaway of Thai green curry and sticky rice.

'Thought you might like a housewarming meal,' he says. 'You look amazing.'

'Thank you,' I say, kissing him. 'A tall, handsome man as my first visitor, isn't that good luck?'

'Only at New Year I think but a new start probably counts. You smell gorgeous too.'

I lead him into the kitchen and while he's opening the champagne, I put the cork back into the wine I've just opened (*aah — that's why people have bottle-stoppers, for when a better bottle comes along*). He hands me a flute, which I sip flirtatiously and he drinks his rather too quickly. He looks like an anxious puppy dog about to get a juicy bone. If he hasn't got one already.

'Shall we start with the guided tour?' I ask. He just nods and tops up the drinks.

We take our champagne glasses and I start by leading him to the window, pointing out the extent of the grounds. Michael politely asks a whole range of questions I have no chance of answering. I promise to introduce him to the gardener when I meet him. We then move through each room on the ground floor with me demonstrating all my new gadgets and him murmuring his approval. The tension is building. My room is on the mezzanine level, up a small flight of stairs, and as I lead him up, my heart starts to race with expectation. I replay the day in the furniture shop when we said all we were waiting for was for me to have my own place. Well, I'm here now.

We finally enter the bedroom and I try to make light of things. 'And this luxurious space is the boudoir for the lady of the manor,' I say.

'Very fitting.' He sits on the edge of the bed and pats the space beside him. Nervously, I sit down and we clink glasses.

'A beautiful room for a beautiful woman,' he says.

I'm sure he must be able to hear the thudding beat from my chest. My mouth is dry and I don't feel at all ready for the kiss I know is coming my way.

Suddenly, I feel thirteen years old again, getting ready for my first real kiss from Gary Marshall. I didn't want him telling all the boys I had a mouth as dry as a bin of pencil shavings but didn't want him to see me wetting my lips either. I learned the difference between boys and girls at that moment. As I was struggling to make myself more luscious, licking my lips as discreetly as I possibly could, he pulled his sleeve down his arm and dragged it across his mouth before asking, 'Ya ready?'

Not that this scene bears any resemblance to my old schooldays. Michael is making every effort to create the perfect moment he knows I've been dreaming of. He takes

145

another sip of champagne and I do the same, then, just like a scene from a movie, Michael leans forward, kissing me and simultaneously putting our glasses on the bedside table. He places his hand on the small of my back and gently lowers me down.

CHAPTER TWENTY: LOVE POTION NO. 9

Come Sunday morning, the buzzer gives me the fright of my life yet again. It's been two days and I'm still not used to it. Although that may be because I seem to have a set of friends and family who think they need to press it for as long and as hard as they can to get my attention. I run over to the intercom.

'OK, OK, I'm coming, you can stop buzzing.'

Patty's face stares into the camera, bearing a daft smile. At least she doesn't have her eyeball pressed up against the camera like Mum did when she visited yesterday. She thought it might have iris recognition like on *Mission Impossible*.

'But even if it did, I'd have to programme it to recognize you and you know I haven't done that,' I told her.

'If it's as clever as they look on the films,' she replied, 'then it'll know I'm your mum. You've always had my eyes.'

Obviously I didn't argue the case further.

Patty reaches the door, armed with flowers, chocolates and prosecco. Everything a girl could possibly want. If it doesn't work out with Michael, I should seriously consider dating this woman — it would probably work now we're not living together.

'Is the coast clear?' she asks as she peers into the living room. 'Ooh, this is very nice, Ange. Very, very nice.'

I hold up two flutes and the bottle she's brought.

'Too early?'

'Not if we call it an early brunch.'

'Isn't that just breakfast?'

'Whatever.'

I pour a couple of glasses and hand one to her.

'Cheers,' says Patty, 'to you and your fabulous new love shack.'

I shake my head but clink anyway. I know what she's here to ask but I'm not going down that route until I have to. We sip our drinks quietly for a moment.

'By the way, I didn't get that shopping channel thing,' she says, breaking the silence, her face betraying nothing at all.

'Oh, I'm sorry. What happened?'

'Same old. They went for a young skinny bird and an old chubby bloke. Apparently food doesn't sell if the presenters are the other way around.'

'After all that contouring too,' I muse. 'Do you think there'll be any other opportunities? They seemed quite keen on you.'

'Between the lines, they basically told me if I wanted to be on TV, I'd need to diet.'

'And are you prepared to?' I ask as she refills the glasses and opens my chocolates.

'Nah. If diets were any good, they'd all say the same thing and there'd only be one of them, but they're all completely different and confusing. For example, if you want bacon for breakfast then go on the Atkins diet because you can't have it on the whole foods one. Then you need to switch to the F-Plan at lunchtime so you have a big jacket potato or sandwich, and if you fancy olives, pasta and wine for dinner, then it's time for Mediterranean eating. The perfect plan would be a combination of all three.'

I have to say that makes sense to me. I particularly like the sound of the Mediterranean one. There doesn't seem to be any cooking with that one, either. I know my friend is trying to stay poker-faced about this rejection but the dismay is coming through in her voice.

'Sod 'em,' I say. 'They don't know what they're missing.'

We clink glasses again.

'I do have some good news though. Yesterday I got an offer on the house.'

'Blimey, that was quick — I was hardly out of the door had it even been advertised?'

'No but the agent was all ready to list it and a cash buyer walked through the door. Apparently they were all ready to complete on somewhere else but it fell through, so they wanted somewhere with no chain and where the seller was definitely not going to change their mind. He brought them round at lunch time and early afternoon they made their offer.'

'And you're sure about selling?' I ask. 'You're still happy about living with Jack?'

'Yes, I am. I'm very sure. If it hadn't been right I'd have known when I started clearing out all the old stuff. I couldn't part with any of it before, but this time I could wave it good-bye as a happy memory.'

'That's good.'

'So it's all systems go. Jack won't know what's hit him, me full time.'

'Poor soul. I'll tell Michael to make up his spare room.'

'And you can make up yours for me. Talking of which, can I have a nosey of the rest of the place?'

It's unlike Patty to ask, so I lead her on my now well-rehearsed tour, which naturally ends in my bedroom. She seems to be studying every inch of it. She even lifts up a pillow.

'What are you looking for?'

'Evidence. That he's staying here. You know, PJs under the pillow, a watch on the bedside table. Come on, spill the beans. How did it go? The perfect night? I've stayed out of your way for two days in case you were still in here all loved-up but it's been killing me. So 'fess up and I want details.'

149

She plonks herself on the bed but I lead her back downstairs and straight onto the sofa. I top up our glasses and take a glug. I pause for a moment wondering whether I should make something up but if I can tell anyone, it's Patty.

'It didn't happen. Coitus interruptus, you might say.'

'What happened?'

'Mum and Dad.'

I set the scene for Patty: my lovely shower, body lotion and sexy robe. How Michael came round on Friday evening bearing food but when we started the tour, it kind of got stuck in the bedroom. Things were getting going and then the buzzer went. After the initial shock, we tried to ignore it but it kept going, being pressed harder and harder. Then my phone rang and I could see it was Mum. I apologized to Michael but he just shrugged at the inevitable. We reassembled our clothing and I went to let my parents in.

'They must have realized what they'd interrupted.'

'Who knows, but the moment was over so we just heated up the takeaway and shared it out. Michael showed Mum around the grounds and after about two hours of her asking about every device in the place, they eventually left and insisted on giving Michael a lift home.'

'He didn't stay? Why didn't you make him?'

I just shake my head and will Patty to read my mind so I don't have to say it.

'Oh no,' she guesses. 'It wasn't happening was it? Earlier in the night, even before your mum interrupted?'

Again, I just shake my head and sigh.

'Girl, you have to do something about this,' cries Patty. 'I know he's a patient man — hell he courted you by leaving bloody gnomes on your doorstep — but even he must have a limit. Let me ask you this honestly and I promise I won't judge, do you actually fancy him?'

'Yes,' I cry. 'I do, I really do and believe me, I'd done everything to make the night perfect. I was *willing* my body to relax and enjoy the moment but it just wouldn't. It's like my pilot light's gone out.'

'Ange — I have *never* known you to give up on something that matters to you. Have you looked at that card I gave you?'

The card had turned out to be a discount voucher for a well-known adult shop.

'I can't go in there Patty, it's just not me.'

'You don't have to go in, you can shop online. And whatever you're thinking, it's not just underwear and vibrators: they have supplements you can take. Honestly, Ange, you're not the only woman going through this. It has to be worth a try even you could manage a super-charged vitamin pill.'

'Have you taken them? I thought you and Jack were swinging from the rafters.'

'We might be now but I needed help. It's not easy for women our age. Come on, fire up that tablet.'

I hand it over and she types in the website address. She shows me a picture of some pink pills. Pink oval-shaped pills obviously designed to look like the female equivalent of Viagra.

'See, it says they're herbal.' Patty tries to reassure me. I scroll down and read the ingredients.

'Ground-up oysters and guarana, even you can't object to that. Unless you're thinking of dining on oysters anyway,' she adds, knowing full well that the one thing I cannot bring myself to eat is slimy seafood. These tablets have a four-star review, meaning that other people have at least tried them.

'Can we look at what they say?' I ask.

We click on the reviews and see hundreds of women describing what I'm feeling.

'You could have written that one,' says Patty as we read the first review.

I am a fifty-four-year-old woman who had lost all interest in sex since hitting middle age. I had to do something, as I was worried that my new man would give up on me. I don't normally do this kind of thing but they worked and I am truly grateful.

151

'Then that one definitely has your name on it,' I counter, pointing to another.

I'm fifty-seven years young and have always been irresistible to men. My mind is still willing but my body had started letting me down. Thanks to these supplements, I'm back to being irresistible and now have a twenty-three-year-old toy boy. They may work on less attractive people too.

We have a giggle, imagining what she looks like. There are lots of people saying the same thing.

'Shall we buy some for you?' asks Patty.

'I don't know, Patty, this just isn't me.'

'OK, so in the past few months,' reasons Patty, 'we've both found out that we're not exactly the people we thought we were, haven't we? I'm not a movie star and you're not a femme fatale.'

I never ever thought that of myself and I'm not sure where this is going but I sense there's a bargain about to be made.

'So why don't we make a pact. I will go on a diet to try and get my career on track and you will take these vitamins to see if they help your love life. No one need know.'

I blow out my cheeks. I can't believe I'm about to do this but I nod and with a click it is done.

'I've had them sent to my house, so I'll pop them in when they arrive,' says Patty. 'Now is there anything left in that box of chocolates?'

'What about the diet you're starting?'

'You're still so gullible. If they don't love me as I am that's their problem. You can fill the glass up too while you're at it.'

I fill both glasses to the brim and then drink mine far too quickly and start giggling. I can't quite believe what I've done but I'm more than a little bit excited about it. Now I know what they mean by a placebo effect.

* * *

Two days later and Patty is back bearing a packet in a plain brown envelope. I take it from her and slip her a few notes — the deal is done. She leaves the scene with just a nod.

Back in the flat I open the packet and read the instructions twice over, even the ones in Japanese. I'll invite Michael over in a couple of days and I'll be ready this time.

I'll take the batteries out of that damned intercom for a start.

CHAPTER TWENTY-ONE: GIVE PEACE A CHANCE

The packet instructions advise taking the supplements for a week or so before the night of passion, so I'm doing as I'm told and come Monday, I think they're starting to work even if it is all in my mind. The words of 'Sex Bomb' are on a never-ending loop in my head and I have to say, I had a new kind of glow about me in the bathroom mirror this morning. I only hope I'm not glowing so much that Charlie and Josie guess what I'm now dreaming about constantly. As it turns out, I've no need to worry about that. When I walk into the office, a warm sugary bliss stops me in my tracks. I look around to see the source of this bewitching aroma. Lorenzo is standing in the middle of the room with a big box in his hands while Josie, her arms stretched out either side of her, guards the PC screens as if trying to stop him copying her homework.

'Err, hello,' I say somewhat inadequately.

'How can we help you?' asks Charlie coming back from our kitchen with coffees in his hands.

Lorenzo puts the box down and opens the lid. Inside is a selection of freshly made cakes and pastries.

'Perfect timing then,' he says, indicating the coffees.

Charlie hands Josie and I our drinks. I take my coat off but everything seems to be happening in slow motion at the moment and I don't know what to do. 'Sex Bomb' has screeched to a stop and I feel as if I'm facing the male equivalent of Snow White's stepmother (her stepfather I guess, but I don't think she had one of those). He's holding out his equivalent of a delicious basket of juicy red apples and you know you'll die horribly if you take a bite. Mind you, if I'd been in the story I could have resisted apples — that stepmother should have taken Snow White a bar of Galaxy. Anyway, it just feels wrong. Josie seems to have read my mind as she picks up one of the pastries and sniffs it. I know arsenic smells of almonds from the many murder mysteries I watch, but then again so do almonds and some of these have nut toppings, so I'm not sure what she'll be able to tell with a sniff. Josie puts it down inconclusively.

'They're perfectly safe, I promise.' Lorenzo smiles, picking it up and taking a big comedy-style bite which leaves icing on his nose. He leaves it on trying to get a laugh from one of us. He looks more sinister than comedic, so it doesn't work. It takes Charlie to break our group silence and act professionally.

'Thank you, they look delicious. So what can we do for you?'

Lorenzo sits on the edge of Josie's desk. If she were a cat, her back would be arched and she'd be hissing.

'I want to apologize,' he says, sounding quite genuine. 'I think we've got off on the wrong foot and I wonder if we could start again, be comrades in business.'

Sideways glances pass between the three of us but we say nothing.

'I know I've been a thorn in your side but it's just how I was brought up. When I was a boy growing up in Puglia, I always wanted to be an astronaut and thought when I was an adult I'd be flying in spaceships, travelling around the universe.' He smiles at the memory. 'And when I realized that wasn't going to happen, I still wanted to explore, so I thought I'd open a travel agency. I had a vision of how it would look and I also knew I would call it Launch because it's the closest I'll ever get to that childhood dream.'

I'm not sure why he's telling us any of this but I'm curious to find out more, so I follow Charlie's lead and sit down to hear the rest of this tale. He'd already told us his family were Italian, which explains why Peter hasn't heard of the name. I wonder if he has any contacts in Puglia and can do more digging.

'My dad was a hugely successful businessman and he always encouraged me to follow my dreams, although he didn't think I had it in me to make it as an entrepreneur. He always said I was too soft, that I didn't have the cut-throat competitiveness I'd need. He died before I could show him he was wrong, that I could make it work. I started Launch with the money he left me, so it has to be a success for his sake.'

He pauses and I'm sure this is the part we're supposed to say something so I give it a go. 'Sorry to hear about your dad,' I tell him.

He nods his appreciation. 'Thank you, although actually it's sort of his fault I behaved the way I did. If he'd had a competitor he would have tried to take them out straight away. I wanted to show him I do have what it takes, but it's not the only way to do business and I apologize.'

What can we say now we know it's about a childhood dream and a dead father haunting him from beyond the grave? Even if it's all a bit convenient, he's made the effort to talk to us and perhaps this means we can both get on with competing fairly.

'Apology accepted,' I say, holding out my hand and getting a furious glance from Josie. His story obviously hasn't tugged at her heartstrings at all.

'Puglia?' says Charlie. 'I've been there — it's very beautiful. I have to say you don't sound very Italian, actually I can't place your accent at all.'

'That's not surprising,' Lorenzo says. 'We left Italy when I was very young and with Dad's business we moved around an awful lot, but you might be hearing a bit of Brum.'

'That's it,' declares Charlie. 'I couldn't place it but it's Birmingham.'

'I've got a Brummy friend staying and I just pick up accents so easily.'

I've always had an irrational hatred of people who say this. OK, so he might be telling the truth, but it sounds so phoney. To me it's like saying, 'Oh wow, I'm so cosmopolitan.'

'What's that shopping centre in Birmingham?' coughs Josie, 'Bull . . .'

I throw her a look, despite agreeing with her — it's best for us all to get back to acting professionally, although that doesn't mean being a complete walkover.

'What you've been doing is unfair,' I tell him. 'Even if we were in the wrong not protecting the email addresses, you were wrong to use them. And your discounting is completely unsustainable — surely you know that by now. If we're going to work alongside each other then you have to stop all of this.'

'I will,' he says, placing his hand on heart. '*Prometto* — I promise.'

He offers to help us in any way he can as recompense but we can't think of anything he can do for us.

'Do you want me to look at your technology, see if I can offer any upgrades?' he asks.

We all simultaneously shout 'No' and shake our heads vigorously. Despite this new truce, we're not letting him anywhere near our computers.

'There is one thing,' says Charlie. 'You can tell the newspaper to allow us to start advertising again.'

'I will ring them as soon as I get back to Launch,' says Lorenzo. 'In fact there is only one more week's advertising paid for, so I will give it to you for free as my apology.'

'That's extremely generous,' says Charlie. 'We accept your offer and in this spirit of reconciliation, we'd be happy to do a favour for you.'

I may have offered a hand of friendship but I hadn't been about to offer any favours and Josie looks positively furious with Charlie. Lorenzo pounces on the offer before he gets the chance to rescind it.

'Actually there is,' he says smiling. 'I've got a local news interview at lunchtime and I'd like to show how we're getting on as two local businesses in a tough market. Maybe Josie could be in the interview too, to represent your side of the story.'

'No way,' protests Josie, and I have to say my spidey senses are flashing red, but if this is the gesture that would just mean us all getting back to respectful business, I'm not going to say no. I'll do it myself if I have to.

'I know I've been worst behaved towards you Josie and I'm completely and utterly sorry,' continues Lorenzo. His hands are now cupped in a begging gesture. 'But you're right, I have a lot to learn and it would make me feel so much more confident in front of the cameras.'

'Garbage,' mutters Josie.

'She'd be happy to,' says Charlie, giving her a nudge.

'Thank you so much,' Lorenzo says, walking towards her and taking her hand — well, trying to, because as soon as he does she pulls it away as if she's been burnt, which I guess we all have by this guy. He says his goodbyes and leaves the shop, taking the biggest and creamiest pastry with him as he goes.

Although I think we might all end up like the frog that was stung by the scorpion in a real-life version of Aesop's fable, I can't let Josie see that. I try to reassure her.

'Come on, girl,' I say, 'it won't be all that bad. Just make sure you're interviewed, too, and that you mention Mercury.'

'I can't believe you're letting me do this, never mind forcing me to,' exclaims Josie.

'We can't keep looking over our shoulders,' I say. 'If half an hour's worth of interview means we can get back to business as usual then it'll be worth it.'

'But don't worry,' adds Charlie, 'we still don't trust him. You know what they say — keep your friends close and your enemies closer.'

'Yeah, I'll have a dig around while I'm there,' says Josie, 'try to get some info on how he's doing and what trips he's planning.'

They high-five their pact of espionage and then we all get back to work. The remainder of the pastries now seem rather unsavoury, so they remain untouched. I imagine they'll stay that way unless my mother or Patty decides to pay us a visit.

* * *

The hour of the interview arrives far too quickly and Josie, who has been clock-watching all day, sighs then gets up and is about to head off without making any effort to tidy up.

'I'm not putting slap on for him,' she tells us.

'It's not for him, you're representing us. Now go and have a lovely long lunch afterwards.' I cup her face and apply some lipstick to her petulant pout. She leaves the shop as if we've asked her to walk the plank into shark-infested waters.

The interview will be on the local business lunchtime programme, so we'll have to see it on catch-up as the shop is usually busiest then. Josie doesn't come straight back, which I hope means she's building some useful bridges or enjoying that lunch. Come early afternoon when we're having our coffee break, Charlie and I turn on iPlayer and gather round, curious about what Lorenzo will say. Peter walks into the store just as it's about to start. The story gets a headline mention before Lorenzo even appears, with the presenter telling us that we're about to see an interview with a local business-man who's donating five per cent of his profits to helping young carers go on holiday.

'We all need a break,' says Lorenzo to the camera when the interview starts. 'These young people work incredibly hard and most of it is invisible, I know from caring for my dad.'

Apologies, reconciliation and now holidays for young people? Have I got this guy completely wrong? Is he actually a saint? Charlie puts his fingers down his throat pretending to gag.

I ignore him and continue watching. The interviewer tells him this is such a generous thing to do and asks him how business is going.

'Well, things are always tough in travel, especially for the small players,' replies Lorenzo, 'but I think we've got a pretty unique proposition here.'

He puts his arm out to show the shop, which is filled with bearded hipsters and trendy young women using the iPads and flicking images of the exotic locations onto the screens. The interviewer asks one of the customers what he thinks of Launch.

'Yeah, it's really cool,' says the customer, 'good to see someone actually maxing out the technology that's available but making it so easy you don't need to be a geek to use it.' Lorenzo does that punchy-handshake thing with him and turns back to the camera.

'It's not about the technology though, that just makes the booking process a little bit easier. The unique thing about us is the number of ideas we come up with. We're not just a sand, sea and sangria business — we want to inspire people to travel and have adventures.'

He signals Josie to join him. Her reluctance looks more like nervousness in front of the camera than the distaste we know she feels for him. Charlie and I simultaneously inhale deeply, hoping she gets the chance to mention us.

'And this is the lady who's been coming up with ideas for years,' says Lorenzo. I've gone cold — you know that feeling when you watch a glass that is about to fall to the ground and smash to pieces but you just can't reach it in time? I feel it now.

'And we're delighted she's here,' he concludes before giving her a hug then pushing her gently out of shot. For the brief moment she's on TV, our open-mouthed Josie has been stunned into silence. The interview over, we look at each other puzzled.

'Did that just sound the way I think it did?' I ask the others.

'It certainly did,' Peter says. 'I need to find out a bit more about this guy.'

I call Josie immediately and she answers in tears. 'I'm so sorry, I've messed up again. It sounded as if I worked for him, didn't it?'

I assure her I didn't think that at all — although that's exactly what it did sound like.

'You'd be better off without me cocking things up every time I open my mouth.'

'You didn't get the chance to open your mouth,' I tell her, wishing I were with her and able to give her a big hug. 'Forget the interview, did you find out anything?'

'Well, everyone claiming to be a customer that night was being paid to be there,' she tells me through the sobs. 'Recruited from the bar next door to come and play on the technology for an hour.'

That's reassuring at least, although it was another painful lesson. I don't know what Richard would say about competing with someone who plays dirty but I'm sure he wouldn't let them walk all over him. The time for *Respect* is well and truly over.

'We've all been played,' I tell Josie, 'so the only thing we can do is to try and sleep tonight then be ready for battle tomorrow, because we will win this. I'm more determined than ever.'

'When we win that Formentera bid, we'll be leagues above him. I wish we had it now,' she says.

'We can only fight with the weapons we have,' I tell her, worried that we'll all just give up if we don't win.

After a few more calming words, I tell her to try and relax for the day, then put the phone down. Josie was right: we do need another weapon in our armoury whether we win the bid or not. I need to give my dad a call to ask how he's getting on with the treasure trail.

The phone rings a few times and I picture the debate between Mum and Dad about who's going to answer it. I pray it'll be Dad so I don't have to explain to Mum why I don't want to talk to her this afternoon. My prayers are answered.

'Hi, sweetheart,' he says. 'I've just seen that competitor of yours on the news. What's he up to then? Josie hasn't gone to work for him has she?'

I sigh as this pretty much confirms the impression that many more people will be getting from the interview.

'No she hasn't but he is proving a bit of a nuisance. That's why I'm calling. The treasure trail isn't ready by any chance, is it?'

'It will be by tomorrow,' he assures. 'I can bring it round to the shop if you like? Around closing time?'

I thank him, hopeful that we might have something to save the day.

'Don't worry,' Dad adds, 'I know my Ange and she's invincible.'

If only.

CHAPTER TWENTY-TWO: HUNTING HIGH AND LOW

The next day, the whole gang gather in the shop kitchen after hours to hear the idea and prepare to do battle on behalf of Mercury. The mood we're in, we might as well be wearing camouflage paint. Mum and Michael have come along to add their strength to the platoon.

Mum is in her element fussing around everyone, delighted to have so many people locked in one room. She's raided the clearance shelf of the supermarket and has arrived armed with an enormous mismatched smorgasbord of food tottering on the edge of a sell-by date.

'Microwaveable cottage pie, falafel wrap and cream cake?' I query, picking through the packets as she unloads them.

'You have to eat them to keep your strength up,' Mum asserts. 'And they'll go to waste otherwise.'

'Not if you'd left them for a small army to buy,' argues Dad.

'But they were a bargain and besides, we're an army and an army marches on its stomach.' Mum folds her arms, very satisfied at having found a justification for her purchases. 'Now who wants the cottage pie?'

No one responds, so, probably attempting to be polite, Michael raises his hand sheepishly and Mum pounces.

'See,' she tells Dad, 'that poor man would've been starving if I hadn't picked this up.'

Dad is kept waiting while Mum takes everyone's orders. I hold out my palms to Michael and mouth, '*What have you started?*'

He shrugs and mouths, '*Sorry*' back to me while simultaneously burning his hands on an over-microwaved plastic container. I don't want to delay things anymore by waiting for something to be cooked, so opt for the wrap, which tastes as dry as it looks. Fortunately, there's also reduced-price fresh juice in her spoils — beetroot and carrot — which is surprisingly good. I feel fortified by my oysters and guarana and despite myself am momentarily distracted by the muscles in Michael's arms. Down girl.

When everyone is fed and watered, we congratulate Mum on her efforts in the hope that's enough to finally settle her down so we can listen to Dad's idea without interruption. We pull up our chairs to form a semi-circle and Dad sits at the centre. He looks like the sage ready to address his worried audience. The storyteller waiting to relay insightful tales that will light the way to better days. Although he can't see the effect he's having, his very calm presence has everyone looking relaxed and hopeful. Even Mum is beaming at him.

Dad takes a folder out of his bag and I can see that it's stuffed with pictures torn out of magazines.

'So imagine,' starts Dad, 'a glorious day, the open road and your first clue — *Gather where the trees read by moonlight, at the library in the woods.* You're looking for this.' He selects one of the images from his folder, placing it before us with a great flourish. I'm not sure what I was expecting and I have no idea where it is, but the image is truly magical. It's a simple wooden hut with a grass roof in the midst of a beautiful forest.

'Wow,' says Josie, 'that looks like something out of a fairy story. I imagine I'd have to wear a red cape if I went there.'

'That's a library?' asks Charlie. Dad nods and shows him a picture of the inside filled with shelves and books, a simple wooden table and chairs.

'Where?' I ask. 'It's not New Zealand is it?' It's so quaint I can only imagine it existing in *Lord of the Rings* land or some-such place.

Dad taps the side of his nose, enjoying the response and the suspense being created. He continues. 'After a glorious night in your luxurious hunting lodge, another clue arrives at breakfast: "*Today we visit the Queen and bask in her golden glory.*"'

This time the picture is a photo of a stunning, endless and completely deserted beach bathed in the glow of a glorious sunset.

'Wow — now you're talking my language,' cries Charlie. 'I want to go there already.'

Peter and Michael keep schtum, trying to work out where this trail is taking place. Given that my job is finding these wonderful places for people, it bugs me too that I can't guess where it is. I say as much to Dad.

'Well, that's the point, isn't it?' he replies. 'You might get it with these next ones.'

Unconsciously, we all edge our seats forward for the next clue we all want to win. If we're hooked just looking at the photographs, I can imagine our Mercury customers thoroughly enjoying this although I am wondering if this location is too far away.

'Today is all about the thrill of the drive,' continues Dad. '*Ascend from the sea to the sky and Bealach na Bà.*' The photo is of a crazy winding road with breathtaking hairpin bends, climbs and drops.

'Wow,' Michael exclaims.

Peter is straight on his phone.

'Aha — the photo might give it away. What was that word — Blachna . . . ?'

Dad shakes his head in a good-humoured refusal. He's not giving anything away.

'And so we reach the end of the week,' he says. '*Rest at the final crossroad for Viking Norsemen.*'

The final photograph is a huge white lighthouse standing on a clifftop with crashing waves below.

They're wonderful and I know this will capture the imaginations of our customers. I hug Dad and tell him so.

'So come on then, where is it?' asks Charlie. 'It has to be Scandinavia somewhere, with the Viking reference — or possibly Iceland?'

'Too green,' I reply. 'Canada?'

He's delighted we haven't guessed it and picking up an atlas, he turns to a page marked with all his notes and opens it to a chorus of wows.

'Scotland?' I'm stunned and just a little downbeat. He nods.

'It's a beautiful country,' he says, 'and for a rally, absolutely perfect. We take in the islands of Arran and Islay before going back to the mainland and zig-zagging our way to the highest point in the British Isles.'

I nod enthusiastically, hopefully hiding my disappointment. The clues are brilliant and the photographs look amazing. I'm sure this would be a stunning trip to organize for yourself but I just can't see a holiday to Scotland saving Mercury Travel.

'There are some stunning castles and stately home hotels that guests can stay in along the way,' Dad says. 'I thought maybe you'd have a convoy of classic cars — all different colours — winding their way up Applecross Pass to a big house on a hill. That would look fantastic.'

'Brilliant!' exclaims Peter. 'I know a car rental company that's branching out into luxury rental — classics with heated seats, if you like — I'm sure they'd promote this to their customers.'

'And aren't the islands famous for their whisky?' adds Michael. 'You could organize a tasting for when your travellers get there?'

'Sounds like I need to get onto whisky bloggers too,' says Josie looking fired up.

'You know this would also be perfect for people visiting the UK, so you could definitely promote it overseas, maybe to Americans already here on golf tours,' continues Peter. 'It really does reach out to new customers for you.'

'I was a bit unsure when you said it was in Scotland,' says Charlie. 'I'd expected somewhere more exotic but I actually think this might inspire our customers. It's worth a shot.'

Maybe they're all right. Many of our customers are old romantics at heart and perhaps this idea could really appeal. There are a lot of people out there who love road movies. However, despite everyone's enthusiasm, I'm still not sure this is the saviour of Mercury.

'It's not enough, is it?' asks Dad, reading my mind.

'It's brilliant, Dad, honest. You can see everyone thinks so. But it's just one trip and if we'd invented it before we met Lorenzo, I'd be deliriously happy, but now I can't help thinking he'll steal this too somehow. We keep having all the ideas but he just copies them a week later and then manages to shaft us somehow. Honestly, there were queues of people in his shop today.'

'Well, he's much cheaper than you,' says Mum out of nowhere and we all look at her.

'How do you know?' I ask, praying she hasn't gone and bloody booked something with him although part of me wouldn't be surprised.

'Moira who gives out the samples is back and she was telling me. Her son went in and they gave him thirty per cent off if he booked right there and then.'

'Thirty per cent? That's just not possible — he wouldn't be making any money at all. He was supposed to be stopping all of this heavy discounting, not increasing it.'

Mum shrugs.

'Maybe he's not trying to make money at the moment,' suggests Michael.

'What do you mean?'

Peter picks up the thread. 'Michael's right, he could be trying to put you out of business. It's not a long-term plan but he'll keep undercutting you until you can't continue anymore. Think about all he's done — the vouchers before Launch even opened that you had to match, then all these offers. As soon as he's the last man standing, he'll hike the prices up. I'll bet he's got terms and conditions that say prices could rise at any time.'

'Moira won't be happy with that,' says Mum, ignoring the bit about her only daughter being put out of business.

'What can we do against that type of plan?' I ask in desperation.

'Keep your costs low,' says Michael. 'Seriously, put everything you have into getting business and staying afloat. It's all about being the one who survives. He isn't expecting to have to hold these prices for long.'

'And stick to your guns,' says Dad in a kind of Dunkirk way. 'Get them blogger people talking about you like Josie suggested. Never forget people love Mercury.'

'I've got another marketing idea actually,' declares Josie, rubbing her hands in glee. 'You've inspired me, Mr Shepherd. Best of all, it's low cost and an absolute cracker.'

I'm so pleased to see her fired up again. We all look at her waiting for her to expand on this idea. She taps the side of her nose.

'Secret strategy I'm afraid but you'll soon know all about it.'

'Well, Private Benjamin, deploy Operation Aussie as soon as possible but get back to the barracks as soon as you can,' I say, trying to keep the army metaphor going and doing atrociously. 'If we're about to go to war, we need our weapon of mass distraction.'

'You do realize that was appalling, don't you,' says Charlie, earning a friendly thump.

* * *

The next day, as I walk into the shop, I spot some bright turquoise signposts that I've never seen before, attached to lamp posts. I subconsciously register the first two or three without really taking much notice of what they say. Then I approach another and I have to stop to read what's going on. I sort of expect that they're giving route details for a fun run, but when I get up close, I see this one says, '*Roll up for the mystery tour.*'

Maybe it's a Beatles exhibition, I think to myself. Unlikely in Manchester, though.

Still, I make a mental note — that Beatles track is a good one to use for our treasure trail. As I look down the street towards the shop, I can see that every lamp post and traffic light has one of these turquoise signs. I get closer to the next one which says, '*Need a ticket to ride?*' Another Beatles track about going somewhere. I positively trot along to see what cryptic message is attached to the one after. Whoever created these has come up with a great idea — I must tell the others. The next one reads, '*Don't worry, it's not a galaxy far, far away.*'

I'm stumped. I was sure they were something to do with songs but this one isn't and now I can't guess what the link might be. I can see there are three more signs attached to posts before I get to the shop, so I mentally challenge myself to guess what they're all about before I get to the third one (not that it matters, I know).

"'*Maybe to the moon and back?*'" I read the next one aloud. My heart sinks a little. If it's referencing space travel then this clever campaign looks like the work of Lorenzo and his childhood dream. It's good and unfortunately has caught my attention, so it's bound to work on others. I bet it leads me right down the high street and stops at his door. I plod wearily to the next one, arrow-shaped and pointing directly to the front door of Launch. My disappointment turns to puzzlement then mild dread when I see what's written on this sign, '*Not this one — it's a black hole.*'

And with that I know this has to be the cracker of an idea Josie mentioned. I sneak past Lorenzo's shop and get to the sign outside Mercury: '*You're here! Mercury Travel — light years ahead of the rest.*' I can't help but smile   it is clever but not very sporting. I know I thought we should start playing hardball but I'm not sure I have that in me. I should have taken down that sign insulting Lorenzo. I don't have time, as Josie leaps out to greet me.

'Do you like it?' she asks beaming.

'I love it, it's so clever. It's a treasure trail bringing customers right to our door.'

'And I've used the signs in our online posts,' she goes on to explain. 'A different one appears every hour. I did think of Scottish-themed ones like, "*Will you take the high road or the low road*", but that would have given the game away completely.'

I agree and we both head into the shop eager to see if it works. It does and throughout the morning, I see Josie smiling as she explains the idea to customers calling in. She tells them about the treasure trail idea, but it's quite a difficult sell when we can't reassure customers about where they'll be going. It looks as if we'll have to work a bit harder to get people exploring these wonderful islands. Ironically, we may have sold them quicker if we'd just told customers the destination. I listen to Josie on the phone and the old cogs start whirring. Peter had the right idea: we're going to need to sell this to a group of people. We need to excite a whole gang, maybe a sales team somewhere, about the idea of a competitive treasure trail. I pick up the directory of local businesses, trying to work out who'd have a big sales force and am lost in concentration when a policeman walks into the shop.

'Oh hello there,' I say, sizing him up and wondering if he's a treasure-trail kind of guy. It's a bit like detective work, after all. 'How can I help you?'

'These signs that are up and down the street,' he replies, raising my hopes that we're about to do business. 'Are they yours?'

'They certainly are,' I reply excitedly.

'Well, they're illegal,' says the policeman deadpan. 'You have to take them down unless you can show me your planning permits.'

I look to Josie and she shakes her head.

'I'm sorry,' I tell him, 'we didn't know we needed permission. We'll take them down straight away.'

'And I need to inform you that there will be a fine,' the policeman continues.

'A fine? Why? Can't we just take them down?' I splutter.

'I'm afraid not.' The policeman refers to his notebook although I'm sure that's just for effect and what he's seen cops on TV do. He can't possibly have any notes about us. 'Another business has complained about defamation of reputation. You told people his business was a "black hole" apparently, so he has the right to prosecute the person who actually posted that notice.'

I knew I should have taken that damned sign down. I can't argue, we did it and although it could hardly have damaged much business in the couple of hours it has been up, I'd be annoyed if he'd done this to us.

'We're sorry and we'll apologize to Lorenzo,' I say. 'We meant nothing by it. How much will the fine be?'

'That's not up to me,' says our boy in blue, 'but I do know that the fine is *per* illegal advertisement.'

'You mean we get fined for every piece of turquoise card up there?' panics Josie, and the policeman nods.

Josie and I sit in shocked silence while he takes my details as the business owner and then leaves, warning us to have the advertisements down by midday.

'I'm sorry,' murmurs Josie. 'I can't seem to get anything right these days.'

'Don't worry,' I reassure her, 'we're all feeling the pressure but we'll get over this.'

I'm thinking of our dwindling accounts, needing to stay afloat to be the last man standing and the fine that's about to land on our laps making that much, much more difficult.

CHAPTER TWENTY-THREE: DOWNTOWN

I didn't sleep last night wondering how much this fine is going to be. According to Google it could be anything between one hundred pounds per sign and one thousand, so that wasn't much help. Then there's the defamation and whatever else he can claim against us. Getting dressed I can't even muster up the enthusiasm to fake it with the power dressing. We're working so hard to come up with ideas and our regulars appreciate them but no one can ignore the cut-prices he's giving out. I switch on the radio hoping there'll be something to cheer me up, even a little.

'*This week only at Launch, two thousand miles for two thousand pounds. Business class flights and five-star hotels in the most sought-after long-haul destinations.*'

I plonk myself down at the breakfast bar, head in hands. He's trying to take out the long-haul market now and at those prices, well, he simply has to be subsidising them, maybe with that inheritance he talked about. I wonder how much money his father actually left him. He has to run out soon surely.

I start the walk to work but I really don't know why I'm bothering going in. He seems to enjoy destroying us. Maybe we should cut to the chase now and surrender or maybe we should just move. I doubt he'd still keep attacking us if we simply relocated, if we weren't directly opposite his shop. The thought of taking on anything else overwhelms me, so I give myself a shake as I open the door to the shop and make an effort to smile.

'Morning, campers,' I say with unconvincing breeziness.

Charlie looks worse than I feel as he puts the phone down.

'That was Josie,' he says. 'She's phoned in sick. She sounds awful and thinks she might be off for the whole week.'

'I don't blame her,' I reply, thinking that maybe a few months hibernating in bed could be another solution to our current situation. Not that I think Josie is faking it. I've never known any lurgy manage to defeat Josie but she's had a tough time recently with Lorenzo. When you've been feeling a bit down, illness takes hold more easily. So if she is having a duvet day, then that's fine with me. A cheesy film and a glass of red wine are such good homeopathic cures (I think they'd count in that category) they make you feel happy and when you're happy, cold and flu have no chance. I myself am an expert in this particular field of medicine. If it brings her back to us in fighting mode then she can take as long as she likes.

However, Josie being off only adds to the sense of emptiness in the shop and after I tell Charlie about the radio ad I heard this morning, neither of us can maintain the fake cheeriness we need to sell holidays for long. We need someone like Josie in the office. Even at her lowest, she has a way of connecting with people on social media and customers are always telling us they look forward to her funny posts. Now more than ever we have to keep up the emails and newsletters to show people that we still exist, if nothing else. If we stop talking about our new ideas, customers might think we've given up. We can't really afford to hire anyone and the only people I know who are at a loose end at the moment are Mum and Patty. Both of them have a knack of staying cheery when the rest of the world is down, although obviously neither of them are known for their tact and diplomacy. I go for the least-worst option, the one who can at least use a PC.

'Stand back,' declares my best friend as, forty minutes after my call to her, she nearly takes the doors off their hinges. 'Your fairy godmother has arrived to save your souls and sell holidays.'

That cheers me instantly. If Patty is responsible for saving souls and deciding who gets into heaven then we're probably all going to get there. Her moral compass has always been fairly flexible.

'OK, Godmother, cast your wand over that PC there,' I tell her, pointing to Josie's desk.

Patty salutes me. 'Absolutely, boss. What do you need me to do?'

'With Josie off sick, we've got no one to do all the marketing,' I explain. 'But she had a really unique style, so we need you to be funny.'

'Not a problem for a world-class entertainer like my good self.' She takes up residence at Josie's computer and switches it on, stretching her fingers like a grand master pianist and running them along the keyboard. Charlie watches her.

'So do you know much about social media?' he asks.

'Charlie, what I don't know . . .' she begins, 'I will soon make up. Now how does this machine work?'

She looks up at us and flicks the screen around. A password box flashes in the centre of the screen.

'Damn, I'd forgotten about that,' I say. 'Josie keeps her password top secret since the email issue. Before then it was always something that she'd like to do to Harry Styles, either sh@gStyles or M@rryStyles. They were two of her favourites.'

'Have no fear, I shall apply all my cunning to cracking this password,' she tells us, leaving Charlie and I staring at each other in disbelief. Since when did she become Alan Turing?

'How?' asks Charlie.

'I'm going to call her and ask what it is.'

We leave her to ring Josie and hear laughter bellowing through the office again as Patty calls her an 'Aussie weakling' and threatens to steal her job if she doesn't get back soon. It's good to have some fun in the place again and I bet Patty is already making Josie feel much better. Patty manages to open Josie's account and with instructions being given on speakerphone, starts to work out where the details are to develop all the marketing. The first thing she does is to tell all our customers Josie is off sick, or as she puts it, '*The Aussie has been flawed by a British cold — what a wuss.*' She encourages customers to send Josie get-well messages to try and coax her back and within minutes we're inundated with them. Josie is obviously reading them as she posts a little '*Thank you*' emoji.

'What's this little thing?' Patty asks me and so I explain the concept and show her a few more on the screen.

She studies them with interest and then gets that look on her face, the one that declares a cunning plan is on its way. The one we all dread and love in equal measure.

'Stand back and get ready to sell holidays,' she says, attacking the keyboard using a single finger on each hand.

Despite the fear and anxiety we feel, Charlie and I leave her to it and try to concentrate on our accounts. We have to seriously review things now to stay in the fight. After about an hour, the door starts opening and the phone starts ringing. Customers head straight to Patty's desk.

'Smiley face, plane, snow-capped mountain, love hotel please,' declares one.

'Romantic break to the Alps when you're ready,' Patty shouts to Charlie.

Charlie gets back to the booking screen and invites the smiling customer to sit down.

'Hamburger, saxophone, quaver, sad face,' requests another customer.

'Blues festival Chicago for you, Angie,' Patty yells again.

It feels as if we're in a fish market rather than a travel agents, but what the hell, we've got customers coming in and they're not asking for discounts.

'What's this one?' asks more than one customer.

'Football, horses, wine?' replies Patty shaking her head in mock disbelief. 'Argentina obviously, now sit yourself down over there and that handsome man will sort you out in no time.'

OK, so it's still only a handful of people but they're laughing, smiling and most importantly, booking trips. The shop feels like Mercury again and we've given people something to talk about — we're innovating again. Online they're sharing the emojis with friends and somehow it's easier to say 'yes' to a pleasure boat and smiley face than to a lengthy holiday description — especially as we're also offering discounts on all the trips booked today. I hope Josie can see it all and that it's cheering her up just as much as us. I drop her a quick text: *You've inspired Patty — hurry back x*

Disappointingly, I get no answer, but perhaps that means she's having a restorative sleep and she'll be back to her old self tomorrow. We have a good day thanks to Patty and I never thought I'd be saying that when she first walked into our office. We close up thinking we might live to fight another day after all. As I'm locking up I can see the lights are still on across at Launch. I walk along the street opposite so as not to be seen and take a discreet glance through the window when I get close. My heart sinks as I see it heaving with people. It's early evening and he's got more people in the shop now than we've had all day. That long-haul offer was incredible, though, and he limited it to this week so no wonder he's crammed. Clever idea to open up later for the after-work crowd though — maybe we should do that. I feel like we're constantly chasing our tails. He seems to outwit us no matter what we do. He even reneged on his offer to give us the advertising he'd booked and now on a day that seemed to have gone well, he's managed to fill both the start and the end of it with angst and misery.

I get home, throw my coat and bag down then head for the fridge to pour myself a glass of wine. I go over to the mantelpiece and pick up the People's Champion trophy. Some businesswoman I've turned out to be. I take it down and stuff it in a drawer. I sigh. I should tell Charlie about the evening-opening idea. I dial his number and he answers immediately.

'Has she called you too?' he asks before I can get a word in.

'Who?'

'Josie. She's just emailed me and resigned.'

Like a demonically possessed woman in a horror film, I open my mouth and a splurge of every single expletive I know (and a few I didn't know I knew) leaves my mouth. Fortunately, my head isn't spinning through 360 degrees — yet.

'This has to be down to him,' I say, 'you know it does. Josie loves Mercury and would simply not do this. I'm calling her.'

Charlie rings off and I start stabbing at the numbers on my phone.

'Josie, please call me.'

'Josie, you have to call me.'

'Josie, I know something is up and whatever it is, I'll help. Just call.'

I must leave twenty messages, some encouraging, some desperate, but I get nothing. I think about calling or emailing Lorenzo. I'm dying to unleash torrents of abuse on his Facebook page but I know he'll use it against me. Common sense gets the better of me and needing to keep myself busy, I call Zoe.

'Hello there,' she says. 'I don't normally hear from you on a weekday. Is everything OK?'

I'm about to say yes but I can't form the word and I end up telling Zoe all my woes.

'Oh, Mum, he sounds awful. You must be really stressed out.'

'Sorry, I didn't mean to burden you but yes, it has been horrendous. Part of me just thinks I should give up. There have to be easier ways of making a living. Maybe I'll go and work for him,' I snort.

Zoe takes a deep breath and I can tell she's choosing her words carefully.

'I remember when Dad left,' she eventually says. 'You didn't know how things would turn out but you just kept pedalling. That's what you used to say in any sticky situation — just keep pedalling. That's the only way to keep the bike upright. That's what you always tell me, Mum.'

I smile at her words. The advice was given to me by my life coach at the time and it served me well. Sometimes the bike wobbled but as long as I pedalled, I didn't crash.

'So I guess that's all you can do now, Mum,' continues my wise and mature daughter. 'Just pedal and, somehow, you'll get there.'

CHAPTER TWENTY-FOUR: I'M TOO SEXY

With Zoe's words ringing in my ears, I try to keep pedalling, I really do. But all week I can't stop myself staring out of the window, watching the people flow in and out of Lorenzo's shop.

'The offer will be over soon,' says Charlie joining me at the window.

'There'll be something else to follow.' I sigh and he hugs me.

'You really should call this business Mercury Funerals,' says Patty. 'Will you get your ugly mugs away from that window.'

She's right, moping isn't pedalling. I try to focus on work, answering the small amount of queries we have. Just then, there's a sound we haven't heard for a while — the front door opening. I perk up with expectation but then fall flat when I see it's just the postman.

'Recorded delivery for the directors,' he says.

My heart sinks, thinking it's probably the summons for our fine. Do you go to court for putting up signposts? Charlie signs for the letter and looks at it.

'Oh my God,' he says. 'Ange, it's from the financial advisors. It must be about the bid.'

He holds it out to me but I just shake my head.

'You open it,' I tell him while Patty and I grip hands. I'm not sure whether it's good news that it's arrived by recorded delivery — does that mean we have it or have they sent all responses that way? Charlie opens the envelope far too slowly. I'm wound up tighter than a Boudicca bodice on my best friend as I watch him read the words to himself and then read them again. His lips are moving but I can't tell what they're saying.

'Do you want the good news or the scary news?' he says eventually, and I look at him puzzled. He pauses dramatically and then cries, 'They're both the same — we got it!'

We holler and jump up to hug each other, then after a few minutes of congratulations and joy, the reality starts to sink in. Every single goose pimple along every inch of my skin is tingling. Charlie was right. I feel fabulous and terrified all at the same time.

'Oh my word, I don't know what to say,' I tell him, wiping the tears from my eyes.

'I'm just so relieved,' says Charlie. 'I couldn't have coped with more bad news this week. At last we'll finally have something Mr Launch Pad can't offer.' He pauses and mock bites all his fingernails at once. 'But holy holidays — we've actually gone and done it — can you believe it?'

'I know. Whose idea was this? Are we mad?'

Half of me is thinking that this is the stupidest thing we could take on right now. We have our hands full with Lorenzo. The other half knows Charlie is right. This gives us something he can't compete with. That's what Branson would advise. Or I think he would anyway. I wonder if he's ever just called it a day at any time. I hope we're doing the right thing. Charlie seems to think so.

'Well, yes, we're mad but that's beside the point,' he's saying. 'We need to get moving on our plans to have everything up and running quickly. The sooner we can get out there to the media with something really new, the better for us. And whatever we do, no leaks on this. We can't have him cobbling something similar together before we're ready.'

So Charlie is definitely pedalling and as fast as he can by the sound of it. Right then, I can certainly do the same. So first of all we have to work out how to deliver everything we said we would. If I'm honest, I wasn't really sure we'd actually win the bid. Not because it wasn't a good plan. It was or it wouldn't have won. It's just that people like me don't run exclusive resorts. Well, I guess they do now. We'll have to ring the bank and tell them that we won the bid. They'll release the funds we need when the contracts are signed. There's so much to do, but strangely, it's come at exactly the right time. When you're not busy, you've time to get gloomy. Now that we have this ray of sunshine in our lives, who knows, it may rub off onto Mercury too. Here's hoping. Charlie is already beaming again.

'This is brilliant.' He glows. 'We're really going to do it. We're going to have our beautiful yurts, our gorgeous bar and the most fabulous wedding venue ever. Peter and I might have to renew our vows when it's all set up. I'd love to be the first couple celebrated when it's finally ours.'

I don't like to tell him that it would be a bit odd for him to renew his vows within the first year of marriage. Still, his joy is infectious and I relax a little. I drift off and start wondering if everyone had to renew their vows every year, whether they actually would. I can imagine it would be an ideal time for couples to split up if they wanted to:

'Do you take this person for another year?

'Err no, I think I've had enough of them. I'd quite like a younger/ richer/ sexier model now.'

It would be a lot more honest and would save a fortune in legal fees. I'm going to have to be far less cynical when I'm selling these weddings.

Enough daydreaming, Charlie is proposing a planning session at his house tonight.

'I think it might be useful to have Michael there,' I tell him. 'He does know a lot about building and planting — he would probably be a real help.'

'And I'm coming, too,' says Patty. 'I might have to help you sell it and I'll stop you both making it either too dull or too kitsch.'

'Cheeky mare.' I wonder which of those hazards I represent but already know the answer.

* * *

Come the hour we gather at Charlie's and divide up the tasks: Michael reviews the tents and their construction while Patty finds out what the wedding bloggers are recommending at the moment. Charlie and I make a Skype call to our new resort manager to say hello.

A rather beautiful woman appears on the screen. She looks like Halle Berry's big sister and she greets us with the most stunning smile. I try to smile back enthusiastically without revealing my typically British teeth. *Note to self* — get them whitened before you go over.

'I'm so delighted you won the bid,' she tells us. 'I remember Charlie and Peter well. You were my favourite visitors.'

Charlie blows her a kiss and introduces us. 'Lucille, this is Angie, my partner and the woman who introduced me to Peter. Angie, meet Lucille who I'm told is the most resourceful person in the whole world.'

If we'd met in person, we'd have been able to assess each other with one discreet glance. With only our heads on the screen we both stay in a fixed smile — mine obviously with mouth closed (which is difficult to hold with any sincerity for any length of time). It's not just idle curiosity, I try to convince myself: this is the woman who'll be looking after my guests and my money.

'You are staying on there, aren't you?' asks Charlie and she reassures him that she is. 'That's brilliant news — the place just wouldn't be the same without you.'

'So what are the plans? Tell me all about them. The finance people wouldn't say a thing,' she tells us.

Charlie talks about the wedding packages, the yurts and the beachfront ceremonies. Lucille is nodding at each of the suggestions, so before Charlie gets carried away, I ask what she thinks.

'I think they'll sell well,' she says. 'Of course beach weddings are not new but couples are starting to want something a little different from the big packaged tours. We can help people personalize their day. Clients don't necessarily want to sit down and dance to cheesy music all night — although that too we could provide if they wish. I will find out what we need to do over here to become a legal and proper place for weddings.'

I'm impressed. She's obviously been watching out for what customers want and her thinking is in line with ours. She doesn't stop there.

'But don't just think about weddings — there are many other opportunities. We're seeing lots of older people celebrating anniversaries or retirement. Apparently our island is on the "bucket list", I think it is called.'

'And what about people renewing their vows?' asks Charlie like an eager pupil.

'Not so much, but we could certainly try them.' Lucille is shaking her head. 'However, divorce parties are big, and fresh start celebrations — we're seeing more of them.'

Poor Charlie sighs something about the lack of romance in this world, but I'm starting to feel more confident having spoken to this beautiful and seemingly knowledgeable lady.

'We need to start ordering the new equipment and also ensuring any repairs are taken care of before the season starts,' I say. 'Can you compile a list of what needs doing and get some quotes for the work?'

'I have it here,' she replies, opening a folder and taking out a sheet of paper. 'I'll email it to you.'

I'm determined to find something this woman hasn't thought of — just to make myself feel useful.

'Can you advise on any structural issues we might have with the yurts?' I ask.

She shakes her head and I cheer a little internally.

'I'm not great on building things but I can find someone who does,' she offers.

At that moment Patty and Michael walk in, so we introduce them and I tell Lucille that Michael is the person who might be helping us with construction.

'So if your structural expert could liaise with Michael that would be fabulous. It'll probably go completely over my head too.'

Michael spends a few moments explaining what he's looking at and what questions he has about the terrain and planning permissions we'll need. Lucille studiously takes notes of all his points and at the end flashes him one of her beautiful smiles: 'I'll get back to you as soon as I've found out about all of this.'

Michael thanks her and leaves us to our conversation.

'Are you going to handle that yourself?' I ask. 'I thought you were bringing someone else in.'

Lucille raises her eyebrows and leans into the desktop camera. 'I was, but that silver-haired gentleman — yum — he could be my Hugh Grant — no? I could definitely become interested in foundations and those joist things if he's handling them.'

Of course she doesn't know Michael is my other half and I don't tell her. Charlie muffles a snort of laughter and takes over the conversation, telling Lucille we have to hang up now as we've a marketing meeting to chair. As soon as she signs off, Charlie releases that muffled snort full force.

'I'm sorry but you should have seen your face,' he teases. 'But I'm warning you, if we have to pimp Michael out just to keep Lucille, we're going to do it.'

I scrunch up a piece of paper and throw it at him in mock indignation. 'Too right we are,' I agree.

Either the sexy supplements or that session with Lucille start kicking in, but I feel a desire to become just a little more exotic. Next to her anyone would look a bit humdrum. I mean she was older than me, yet even via a long distance call with her I felt like a bowl of Weetabix on a breakfast table laden with juicy mango and pineapple. However, it isn't just that she's gorgeous, I tell myself. For goodness' sake, we're just about to take out a lease on a beautiful island and I'm sure I shouldn't be facing this brand new start in my twinset. If I can take a risk this big, surely I can manage a plunge neckline. I think ahead to when we announce this new venture — won't the journalist and photographer be expecting someone just a little more — well, colourful? I think about all the famous women entrepreneurs — Karren Brady, Arianna Huffington — they're all very ballsy of course, but there's also something just a bit glamorous and bold about them. Maybe I need to start looking the part.

* * *

When I walk to work the next morning, I take sideways glances at everyone I pass. Who seems completely at home in this summer sunshine? Who looks stylish? If I were a photographer, which ones would I want to photograph? Some people — and I would have included myself in this group pre-Mercury — obviously have a work wardrobe which doesn't really change whatever the weather. Generally navy or black and sort of shabby looking as it's worn day in, day out. I guess they're thinking it doesn't matter what you wear when you're in an office with those awful cubicles. I can spot the people who are going places and those who never will. It's not about the most expensive clothes: it's about flair. Patty would tell you that, as a performer, when you step into your costume, you become that character. I look down at my sensible courts and know this character is definitely not an exotic international entrepreneur.

All day long I assess the outfits coming into the store. Charlie spots me.

'Why are you staring at all our customers' shoes?'

Rather than answer the question, I ask, 'Do you think I could wear bright colours?'

'Definitely — you're dark like Peter. Do you want to see his colour swatch?'

He pulls out two little wallets of mini fabric swatches. He tells me that they've both had their 'colours done' — which involves going to see an expert who tells you what you'd suit and what to avoid.

'You see, I'm a summer so I wear blues and greens, but Peter, he's winter, like you,' explains Charlie.

This means I can wear yellow and aqua, Charlie tells me as he holds the colours up to my skin. I ask to borrow the swatches and plan to go shopping tonight. Now that things are finally looking up, it wouldn't hurt to try on something a little more adventurous would it?

* * *

Later that evening, the assistant in the store agrees completely. She tells me I'm definitely winter and brings me a selection of outfits to try. I have to say the raspberry-coloured short-sleeved top she gives me brings a glow to my face that I'm sure isn't just a reflection of the colour. I swirl around in it, checking out my reflection. This looks good and is certainly more international entrepreneur — if only I didn't have such pasty arms. The tone isn't too bad but I should probably stop off at the sports department and get some weights to exercise them more.

After buying the top, I look at the store directory trying to find the sports section. Instead, I'm drawn to the beauty salon on the same floor. Perhaps I should have a facial while I'm here? After all, I might as well go the whole hog — Michael is coming round later. I've been religiously taking my supplements and it wouldn't do any harm to look every bit as exotic as Lucille when he arrives — although I can't imagine her ever seizing up at the crucial moment.

I'm disappointed to find there aren't any more appointments for facials and am just about to leave when I spot the special offer running — half-price spray tans. Now, I have never had one of these before but lots of our customers tell me they always get themselves a little colour before they go away as they don't want to look like the Brit on the beach. I look down at my arms — I imagine they'd look more toned if they were tanned and then I might not need to do the exercises after all. It could be the upper arm equivalent of contouring. Nothing ventured, I ask if there's a free appointment and fate must be intervening as there is, if I'm prepared to get my treatment from the trainee.

Everyone has to start somewhere, so I go into the changing room and put on the horrid paper knickers they give me without any fuss — I don't want to look like a tanning virgin. As instructed, I take off all my make-up and put on the shower cap — the end result better be glamorous because this bit sure as hell is not. Stepping into the cubicle, the assistant asks me how dark I'd like to go.

'As if I've just stepped off my very own private island,' I tell her.

I move round as I'm told to and before long, it's over. I look in the mirror and I'm slightly disappointed — I don't look very different at all.

'Could I go a little darker?' I ask, 'please?'

I think the trainee is frightened to say no to her first customer, so she reluctantly agrees and repeats the process. She then tells me the colour will develop over the next couple of hours and that I shouldn't go any darker. I still don't look too dark but take her word for it, get dressed and leave.

I can't get washed tonight, so put on my new exotic raspberry top and chill the wine. I feel fabulous and know that Michael is going to find a very different woman here tonight. I even put on some slow and sexy music just to put us in the mood. The doorbell rings and I turn the music up and fling the door open.

'Welcome to the new me,' I declare.

Michael stands transfixed. 'What on earth?'

It wasn't the reaction I was hoping for.

'Thought I'd give myself a little sun-kissed glow,' I tell him. 'In celebration of the island.'

'You're orange.'

Horrified, I rush inside and he follows me to the bathroom. I stare at the creature in front of me. The colour certainly has developed over the intervening hours and I definitely didn't need that second coat. I sink onto the toilet seat, my head in my hands.

'I was trying to look exotic for you.'

'You've certainly achieved that.' Michael laughs, lifting my face up to his 'You're like a glorious tropical cocktail — or the juiciest ripe mango.'

He strokes my hair and kisses me. At least I'm no longer the Weetabix.

'In fact from now on, I'm going to call you my little Or-Ang-Ina.'

I give him a friendly punch then fall into his embrace. He gently strokes my arms.

'Now,' he says, 'shall we go and get fruity — you sexy little citrus.'

CHAPTER TWENTY-FIVE: SMOOTH CRIMINAL

After a weekend of lurve (as Patty would call it), I can't stop smiling. I have re-established myself as the juicy temptress of Manchester and I feel completely re-energized. I am glowing with gorgeousness and I'm sure it isn't just that the fake tan hasn't worn off yet (though I have scrubbed it several times in an attempt to look less Oompa-Loompa like). Today I feel like I can do anything at all. I am woman, hear me roar and all that gubbins. And the first thing I'm going to do as mistress of my own destiny is sort Josie out. There is no way that bundle of rude health was ever ill and there's equally no way that she'd just resign, especially not via email. If she really were unhappy she'd come in and tell us to stick our job where the sun didn't shine. Nope, this is just not the Josie we know and love.

I know in my bones Lorenzo has something to do with her resignation, so I get up early and park on the street opposite his shop before he opens up. I lie low in the car as if I'm on a stakeout and wait. Sure enough, within half an hour, Lorenzo walks up the street dragging a reluctant-looking Josie behind him. I hold my breath, poised to pounce as soon as I'm sure she's going into Launch. They both look around to see if anyone's watching, then Lorenzo takes some keys out of his manbag and starts to open the locks. I slam the car door and rush across the road, yelling her name.

A couple of years ago, I was driving to the shopping centre to get some tights and news broke on the radio of a military coup somewhere or other. It was a very dramatic report. The rebels had roused a crowd, they were well-funded and organized and all the while I was parking the car, the reporters were very excitedly telling us that they were going to witness the birth of a new nation.

In the time it took me to select a pair of tights (to my defence, they didn't have my usual colour so I had to keep taking the boxes into the sunlight), the rebels had broken into the Presidential suite, declared sovereignty, been attacked by loyalists, had a huge battle, lost the war and been imprisoned. And all of this happened while I bought a pair of ten-denier nearly nudes.

It feels like my own uprising today.

I reach the door and try to grab hold of Josie. Lorenzo blocks me, pushes me away while frantically trying to get all the locks open. He finally gets the door open and tries to push Josie inside. I get hold of her sleeve and pull her the other way. She's being torn between the two of us and just starts sobbing. She breaks away from me and runs into the shop.

'What's happened, Josie? Tell me what's happened!' I shout through the glass door. 'I know you wouldn't just resign, this isn't like you.'

'Please, Angie, just let me go. It's better for you if I go.'

'No, don't say that. We need you and you can't prefer this place to Mercury.'

'It's not that, just go, please. I'm begging you.'

'If you don't leave my employee alone I'll call the police — again,' snarls Lorenzo before shutting the door in my face.

Like a Victorian urchin I stand for a while with my face pressed up to the glass. I watch as Lorenzo pushes Josie into the back room out of my view. He comes out once more to tell me he'll have me arrested if I don't leave, so stunned and confused I start up the car and drive round to the parking spaces at the back of the Mercury Travel shop.

Charlie is already there when I walk through the door. He stares at my dishevelled appearance.

'What on earth have you been doing? You're bright red.'

That'll be the combination of fake tan residue and frenzied warfare, I think to myself.

'Josie's working over the road,' I tell him. 'I tried to get her back but she wouldn't come. I don't know what hold Lorenzo has over her but I really don't believe she's there of her own free will — she was in bits.'

'What exactly did she say when you asked her?'

'That we're better off without her.'

'Do you think she's done something illegal? Maybe her visa has expired and he found out.'

We both shake our heads and sit in silence. We smile politely at the handful of customers who walk through the door but I can see Charlie's heart is as heavy as mine. Last week ended so well with the bid win and everything, but with him over the road, we always seem to have to pay for any moments of joy. I don't know how long I can keep this up. Or whether I actually want to. Maybe Zoe's wrong and there is a moment when you simply have to stop pedalling and park your bike up against the wall. I love Mercury but maybe it's time to call it a day. If we sold the business, Charlie could use the meagre proceeds to invest in the island, anyway. He could move over there, his dream would be safe. I'd still have the apartment and Michael, and as it says in the song, *two out of three ain't bad*. Maybe I should retire and spend my days lunching with Patty. Lots of businesses fail when there's new competition. I'd just be another statistic. Even Richard has closed businesses. I don't think Virgin Brides lasted long, which is a shame really as we could have partnered up. That's the thing though, I'm always thinking of ideas for the business. I don't want to let it go, especially not because of some upstart toe-rag. I wonder how Charlie's feeling.

'Come on, let's go and get a coffee or something,' I say to him. 'We need to talk.'

Closing up while still desperate for business isn't the best idea in the world but I need to get out of there. We stick the 'out to lunch' notice up and head to a coffee shop. We don't talk until the cappuccinos have been served, and after a sip of froth, which seems to soothe my soul, I sigh. 'So how are you feeling about all this?'

Charlie pauses then begins. 'We've had some great times together . . .' I go cold as this is sounding distinctly like a break-up conversation. If he suggests it, I'm not sure I'll have the strength to protest.

'I remember when you first joined Mercury,' he continues. 'You were really smartly dressed but you had on these amazing pearlescent stilettos. I remember thinking you might be some sort of eccentric — sensible on the outside but glamour puss underneath.'

'Trust you to notice the shoes,' I reply. 'I'd put on sensible shoes for the interview but five minutes down the road got my heel stuck in the kerb and the whole thing came off. Those stilettos were the only clean pair I had but they crippled me with every step.'

'So you were grimacing, not smiling.'

'Have been ever since.' I laugh and he punches me.

We both fall silent and then I pull myself up.

'This feels like you're trying to tell me something, Charlie.' I reach out to hold both his hands. 'You're not thinking of giving up are you?'

'If he were playing fair,' Charlie replies after a long pause, 'I'd fight. No one has a right to customers and so we'd just have to pull our socks up and compete. But this is plain nasty and I don't know what he's going to do next.'

I nod throughout just letting Charlie talk.

'If we hadn't lost Josie, it would feel different. It's as if he's picking us off one at a time,' he continues. 'Sometimes I wonder if we're in actual danger. I don't want to wake up one day and find he's taken Peter just to spite me.'

'You know that would never happen,' I tell him, but I agree with all he's saying. It does feel very personal.

'Do you still want to invest in the island?' I ask after a few minutes of silence.

'It's probably the only thing I'm still sure about. It's the only thing unsullied by all of this.'

I nod, totally getting that.

'Okay, partner,' I say, sitting upright and releasing Charlie's hands to punch my fist on the table. 'Let's pack all these thoughts about giving up away and unpack the Mercury fighting spirit. We've risen before and I'm sure we can do it again. First of all, I'll see if Josie will talk to Patty and tell her what's going on.'

'Oh please do — it would be so good to hear from her.' Charlie finishes his coffee and exhales deeply. 'Come on then partner, let's get back to the office and try to make it through the day.'

I drop Josie a text wishing her every success but asking if she'll meet with Patty. I don't expect an answer and I don't get one.

We walk slowly back arm in arm and as we turn into the high street the first thing we see is a police car screeching to a halt outside Lorenzo's and an angry mob surrounding the shop. Josie is trying to hold back the furious group of people who yell and push her. She looks tiny and defenceless against their efforts. Without thinking, I rush to help her, picking my way through the crowd until I can grab her hand and pull her to me.

'What's going on? Where's Lorenzo?' I ask over the shouting.

'He's gone.'

'With our f-ing money,' says one of the mob. 'And she must've known about it.'

'I didn't, I didn't, I promise,' whimpers Josie.

One of the policemen eventually parts the crowd and gets to us. He asks Josie to open the door and pushes us in. Charlie squeezes in with us while the other policeman gets the crowd to calm down. I find a glass of water for Josie and then we're asked to state what we know, but Charlie and I have to shrug our shoulders. We're as confused as everyone else. Josie shakily takes a sip and then tells us through the tears.

'I didn't want to work here,' she says, 'but he said he'd bankrupt you if I didn't. He said I'd committed a huge crime sending out those email addresses to everyone and then even worse with the road signs. He said he'd sue Mercury but it wouldn't be me that would go to prison even though it was my mistake. It would be you as directors. I couldn't risk that happening to you guys. I care too much about you and he's such a bastard I thought he'd really do it, so I eventually agreed. I thought if I just came into the shop and didn't do any work, he'd get fed up and let me come back.

'Then today, a customer came in to check their booking. They'd bought one of those long-haul offers and paid the full amount to get a bigger discount, but when I went on the system I couldn't find it. I asked Lorenzo and he fudged it saying the system wasn't up to date but I knew that it was. I promised to call the customer when things were updated and left it at that.

'Then I started checking a few more and I even rang the hotels, but they hadn't heard of him or Launch. I found over a hundred customers who'd paid the full amount and for who he hadn't even reserved a place.'

'What did you do?' Charlie asked.

'I confronted him,' Josie says. 'I mean there could have been a logical explanation but with him I just had the feeling there was something dodgy going on. I thought I had found some leverage to get back to you, but he's a crook and as soon as he realized I'd caught on to him, he scarpered.'

'With how much?'

'Over a quarter of a million pounds I think.'

I sink my head into my hands. This isn't our problem but we're travel agents and we're here, in his shop, when the fraud is about to be announced. Outside, the local press have got wind of a commotion happening and have a photographer trying to take pictures of the people inside. Whichever way you look at it, we look involved. The crowd outside are getting restless and the one policeman doing his best to hold them out eventually loses control and someone gets through. He's followed by the others.

'We've a right to know what's happened,' he says with the calmness that usually precedes a storm.

Josie chooses her words carefully and tells him that it looks as if Lorenzo has taken their money but not made the bookings. The storm erupts when they hear this. The crowd start grabbing the iPads, the computers and even the espresso machine as some form of recompense. The police try to grab them back and it's starting to turn nasty, when Charlie stands on a chair and calls order — literally.

'Order, order,' he shouts. 'Look, this is bloody awful but no one in this room had anything to do with it.'

There are a few shouts of 'Yeah, right' and 'All right for you', as Charlie continues.

'Honestly, we don't work here but we'll take your names and I promise you, when we get back to Mercury, we'll check exactly what's happened and we'll see what can be done. We're not going to solve anything here this afternoon. Please let us try and help.'

Fortunately, the ringleader accepts this and holds out his hand to thank Charlie. The mob form an orderly British queue and start giving Josie details of the holiday they thought they'd booked.

'So he didn't just play dirty with us,' I say as the last of the crowd leaves the shop.

'We have to help sort this out,' says Charlie.

'But why? We had nothing to do with it,' Josie says.

'Because right now, all people will remember is that a small high-street travel agent went bust and took customers' money,' Charlie tells her. 'If we don't help sort it out, they'll never trust us again.'

CHAPTER TWENTY-SIX: BOULEVARD
OF BROKEN DREAMS

'Somehow we have to emerge as the heroes of this story,' I say the next morning as Charlie and I gather early in the shop to try and sort things out. We have yet to work out how to make that happen.

The door opens and Josie walks in. She hangs her head, avoiding eye contact, and I guess she's wondering where she fits now. I rush up to her and put my arms around her shoulders.

'It wasn't your fault, you have to know that,' I tell her. 'Now do you want to come back to work? I think we're going to need you.'

She squeezes me so tightly I'm in danger of popping. I nod at Charlie to join us and we have a big Mercury hug before settling down to the task at hand.

Charlie calls the local papers. They've inevitably picked up the story and want to know if we're involved. They ask whether our customers are safe: Charlie was right — this is an issue that affects us, too. He reassures them that we weren't involved and says our customers are completely safe. The police are really helpful with this. They let the newspaper have a picture of Lorenzo's leather manbag, which he left behind in the rush. Fortunately, it contained his passport, so when the papers found out that he wasn't even called Lorenzo — he was a conman called Larry Maxwell from Wolverhampton — it all added to the frisson and took the attention away from us a little.

Nevertheless, we need to do the right thing. My first job is to call every single person who has booked a trip with Mercury. I tell them Launch has gone bust but we are safe and their holiday is safe. Then Josie gets in touch with Launch customers to find out if there's anything we can do to help them. We ask the local paper to include a bold paragraph stating that Mercury has offered to help and that if they've been affected by Lorenzo, they should call us.

It's an emotionally draining morning, listening to people telling us how they'd saved up for months to pay for their holiday or how the break was their once-in-a-lifetime chance to visit family overseas. I've always known that I'm selling more than simply a few days away but these stories really bring it home. We're shattered by the end of the day. I invite the guys back to my place for some food and wine. We can't go out locally in case someone corners us about their trip. After today we all need a break.

I order a takeaway and open the wine. We toast 'survival', then all three of us empty our glasses without coming up for air.

'I suppose this makes us the last man standing,' I say, filling them up again. 'So why doesn't it feel better than this?'

'It's like winning a silver medal in the Olympics against a drugs cheat,' says Josie and she's right, it does feel like that.

The next day, the local newspaper article is out and spreading across social media. The phone never stops and we work another twelve-hour day. There isn't much we can do — the money is gone — but we do try to find cheap alternative trips if people want to book them and we help them apply for compensation if they've booked by credit card or have travel insurance. Unfortunately for many, Lorenzo encouraged them to just transfer the money and said he'd sort the insurance — which of course he didn't. In a few instances, we can't stop ourselves: the story is so sad that we just have to help the customers out ourselves. It might be bad business but I'm hoping that karma will come into play, too. We're trying really hard to sort out this mess. The poor charity Lorenzo pretended he was supporting (I still can't get used to the idea that he's really called Larry. Patty was right, I'm far too gullible) got nothing, so with another few calls, we persuade the local business community to come together and put collection boxes in their shops and reception areas. I think people are starting to understand that we're not to blame. As the day ends, Charlie and I get an email from the bank asking us to come in tomorrow to discuss the resort financing.

'Well, at least he can't say that we've too much competition on our hands now,' I tell Charlie.

I ask Patty to help Josie in the shop while Charlie and I head into town. We've got the very last appointment of the day so that we don't have to close up. Closing the shop, even at four o'clock, would look dreadful right now and I'm still wary of leaving Josie on her own. She's prone to spontaneous sobbing outbursts despite the number of times we've told her she's not to blame. I doubt Lorenzo/Larry is crying over this. The truly guilty ones never do.

This time, I haven't even thought about how I look. I'm the competent travel expert who's sorting out a mess left for customers, not the smooth talker who was here last time. If I had sleeves to roll up, they would be. Charlie's are and his tie is relaxed as he throws his jacket on the back of his chair while shaking hands with the bank manager.

'You've had quite a time recently,' starts the manager, holding up the front cover of the *Evening News*.

'You can say that again,' Charlie says. 'But it goes to show — if the offer looks unbelievable, it probably is. At least we won't see discounting like that anymore.'

The manager nods and pulls up our most recent bank statement.

'It's a good job really,' he says. 'You were getting pretty close to the edge, weren't you? It's a shame he didn't go bust earlier.'

I'm quite shocked but keep quiet. To me his going bust has meant lots of customers lost out. Yes, of course I'm glad he's gone but I'd rather people hadn't suffered on his way out.

'Certainly, there'd be fewer innocent victims if he had,' says Charlie, obviously biting his tongue. 'Still we've survived and we're relatively unscathed.'

The manager stops scrolling through the statements and looks directly at us, his hands folded in front of him. 'I'm afraid there's no easy way of saying this.'

I sit upright, not sure what he's going to say.

'The business loan to finance the new resort expansion was secured against the core business as you know. The terms always required that the loan would be reviewed directly before drawdown to ensure the collateral was still a sufficient guarantee.'

I'm following it, just.

'With the downturn in deposits and now this collapse of a competitor, the bank does not have enough confidence in the independent travel sector to approve the release of funds.'

What exactly is he saying?

'The competitor didn't collapse,' argues Charlie. 'He defrauded customers and ran off with their money. It had nothing to do with us.'

The bank manager closes the file on his desk to show unequivocally that the conversation is over.

'I'm sorry,' he says. 'If the bank over the road went bust, we'd experience a run on funds, and you've yet to prove you can recover. We cannot lend you the money for the resort.'

CHAPTER TWENTY-SEVEN: LIVIN' ON THE EDGE

'We don't need them, think about it,' Charlie calls after me as I get out of the cab.

I'm in a daze as I walk through the main entrance of this mansion house. Although I only have an apartment in here, I always get a rush of excitement coming through the doorway into the enormous hallway with its beautiful chandelier and Hollywood-style staircase. I head to my front door and turn the key. The late-afternoon sunlight streams through the patio doors like a pathway to the garden. I follow it, open the doors and step out into the fresh air. I sit down on one of my garden chairs. Despite the sun, the seat is cold and the cushion slightly damp. Summer will be officially fading into autumn in a few weeks. I must remember to start bringing the cushions in. I love autumn, or at least I always did. This year it seems to have come around too quickly and I can't help but think of the trees stripped bare as some sort of symbol of this year. It started so brightly.

I sit until the sun fades further and I'm immersed in shadow. It's chilly, so I head indoors. I love this apartment. I love it. I love the space, the beauty and the freedom it gives me. It tells me I survived the divorce, not only survived it but bloody well kicked ass. It represents my independence. I pour myself a glass of wine and sit down. I stroke my hands over the fabulous damson velvet. This sofa is huge, sumptuous, indulgent, glorious and huge. Where else would it fit if it all went wrong? Where would I live if I didn't have this place? Because that's what Charlie has suggested, remortgaging our houses to fund the Caribbean investment.

The doorbell rings and reluctantly I drag myself to the intercom. I could really do without any more decisions or pressure or trouble tonight. Mum and Dad are at the door and I buzz them in. Mum bustles straight through to the kitchen as I hold my front door open for them but Dad pauses and looks me in the eye. He gives me a big, knowing hug and I have to hold back the tears.

'It'll get better, kiddo,' he says.

'We thought you probably needed cheering up . . .' says Mum, unpacking a carrier bag. Lord knows what she has in there but I can't say that a reduced-price cottage pie has much chance of cheering me up, if that's what she's brought.

'So I brought wine,' says Dad. He knows his daughter well.

'And I brought this linguine that you like — you know the one that's just fancy spaghetti. And some of these scallop things, nice salad and the naughtiest tub of ice cream I could find. All your favourites and none of them were even half price.'

'I am truly honoured.' I smile at her, despite my mood. 'There's rather a lot there though.'

'Oh we rang Michael on our way round. He said he was coming anyway to sort out your weekend away.'

Oh blimey, I'd completely forgotten about that. Michael's trip to Lords. I don't think I can cope with that right now. The intercom buzzes again but Dad sits me down with a replenished glass and lets Michael in. I'm in a kind of daze as they busy themselves in the kitchen making food and setting the table. I may have only lived here for a few weeks but all three of them already look very at home. And that's the key word — home. This is my home. It feels like mine already and I can't risk it. I simply can't. I'll work day and night to save Mercury, I really will, but I can't risk this place. I know this resort is Charlie's dream and I hate to let him down but I can't do it. I leave the chefs to their masterpiece and head into the bedroom, closing the door behind me. I call Charlie's number.

'Hi there,' I murmur, hoping the tone of my voice prepares the ground for what I have to say. Charlie pre-empts me.

'You can't do it, can you?' He sighs as I pause trying to work out the right words.

'I can't, I'm sorry.'

'OK, I understand. I really do.' He rings off.

I'm called to dinner and get through it as best I can. The people I love most in the world have made such an effort to cheer me up, I owe them that at the very least.

* * *

The next day, I walk to the shop slowly, dreading actually getting there. It won't be a happy day today. I didn't sleep last night but not because I'd made the wrong decision. As I lay in bed, I knew I'd made the right one, but I also know I've destroyed Charlie's dream and it was a good dream. I reach the shop door and push it open slowly. Charlie and Josie are already there and I can see from their expressions that he's told her the news. She gets up and hugs me as I walk in.

'There'll be another chance,' she says. 'We'll get through this.'

'I shouldn't have asked you to risk your home,' says Charlie, taking my hands in his. 'It was a big ask. Maybe there will be a chance next year when Mercury is back to fighting fit.'

His kindness and empathy somehow makes it worse.

'When are you going to tell them we're backing out of the bid?' I ask.

'Not yet,' he says. 'Maybe next week. I can't bring myself to say the words right now.'

I nod and completely understand what he means. I offer to make the call when we have to.

We each retreat to our desks to get on with the main task of sorting out customers' lost holidays and selling new ones. It's pretty difficult to sound and look cheery when you just don't feel it, but we have to. Our dreams might be shattered but we still have to sell people their dreams. Lots of them.

CHAPTER TWENTY-EIGHT: A FINE ROMANCE

'We don't have to go,' Michael says. 'I know you've got a lot on your plate.'

'There's not a lot more I can do. The police are investigating the fraud, Charlie is telling the investors next week and we've helped as many people as we can. The shop is now closed for the August bank holiday. Besides which, Jack's changed a shift to be able to come. We can't let them down. Life has to get back to normal at some point.'

I continue to pack for what is predicted to be a gorgeous weekend weather-wise. I do need to get away. I really need to have something to take my mind off recent events and although I doubt the cricket will do that, I imagine Patty will.

Once we're in London, we head to a real ale pub just outside the ground. I walk in and look around. I can't help but laugh — the place is full of men with shiny brown foreheads and noses. Everyone looks like a little gnome. They all have the same cricket-lovers tan that Michael sports.

Michael is glowing: this is his territory. He heads up to the bar with Jack and they assess the ale on offer. Patty and I tell Michael we'll stick to gin and tonic and he calls us cowards. Michael spots someone he knows in the crowd and they have a man hug. He introduces his friend to Jack. Seeing him so happy makes me think we'll get through this. Maybe I should try and take an interest in his hobbies, too. Michael loves all sport and is really looking forward to the game. I know as much about cricket as Patty does (and that consists of knowing the men are often rather gorgeous and by the end of the game they have nasty red streaks down their trousers), but I always think that if you're with friends, it doesn't really matter what you're doing. I bet I could do the commentary, though. I've heard it on the radio and it seems to consist of saying, 'what a shot' and something about 'overs'.

Come the hour, we finish off our drinks and follow the stream of people out of the pub and into the ground. We're soon squeezing our way along the terraces to get to our places.

'Fabulous seats,' says Jack, congratulating Michael.

'Not much cushioning in them though,' complains Patty of the moulded plastic seats. Much to our collective amusement, she adds, 'Good job I brought my own.'

The teams run out onto the pitch and Patty takes out her binoculars. I'm sure what she's doing could be classified as harassment.

I've watched cricket on TV with Michael, or rather I've sat in the same room while it's been on. I know they throw the ball and hit it — a bit like rounders at school — then they run but sometimes they don't and I think they only get so many throws each. On TV things are much closer and it's easier to see what's going on. If it weren't for the cheers and groans of the crowd, I wouldn't have a clue who is winning.

'That one over there is my man of the match,' declares Patty.

'Why? What's he done?' I ask.

'Oh, I have no idea but you should see his stubbly jaw-line. Here, take a look.'

I might as well and yes, he's a handsome chap. I decide to join Patty in checking them out.

'Who's the equivalent of Freddie Flintstone here?' I ask the boys, as I recall the only cricket player I've heard of.

Jack bursts out laughing and Michael shakes his head.

'It's Freddie Flintoff. His equivalent would be that guy there,' he tells me, pointing him out.

'He was very handsome,' I tell Patty, 'so big and muscular.'

She grabs the binoculars back and takes a look. The current Mr Flintoff is just as handsome. Patty nods and murmurs with approval.

A break is announced and the crowd starts shuffling about, heading to the bar.

'Are we getting up?' I ask Michael.

'You sit here,' says Jack. 'We'll get some drinks.' He nods to Michael who gets up to follow him out.

'Now those men know how to treat a lady,' says Patty. 'Get some snacks too.'

The guys are still not back as an announcement sounds that play will resume in ten minutes.

'I imagine the queues are pretty long,' I say.

'Well, here's hoping they've bought two drinks then. The first won't touch the sides.'

Finally I spot Michael but no Jack.

'Patty,' Michael says, 'can you take a look at the screen up there.'

We look up at the screen that has been showing shots of the match and the crowd. Jack is up there.

'What's he doing up there?' Patty asks.

'We now have a special broadcast,' the tannoy announces and everyone starts looking up at the screen.

'Patty,' starts Jack, 'you are the loudest, funniest, naughtiest woman I have ever met. How on earth I fell in love with someone who dressed up as Cyndi Lauper for a living I will never know, but I did. I fell head over heels in love.'

There's an 'aah' from the crowd.

'Every day I spend with you I spend laughing and I want to laugh for the rest of my life. Patty, my darling, will you marry me?'

The camera is obviously somewhere in the air as it pans onto Patty who has tears streaming down her face. She starts nodding frantically.

'Yes, yes of course I will.'

The crowd erupts into a huge cheer and the camera pans up to a row behind Patty. Jack had been standing there all along and he's now holding out a ring, which he puts on Patty's finger. They kiss and Patty waves the ring at the camera. There's a collective '*Ooooh*' from the crowd this time. They sit down and a waiter appears with four glasses of champagne. We each take one and clink glasses. What a glorious afternoon.

And it just gets better. Our hotel for the night is a fabulously decadent place overlooking Hyde Park. We jump into a cab and head around Marble Arch to the grand entrance of the Mandarin Oriental. A doorman greets us and our luggage is taken from us as we stand marvelling at the sheer opulence of the atrium. I have stayed in many beautiful hotels over the years but this is really something special. Our rooms are beautiful, too. A king-sized bed graces the elegant décor without dwarfing it   tasteful peony wallpaper that would only work in a room of this size reaches up to the mouldings, which in turn frame a glorious contemporary chandelier. A bottle of champagne sits chilling, so we forget about unpacking and take a seat absorbing the luxury and peace.

'This is stunning,' I tell Michael. 'What made you choose it?'

'I've a confession,' he says. 'I could have chosen somewhere closer to the cricket ground or the river but I just love the gardens in Hyde Park and thought we might get the chance to take a stroll.'

I shake my head, smiling — this is so typically Michael.

'So do you fancy a stroll before dinner?' he pleads.

'Nah, not really.' I prod him as his face drops. 'Only kidding, come on then.'

The colours are glorious and I wonder what Charlie is doing right now and whether he's forgiven me. I must stop thinking about it and just enjoy the moment. I link arms with Michael as we walk through the gardens and I imagine myself in an elegant costume drama. I look up at my Mr

Darcy and smile. He suddenly yanks me to one side. 'Watch it,' he yells pointing at the ground.

I look down and see a horrible brown slug, which would have been a brown smudge if my wedges had landed on it.

'*Arion vulgaris*,' says Michael.

'What?'

'The slug. It's an *Arion vulgaris*.' He then points at a shiny black one. 'And that's an *Arion circumscriptus*.'

OK, so he loves his gardens but this isn't the romantic stroll I was expecting.

'Some men would be telling me the names of the flowers not the slugs,' I say.

'I could do that too if you like. That one over there — it's an Agapanthus "Black Pantha".'

So much for Mr Darcy. 'Not quite what I was hoping for,' I say. 'Aren't they called things like Wonderful Lady? You know something that might sound vaguely romantic.'

'OK, Miss Needy—' Michael laughs — 'that rose at the back — it's a "Carefree Beauty", which is how you look now you've relaxed a little.'

'Is it really called that?' I ask, snuggling in a little closer.

'Honestly? I have no idea but it does the job doesn't it.'

I give him a little punch. 'OK, we'll stick with slug spotting you crazy romantic fool.'

'Extra points if you see a *Limacus flavus*.' He smiles.

It's a tough life, all this strolling around beautiful parks in the late summer sun, and I'm soon ready to avail myself of the luxurious bathtub and the exotic smellies provided. Michael leaves me to it, opting to sit in our lounge reading the news from a real paper. That seems as much an old-fashioned luxury as the linen napkins or cups and saucers.

He picks up a broadsheet and the simple rustle of the pages transports me back in time to a slower pace of life when you couldn't just right-swipe through the headlines. Although it's been a long time since I ever bought a newspaper, it used to be one of the simplest of pleasures. I remember the weighty tome of the Sunday papers and dividing out the supplements. Zoe would take the book reviews first while I always read the travel section. We'd be listening to the radio, enjoying pots of coffee, sometimes with a croissant, and we'd take hours over this. A full morning taking in the news and views of the world. Does anyone take an hour perusing a newspaper on their tablet or phone? I barely skim the headlines now.

I fill the tub and pour in the entire bottle of bubble bath. I want the sort of soak you see in films where the heroine's modesty is entirely protected by a foamy barricade. Should Michael walk in, he'll see a playful bathing beauty not a middle-aged woman tackling the forest on her legs with a disposable Bic. That's if he can see anything through all this steam, which is another tactic, as I figure it's the equivalent of a soft focus filter. When everything is just as it should be, I take my glass of champagne and step into the tub carefully. I lower myself into the water and as I do so, each vertebrae of my spine relaxes with the heat. Bliss.

I think back through this evening's stroll and smile to myself. In his own way, he's as nutty as everyone else I know. Given my collection of friends and relatives, is it any wonder I get the guy who thinks slug-talk is romantic? He knew this weekend would be difficult for me but he's made it as lovely as possible. And who'd have thought we'd be celebrating Patty's engagement this weekend, too.

There'll be photos tonight, so I better make sure I look gorgeous. The stress of Lorenzo has added years to me and it might be Patty's night but I don't want to look like her mother. More steam is required. I soak the hotel cotton face-cloth in very hot water (trying not to recall what Patty did with mine) and lay it across my forehead and crows' feet, willing it to plump out the lines and take years off me.

Bathing complete, I sit in my fluffy white robe at the dressing table, perfecting the hair and the make-up while Michael comes in to get ready. Shower, shave, quick squirt of aftershave, then he's dressed and out before I've even finished with the hot brush.

'Shall I wait for you?' he asks.

'No, you go to the bar and I'll be down soon. Let me make an entrance,' I tell him.

'That means I have to notice the dress is new, doesn't it?' He grins.

'You're learning.'

He heads out and I slip into the new sapphire blue (yep, another one of my winter colours) cocktail dress I've bought specifically for tonight. Elegant drop earrings, my pashmina and I'm ready. I do a quick swirl for myself and I have to say, I'm quite pleased with the results. I step into the classic nude courts, which I'm told will make my legs longer, and I'm ready. The hotel has a movie-style staircase, which enables me to make the entrance that I'd planned and as Michael looks up to see me he smiles broadly and gives me a sexy wink. I think every woman kind of hopes that one day, she'll enter a room and the entire crowd will turn to look — mesmerized by her beauty. I don't like to kid myself but I think it's happening now. Certainly more people than Michael have turned to look at me. I smile at them and notice a young, handsome guy waving. I start to raise my hand to wave back, stopping just in time when I realize he's waving at someone behind me. I turn and see the most beautiful young woman in a scarlet prom dress, the kind only youth can get away with. So it wasn't me they were staring at but it doesn't matter: she is beautiful and if I were in the room I'd be staring at this lovely young thing, too. At least Michael still has his eyes on me.

We meet Patty and Jack in the bar. She is glowing, positively lighting up the room with her smile. For as long as I've known her, Patty has managed to raise the spirits in any situation. She makes people laugh and has always been a half-full kind of girl. This is different. This isn't a performance. I'm seeing true joy and adoration dancing across her smile. I can't help but hug her.

'You look absolutely stunning,' I tell her.

We head into the Michelin-starred French bistro and read through the menu. It all sounds fabulous and I wish I could have a little taste of everything.

'Why don't we each pick something different and we'll have a taste of each,' I suggest.

'Good idea,' Patty says. 'Just one rule: no snails.'

'So have you had any thoughts about the wedding?' I ask Patty and Jack when we've ordered. 'When will it be?'

'Pretty soon,' she says. 'Neither of us have huge families. Well, I have no family at all, not blood anyway. So it'll be a pretty small affair.'

She looks at Jack and he nods.

'Actually, I wanted to ask you whether you'd be my maid of honour.'

'I would be absolutely delighted. Who's going to give you away?'

'Oh, I wouldn't hold with all that nonsense even if I knew where my dad was. I'll probably give myself away.'

Her smile fades slightly before perking up again.

'But the biggest question I have to ask is this. Can we be the first to get married in your gorgeous new resort?'

It's my turn for the smile to fade. 'Oh, Patty. I would have loved that but the whole thing has fallen through.'

I tell her everything about the visit to the bank manager and Charlie asking me to remortgage the apartment. 'But I just couldn't.' I sigh. 'So come Tuesday morning, we're formally withdrawing our bid.'

'Wow,' says Patty. 'I am so sorry. I know how much that meant to you both.' She looks pensive and I imagine she had her heart set on the island. She starts smiling again when we're interrupted by the arrival of the waiter bearing a dessert menu.

'Are we sharing again?' asks Michael.

'After news like that?' says Patty. 'You've got to be joking. Ange is getting the chocolatiest thing on the menu and no one else is getting a look in.'

The mood is re-established and we order puddings. I get no say at all. Le Rêve Chocolat, which promises chocolate mousse and chocolate ganache, is on its way to me. My very best friends are easing my pain with pudding — well there are worse things they could do. Just then I turn to see the waiters coming in with a bucket of champagne and a violinist following them. I panic.

They go straight past us to the young couple's table where, on cue, the guy gets down on one knee and holds out a ring box with a sparkle refracted into a rainbow of colours by the dazzle of the chandelier. She looks quite overwhelmed then deliriously happy as she says yes and kisses him passionately. The violinist strikes up and the champagne is poured. A glass is given to everyone in the restaurant and we toast love's young dream.

'There must be something in the air today,' says Michael.

'Bit public for me,' I say. 'What if she wanted to say no?'

I know I snapped out those words. I don't know why I panicked. Did I think Michael was going to follow Jack's lead? Would it have been so bad if he had? I hope he didn't notice. Fortunately, Patty moves the conversation on to wedding music and the worst song you could possibly have to walk down the aisle to.

'"Fat Bottomed Girls" wouldn't be a great choice,' says Jack.

'I can't believe that's the first one you thought of.' Patty thumps him. 'I hope it isn't a reflection of your feelings.'

'Never, ma chère.' Jack is channelling his inner Gomez Addams.

'"I Still Haven't Found What I'm Looking For",' suggests Michael, continuing the game.

'"I Want to Break Free",' I add.

'That'll be my divorce tune if you don't all say something nice,' Patty scolds.

'OK then, "The Most Beautiful Girl in the World",' I tell her.

'That's better, you're still invited.'

At the end of the evening we say our goodnights and head back to our rooms. Michael links my arm as we walk up the staircase.

'Did you think I was going to propose back there?'

'No, I mean not really. Well, I suppose I didn't know.'

'Did you want me to?'

At the top of the staircase I turn to face him and holding both his hands I say, 'Despite everything that happened with the divorce, I do still believe in marriage. But I don't think I'd be ready to do it again yet.'

'Phew,' he says. 'I feel exactly the same but I was terrified for a moment that if I didn't I'd lose you.'

'Never,' I say, kissing him. 'Where on earth would I find another man who knew the Latin for slug?'

'It'd be tough.' He opens the door to our room.

CHAPTER TWENTY-NINE: WE GO TOGETHER

I'm awakened by my phone buzzing away on the bedside table. It takes me a few seconds to work out what it is and then I go into motherly panic — it can only be Zoe at this time of night. I feel relief then confusion when I see it's Patty. I look over at Michael who hasn't been disturbed and is still blissfully dreaming away. I stealthily get out of bed and tiptoe into the bathroom, taking the phone with me.

'It's four o'clock in the morning, what on earth . . .' I whisper.

'Come to our room in ten minutes.'

I get dressed then leave a note for Michael in case, by some miracle, he wakes up. I sneak along the hallway. Hotels at night are very otherworldly. This isn't the type of hotel to have been chosen for a girls' weekend away or a stag do, so there are no drunken revellers returning from parties and no shenanigans taking place in the lift. Believe me, I've seen a few of them in my time during cabin-crew stopovers.

The hotel night shift are quietly getting on with what-ever night-shift people do. They're surprised to see someone wandering the corridors at this hour but are too polite and well-trained to say anything. When I was an air stewardess, I saw married cabin crew and pilots sneaking into each other's rooms thinking no one knew what was going on. You just learn to look away in the end. Right now, the guy delivering newspapers to the rooms does precisely that. He politely nods at me, then discreetly looks away as I quietly tap on Patty's door. Jack peers down the corridor before dragging me inside.

* * *

The next morning we set off after a quiet breakfast. None of us talk much on the journey home either and I suspect we're all deep in thought. We drop Patty and Jack off to get changed, then head back to my apartment. I call Charlie and Josie and ask them to meet us there. When we reach the apartment, Michael gets the coffee cups ready and I pace anxiously until everyone arrives. Charlie and Peter arrive first.

'So, what's the mystery?' asks Charlie. 'What have you two been up to?'

I shake my head, indicating we have to wait. They take the hint and sit down at the dining table, cups of coffee in hand. Josie arrives next and looks around. She notes the atmosphere and sits down beside the guys. 'I'm guessing this is serious if you're serving coffee rather than wine,' she says. I smile at her.

I'm not sure how long I can hold out without saying something but I'm saved by the bell — literally. The buzzer goes and I hurry to let Patty and Jack in.

'Ooh, this feels very tense, like the moment before the Oscar is announced.'

'Well, Angie won't tell us what's going on,' says Charlie.

I join everyone at the table and am relieved that I can finally say something. 'Patty has some news.'

She takes centre stage, pauses for a dramatic moment and then begins. 'We've had a truly glorious weekend and the highlight for Jack was me agreeing to be his wife.'

'It most certainly was,' he says moving to stand beside her and kiss her.

Afterwards Patty flashes the ring to lots of 'oohs' and 'congratulations' from everyone.

'But we didn't get you here to tell you this. Angie told me what happened at the bank last week and I'm gutted, I really am. When Jack proposed, I couldn't think of anywhere I'd rather get married and I can't believe it might not happen.'

My best friend squeezes Jack's hand as she says this.

'So I have a proposal for you all,' she says. 'The sale of my house will go through this week and when it does, the one thing I won't be short of is money. But if the Aussie is actually coming back to work, and it looks as if she is, then I've got nothing to do. You've all got the opposite problem so let me help.'

She takes a deep breath, ready to deliver the finale and beams at us.

'I'd like to invest and become a partner in Mercury. I've loved working with you all and I think I can add something. I promise not to get under your feet. I'll set up in the back room or the dungeon — wherever you want, just let me help.'

Charlie looks at me open-mouthed. I don't know what he's thinking, but my feelings are slightly mixed and they have been since she suggested it last night. It's been fun having Patty around and I'd love her to stay but I don't know whether she could cope with doing the same job day in, day out. Would she get bored? Charlie gets up and gives her a big hug.

'That is an amazing offer, Patty,' he says. 'Thank you. From the bottom of this little heart, thank you. Would you mind if I just have a few minutes with Angie and Josie?'

'Of course,' she says. 'Take whatever time you need.'

The three of us head out into the grounds to walk and talk.

'What do you think?' I ask Charlie.

'I feel slightly overwhelmed,' he says. 'I mean, it is incredibly generous of her but could you work with your best friend for the rest of your days? And would she be bored of being in a shop every day?'

'That's what I was thinking. What do you think, Josie?'

'She's been ace, she really has. The customers love her. She makes them laugh and she needn't be stuck in the shop. She could run the wedding business, and who's to say it has to be based in the shop? It could be all about home visits — we come to you to plan your big day. It would probably be better that way anyhow.'

'But Charlie really wants to work on the weddings, don't you?' I say.

He shakes his head. 'Not really. I like the ideas part, sorting out the décor and design. And of course I'd love to go over to the island more often, but dealing with brides and their mothers? No thank you. I'd much rather leave that to someone else. Patty would be fab.'

I nod. I can see that, too, and I think she'd be brilliant at it. She could develop themes, the entertainment and she knows how to create the perfect stage for every event. She has that instinct and imagination.

'My take on all this is quite simple,' Josie continues. 'You have a dream but no money. Now you've got a chance of the money — has the dream gone away?'

We both shake our heads.

'Then grab this offer before she goes and spends all that cash on hiring some eighties has-been to serenade her down the aisle or some other rubbish.'

We laugh and Charlie looks at me. 'So we're going to say, yes?'

I nod. We most certainly are.

We head back into the apartment and the chatter stops. Bizarrely, Patty looks very nervous, as if she's on *Dragons' Den* waiting to hear whether we're going to invest. She's the one getting us out of a pickle, so we should be the nervous ones in case she changes her mind.

All eyes are on us as Charlie steps forward and takes hold of both Patty's hands.

'You strange and wonderful creature, I don't know what to say except thank you. Thank you for stepping in so often over this awful year and thank you for rescuing my dream. We would all be absolutely delighted to have you as a partner in Mercury Travel.'

Patty squeals and throws her arms around Charlie, then me, then Josie, then Michael, then Peter, then Jack, then Charlie again . . .

Everyone gets hugged to extremes. Michael gets a bottle of champagne out of the cooler and another holler goes up as the cork pops.

'Thank goodness for that,' says Patty accepting a glass. 'I thought I was in the wrong house when I saw you serving coffee.'

'When does the house sale actually go through?' asks Peter.

'Thursday,' Patty says. 'So I suppose we could transfer the money on Friday.'

'You need to read through everything before you sign on the dotted line,' Peter instructs Patty. 'You have to be absolutely sure of this. If you're happy, we'd still be a week late on the investment timetable, but that shouldn't cause too many issues. We're a bit behind on getting the resort up and running for the wedding season, though. You're all going to have your work cut out.'

Michael stands up. 'Well, that's where I can help. I can help you make up for lost time. As soon as the deeds are signed, I could take a few weeks off work and go over to Formentera to supervise the work. You need someone you know to watch the construction of those yurts so that they're in place on time for the health and safety inspection. Someone you can completely trust. Let me do that.'

I hadn't known he was going to do this but I melt a little at his offer.

'Wow,' says Charlie. 'Are you sure?'

'Certainly am. I've been investigating the construction features needed to get that safety licence. They're not onerous if you know what you're doing but there's little room for error so we need to closely supervise the workforce. If I'm there, I can make sure the work is done on time, that you have an update every night, and of course, I can pitch in with the landscaping too.'

'It's a huge amount of work,' I say. 'Are you sure you want to take this on?'

'I'd do anything for you. You should know that by now.'

He leans over and kisses me and everyone sighs 'aah', except Josie who just says, 'Yuk, get a room.'

'In fact I feel so strongly about this,' he says, 'that I just can't sit here and watch the days tick by not knowing whether or not the construction is going to be finished or not. After all that you guys have been through this year, I have to do it for you. I really do.'

I raise my glass and clink it against his. 'Then I thank you from the very bottom of my heart and I'm sure Charlie does too. How can we ever repay you?'

'Well, I'm not sure about Charlie but I'll think of a way that you can.' Michael kisses me.

More *aahs* and *yuks* from our friends.

Josie stands up. 'Before we all drown in drool, let me say this. I have a lot to make up to you guys—' she waves away the protests we make — 'no, I know that I've made some real mistakes this year. So my offer of help is this: I'll work twenty-four hours a day to get back the bookings we lost and I'll get people talking about these weddings. We are going to be booked up and back on track by the end of the year.'

We raise our glasses to her.

'So with all these fab offers, what can we do, then?' I ask Charlie.

'You're going to Scotland,' he says and I frown, puzzled.

'The Americans Patty was flirting with a few weeks back,' Charlie explains, 'they've booked up the treasure trail and after everything we've been through, it has to be absolutely perfect. I'll man the office but you have to go up and recce that first stopover before they arrive.'

'They booked!' cries Patty. 'That's brilliant. I knew they would. Angie, you have to let me come with you.'

'It's your business too now. I'd say coming along was pretty much compulsory.'

Michael brings out another bottle of champagne and refills the glasses.

Charlie holds his aloft and makes a toast. 'Friends, we have all had what you might call, a difficult year.'

'You can say that again,' adds Josie.

'But thanks to you all rallying round, it might just have a happy ending.'

He tilts his glass towards Josie. 'First of all, to our Antipodean colleague, thank you and yes, we accept your kind offer to work twenty-four hours a day.'

She bows and takes a sip.

'Next, to the man putting a smile back on Angie's face, thank you and yes, we also accept your kind offer to supervise our building work.'

Michael follows Josie's lead with his own bow.

'And finally to the lady rolling in cash — welcome aboard. I cannot wait to see what weird and wonderful weddings you conjure up. I'm sure they'll be unique, if nothing else.'

Patty curtsies.

'To Mercury,' says Charlie, 'and living to fight another day.'

CHAPTER THIRTY: WILD WOOD

Michael has to go and catch his flight, so I should let go of him but I really don't want to.

'You'll be away for ages,' I say grumpily.

'It'll fly past and besides, you'll be on your own adventure.'

'Don't you go having your head turned by all those island beauties.'

'Don't you go falling for those rugged Scotsmen and their cabers.' He kisses me and I promise not to. 'Besides which, you want this place perfect for Patty's wedding, don't you? I promise I'll do everything I can to make it spectacular and when your customers see that wedding, they'll book up in no time. And I'll see you when you come out.'

'I can't wait,' I tell him. 'But yes, I know you'll make it perfect. We're all lucky to have you.'

We hold hands like a couple of teenagers until we reach the departure gates and then I stand and watch as he disappears into the labyrinth that is airport security. I pay the extortionate airport parking fee and drive home to wait for Patty. Both Michael and I packed last night, laughing at the differences in our suitcases — his full of shorts and beach pumps, mine, woolly jumpers and walking boots. It might still officially be late summer but I'm taking no chances with the Scottish weather.

Patty is hiring a car so we can share the driving. She will only drive automatics, therefore that rules my old faithful out of the running. I'm rechecking that I haven't left any plugs in (thanks to my mother, I am paranoid about this), when she drives up and toots the horn. My eyes pop.

I grab my case and head out onto the street. 'You don't do things by halves, do you,' I say of the bright red convertible she's chosen for our journey. 'You know it'll probably rain in Scotland.'

'Stop being a killjoy. Anyway, it does have a roof. I just thought we should do this in style.'

'And you're absolutely right,' I say, 'we've been through the mill this year.'

I put my case into the tiny boot and hop in alongside her. This car could make any trip an adventure and I'm ready for one.

'Do we have everything?' asks Patty.

I put my sunglasses on and turn to her. 'You know what Thelma would say.'

'*Sometimes all you need is a great friend and a tank of gas,*' we both drawl in our worst American accents.

'Now let's go test this treasure trail,' I yell as Patty skids out of the drive.

We have five hours of travelling ahead of us, so the back seat of the car as usual looks like a sweet shop. I'm the confectionery waitress with the heavy responsibility of ensuring Patty's sugar levels don't drop — as if that could ever happen.

'Wine gum please,' she calls, 'preferably an orange or green one.'

I dig through the packet to find her choice and feed both to her.

'Extra strong mint,' she calls next.

'You do realize we've only been travelling for forty minutes,' I tell her.

'I know — but they're calling me.'

I get what she means. I'm trying to ignore the tempting siren cries of the Starbursts. If I open the packet they'll be gone before we reach Cumbria.

The M6 isn't the most interesting of roads but we make steady progress and before long we've left England behind us and the Scottish scenery opens out. I'm driving now and it's an absolute joy, as the roads are quieter and sweep through the heather-topped hills. Patty starts shuffling through her MP3 player.

'Be ready to put your foot down. I've loaded some Scottish music for us.'

I'm sort of expecting something about the bonny banks of Loch Lomond but don't really see this as driving music. Nonetheless, I speed up sending our hair flying across our faces. The music starts and I smile at her choice. I turn it up to full volume and we both join in with Lulu belting out the opening bars of 'Shout'. Boy that song should be handed out on prescription — it could make anyone feel better.

On Patty's Scottish medley, Lulu is followed by the Proclaimers who are followed by the Bay City Rollers.

'Aah,' I reminisce, hearing 'Bye Bye Baby' filling the air, 'which one was your favourite?'

'Les,' declares Patty without hesitation.

'It was Eric for me, he had sticky-up hair like one of my gonks.'

'Get you, picking the bad boy at such a young age.' Patty laughs.

After one more change over and another hour we reach the ferry at Ardrossan.

'I think I seriously underestimated how beautiful this trip would be,' I say as we look out over the water glistening in the fading sun.

'Or how clean the air would taste,' adds Patty inhaling deeply. 'It's like breathing pure freedom. I think the Americans are going to love this.'

'Oh damn,' shouts a voice from somewhere behind the car.

We turn to see a man struggling with his motorbike panniers.

'Can we help?' I ask.

'I think it's broken but you're welcome to see if the female touch works better,' he says.

We take a look and attempt to close the catch but it is indeed broken.

'It's going to be a bloody nuisance carrying this on the bike.' He sighs.

'Where are you going? Maybe we could take it in the car and drop it off,' I offer.

'Are you sure? It might have drugs or machine guns in it for all you know.'

'And we might be drug and machine gun thieves for all you know.'

'Nah, you don't look the type.'

I hold out my hand and we shake. 'I'm Angie and this is Patty. We're heading for the hotel near Seal Shore if that's any good to you.'

'I'm Rab and this must be destiny,' he says, shaking his head. 'That's where I'm off to. I suppose you're going to the music festival.'

'What festival?' Patty's ears prick up.

'Och, it's great fun. Bands, singing, real ale — what more could anyone want? But if you hadn't heard of it you must be up to something else — just touring?'

'Far from it — we're hunting treasure,' I whisper conspiratorially.

Rab taps the side of his nose. 'Say no more. Although I'd have put you down for undercover bounty hunters if I were guessing.'

'He doesn't mean the chocolate bar,' I tell Patty and get a backhand slap for it.

The car queue to get on the ferry has started moving, so we take Rab's pannier and load it into the car, promising to meet him at the hotel.

It's a short journey, so we stay up on the deck watching the island get closer and closer. Landing at Brodick has us buzzing — maybe you just have to cross the water to feel as if you're having an adventure. I imagine the first guests discovering that they're leaving the mainland and being quite excited to discover where things are going to end. As the ferry leaves, they'll be wondering when and how they have to leave the island to reach the next destination. I know all the details and I'm excited. I think this is going to work. Before we leave the port, I take a photo of Patty in the beautiful red car with the Firth of Clyde and mountains against the setting sun in the background. This isn't for publicity though. It's to sit alongside all those other pictures of our adventures together.

As it's now early evening, the temperature has dropped, so we put on our headscarves and drive slowly around the island until we reach our hotel on the edge of the shore. Darkness has fallen and we can no longer see the sea, but we hear it lapping gently on the rocky beach as a breeze flicks through the flames of the torchlights bordering the hotel garden. We check in then order a glass of wine, which we bring back outside. The absolute blackness of the evening accentuates the peace as more stars than I've ever seen before start to appear, twinkling away.

'Have you made a wish?' asks Patty.

'For Mercury to get back on track and everything to end well,' I tell her. 'What about you?'

'To have the perfect wedding then never be alone again.'

I squeeze her hand and suggest we go inside to eat. Adrenaline and jelly babies have kept me going so far, but I suspect a comforting meal will have the opposite effect and I'm so looking forward to getting a full night's sleep.

We meet Rab in reception where he's teamed up with some of his friends. They invite us to join them but we decline, saying we've an early start.

'I hope you get your treasure,' calls Rab as we head into the restaurant.

I eschew the healthy local salmon in favour of haggis, neeps and tatties with a whisky sauce — well it seems the right thing to do.

Laden with food we trudge up to our room and slide into our little twin beds. I turn out my bedside light and say goodnight to Patty. She says nothing and when I look over she's flat out, eyes closed and mouth wide open. That's exactly how I want to be and as I snuggle into my soft pillow I know it won't take long.

* * *

When I wake up to sun peeping through the curtains, I realize that I've slept more soundly than I have in weeks and I feel completely rested. I get dressed for the hike we have ahead of us and then I gently shake Patty, telling her I'll just be downstairs. I walk out to the shoreline, tentatively stepping from rock to rock and peering in all the pools in between. Balancing on one, I look out to sea and notice one of the rocks moving. I wonder what it is and putting my hands above my eyes to shield them from the glare of the morning sunlight, I step out to a more precarious rock to get a better look. The *rock* appears again but it's not a rock, it's a seal. How wonderful, I've seen a seal! It's probably not uncommon here but feels like a good omen. I wobble back over the seaweed and barnacles then head back in for breakfast.

'I didn't fall in the water and I saw a seal,' I tell Patty as I sit down. 'Today will be a good day.'

'And this funny square sausage is delicious so I absolutely agree,' she says, waving a slice at me.

The hotel packs us some sandwiches for our trek and so with more food than an Everest expedition would most likely consume, we set off for the woodland. It's a fairly straightforward path to begin with and we meet lots of friendly people walking their dogs.

'I feel a bit overdressed in all this gear with the hiking poles,' says Patty and I nod in agreement. So far this walk doesn't feel much of a treasure trail and I hope Dad hasn't got it wrong.

After a couple of miles, the path becomes very narrow and enters the woods proper. The dark pines tower over us, blocking out the light and making the forest rather eerie. I stop to take a drink of water then freeze as I hear a rustle and something snapping. Patty hears it too and holds out her hand to tell me to stand still. It happens again and it's getting closer. Patty quietly moves to stand behind me — typical.

Then suddenly the rustling sound is in front of us, the lower branches of the tree start shaking and as we shriek and cower, out runs a terrified little fawn. We jump nonetheless and Patty instinctively pushes me towards it.

'Thanks a lot,' I tell her when the 'threat' is over. 'I know where I'd stand if we were ever in real danger — thrust to the front.'

With that deer and the seal this morning, I'm beginning to feel like a Scottish Doctor Dolittle.

We continue through the wood until it opens up dramatically to reveal a huge gorge and waterfall.

'Wow,' says Patty, 'this is stunning.'

The ravine must be hundreds of feet deep with a single plume of water gushing through it. A rainbow shines through and the effect is just magical. We could stand here for ever just captivated by it but we need to get moving. Away from the ravine we go back into the woods and then cross a river. This is starting to feel more like the adventure we thought we'd be having. You can only get here on foot so the Americans wouldn't be seeing all this if they'd just taken a standard package trip. I feel a surge of pride that Mercury might just be back on track. There is sunlight breaking through to the rocks on the opposite side of the river, so Patty suggests we have a break. Gladly I take off my rucksack and lie back using it as a pillow. Patty gets out the thermos and pours us a tea, then unpacks the picnic. She laughs and I turn my head to see her holding up a Farm Kitchen fruitcake provided by the hotel.

'I can't escape these things can I?'

'I hear they're very moist though.'

'Don't know who told you that.'

After topping up our energy levels we start moving again, and reach a small loch. I check my map and the instructions from Dad.

'We can't be that far away now,' I tell rosy-cheeked Patty.

I don't know what I'm expecting to do when I get there. A treasure trail should have some reward when you hit the spot. I guess we'll see what the place is like first.

The map shows the library in a clearing just beyond the woodland boundary. Through the trees I can see that the grass changes from the dark of the forest to the golden of moorland in a few hundred yards   we're moments away from our target.

I have no idea why but I start walking more stealthily like a hunter on the trail of his quarry. Patty notices and does the same. We're a two-trees-width away from the clearing and we bob slowly from one tree to the other, stopping to check we're not being watched. What am I expecting? To actually see the seven dwarves? It's that kind of place, honestly it is. Happy that we haven't been spotted by any pint-sized characters on their way to work, we move out into the clearing and there it stands — the library in the woods.

If the dwarves were real, they'd live here. I can't help smiling at the glory of this beautiful little place. The wooden shack with its grass roof looks just like a prop from a Disney film and it's simply magical, even more so because it's a library. We approach the back of the building and then skirt either side of it, ducking underneath the two little windows at the front. I bob up to take a peak: it's empty. We head inside.

Shelves of books cover two sides of the room. All the classics are here: *Moby Dick*, *Treasure Island*, *Swallows and Amazons* and so many others that just transport you back to your childhood. The air is calm and filled with the smell of pine and paper. In the centre of the room there's a desk and some chairs. How wonderful it would be to camp here overnight, reading by candlelight with the woodland creaking and coming to life outside. On the walls are pictures drawn by the children who have visited here, while the adults have left their thoughts in the visitor's book. I read through some of the comments — people from all around the world expressing their wonder and enchantment with the place. We've come to put a book on the shelves, the book that contains the clue to where our customers go next. I wasn't sure whether guests would be able to find it but now I know it'll stick out like Patty in a nunnery.

I've brought a Haynes manual for building and repairing NASA's Mercury spacecraft. I can't imagine anyone wanting to take it away and I think the guests will spot it straight away. The clue is written on the inside back cover. I wedge the book into the bottom shelf between *Jane Eyre* and *Robinson Crusoe*. At least it's in good company. I want to do more.

'We have to think of something that marks our guests finding this place,' I tell Patty.

'Could they maybe sign the copy of *Treasure Island*? They can't really take anything as a souvenir, can they?'

'No it would be wrong to take from this place. Maybe they should leave something.'

'They leave a gold coin and make a wish,' says Patty, pointing to the donations box.

'That sounds absolutely perfect.' And we both do just that.

Reluctantly we leave this wonderful place and start the long trek back.

CHAPTER THIRTY-ONE: THE HEAT IS ON

The journey back from the library was as dramatic as the trip out with boulders to scramble and gorges to climb. We're grubby, sweaty and tired by the time we get back to the hotel but still glowing with the wonderment inspired by the little library. I still can't believe someone actually chose to build it there but I'm glad they did.

Despite being exhausted, we're going to join in the festivities kicking off in the bar tonight. We can hear the bands starting to set up for the session, so I very much doubt we'd get any sleep if we didn't go along.

I shower first and lie in my pyjamas having forty winks while Patty heads for the bathroom — if I were one of our American guests, this would be a power nap, which sounds far more purposeful than forty winks. Either way, I manage a good half-hour of nod and when I open my eyes, I see the clock ticking onto the appointed hour and I can make my Skype call to Michael. It's funny how I knew to wake up at this precise moment. Eventually, his face appears on the screen and I can't help breaking out into a wide smile. It's so good to see him. The fact that it's only on my tablet makes his absence even more apparent — I can't reach out and hug a virtual man.

'Hello, gorgeous,' he says blowing me a kiss. 'How's it going?'

I explain our fabulous day just as Patty emerges wrapped in a towel. 'Would you like to see my white bits, Michael?' she calls out, pushing her face into the camera.

'I doubt you're getting a tan in Scotland,' Michael says.

'I'm not — *all* my bits are white.' She guffaws and I push her out of the way.

I ask Michael to tell us how it's going and he turns the tablet round so I can see the resort and the work in progress.

'Wow, that's even better than I remember from Charlie's photos.'

'It's fabulous, Ange and as soon as I saw it I knew you'd made the right decision. When you start selling weddings out here, everyone's going to want one.'

'Is the building going well?'

'I did need to be here but now I'm cracking the whip we'll get there. Lucille is brilliant — she has the workforce wrapped around her little finger.'

I bristle a little at the mention of her name but resist saying anything: I trust this man. Just then a boom of drums and bass guitar rocks the room.

'What on earth was that?' asks Michael.

'We've arrived during a music festival — I guess that's the sound check starting.'

'Good luck keeping Patty off the stage.'

Patty appears dressed for the evening and yells, 'She's got no chance — I've been practising my Sheena Easton all day.'

I shake my head and blow Michael a goodbye kiss. He tells me he's off to phone Charlie with the update and I'm relieved we have nothing to worry about. Michael was right to go out there, but it's strange to think of us so many miles apart yet still gazing out on a place of stunning natural beauty, a place we're only visiting because of Mercury. And nevertheless we're able to see each other with a little screen — all quite amazing really. When I think back to those postcards and photos in Patty's house, they were once the only way we could share travel experiences. Now we can virtually be there with each other.

'Come on, missus — get your glad rags on,' says Patty. 'Ooh there's an idea: "Gladrags and Bags" — did anyone Scottish sing that?'

'It's "Handbags and Gladrags" and yes, Rod Stewart did a version.'

'Now you're talking.'

She launches into a version of 'Hot Legs', prompting me to get dressed quickly just to shut her up and get out of the room.

Rab is in the bar with a group of friends. He asks us to join him and Patty accepts before I have the chance to tell him we've had a long day and need a quiet night. I guess Patty has no intention of having any such thing.

The banter is good, and as the wine and food flow, the music seems to get even better and we start to get in the mood. The final band are rather good folk musicians who get the audience up dancing.

'Come on, ladies, time to strip the willow.'

Which, it turns out, is a dance. Rab teaches us the moves. They start out rather sedate but before long we're all whirling each other round in a jig and panting for breath. Never mind all those marathons — Mo Farah should try Scottish country dancing — it's exhausting.

I beg to leave the furore and sit down soaked with sweat. I must have burned off so many calories today I can probably justify opening the Starburst tomorrow. The band eventually says goodbye and our group rejoins the table, bringing liquid refreshment with them.

'You're quite a mover,' Rab tells Patty.

'Oh I'm quite the all-round entertainer,' she says, patting the back of her head. 'I was on the cruise ships, you know.'

'Fabulous, well if you sing, there's an open-mic section next.'

Patty perks up and looks at me as if asking for permission.

'Don't look to me for approval. You know you'll do it anyway.'

'What should I do?' she asks. 'I don't know any Scottish songs.'

'Och, you can't go wrong with a bit of "Sailing",' Rab tells her, 'this crowd'll be carrying you along in no time. Everyone knows the words.'

So that's precisely what she does. When the open-mic session starts, everyone interested has to write their name and the song they'll be singing on the blackboard (Patty put her name right under 'the catch of the day' — it amused her greatly). After a ragtag of singers, some good and some awful, the compere eventually calls out 'Patty' and we all holler her onto the stage. 'Sailing' goes down a storm — I don't think Patty actually knows any of the words but it doesn't matter, Rab was right — everyone else does. Jumpers are waved in the air like flags then people stand up linking arms and swaying together. How wonderful it must feel to write a song that makes everyone so happy for years to come.

After singing this, Patty gets an encore from the rosy-cheeked crowd. Of course she can't resist and as her pièce de résistance she leads the revellers in a rowdy chorus of that other Rod Stewart classic, 'Do You Think I'm Sexy?'

It had to happen and within minutes the makeshift stage is full of men pouting, thrusting their hips and flashing an off-the-shoulder look.

'She has a lot to answer for,' says Rab sitting with me watching the frenzy unfold.

'She usually does.' I wonder if sitting behind a desk at Mercury is ever going to keep her happy.

Suddenly she stops singing but you wouldn't notice if you weren't watching her as the rest of her 'backing singers' onstage keep going. She seems to be looking at something, working it out. I try to follow her line of vision and I see what she's seen at the exact moment she works it out.

'Angie, it's him,' she yells from the stage and dismounts it in a single leap.

Every hair on my body stands up and my head rocks with disbelief. I cannot process what I'm seeing but I am seeing it. It's him. He's bearded, in sunglasses and wearing a completely out-of-place trilby, but there he is, bold as brass. It's Lorenzo.

I knew he'd left his passport when he ran off so couldn't leave the UK, but to end up here? Right now? He probably thinks a small island is a safe bet for a fugitive. He certainly looks relaxed: he's standing chatting to one of the bands looking like he doesn't have a care in the world. He's obviously completely unaware that Patty and I are in the same room. I don't know what to do. Should I approach him? Should I call the police? What if it's just his Scottish double? No, I'm sure it's him. Then he does it, the act that stops me thinking rationally and turns me into a lioness ready to take down my prey. He gets out my pen. My award-winner's pen — the one I gave him in good faith that we could work alongside each other as respectful competitors. The one I want back right now.

Stealth-like but with my heart pounding so loudly I'm sure it drowns out the drums, I sneak up to the group and when I get close enough I shove him and shout.

'Give me back my pen, you swine.'

Well I meant it to be a shout but it comes out a croak. I really must work on my lioness cries. Nevertheless, the band members look shocked and move aside, but Lorenzo just stands there, hands raised.

'Woah, crazy lady, I think you've got the wrong person.'

'Is this the ex you've come up here to get away from, Laurie — or her mother anyway?' One of the band members laughs.

'So it's *Laurie* now, is it? Not Lorenzo and certainly not Larry from Wolverhampton.'

He looks at the band members, spinning his finger in a circle at the side of his head to suggest my craziness and then turns his back on me. Patty and Rab reach me as he does this, which is just as well because I'm seething now and I have a growing urge to start punching him.

'What's going on?' asks Rab.

'This man—' I try to calm myself down — 'is wanted in connection with fraud. He robbed people of their holiday money. He stole thousands from them and just ran away like the big fat coward he is.'

'She's got the wrong person,' Lorenzo says to Rab, 'and if she doesn't stop making accusations, I'm going to call the police.'

'No need,' Rab says. 'I'm here already.' Rab takes his badge from his pocket.

The joy on my face is matched in an equal and opposite way on Lorenzo's. He starts to move towards the door.

'I'm not staying for any of this bullshit,' he says but Rab grabs him.

'Hold on, hold on,' Rab tells him. 'Let's just get the story straight and then you can go. If these ladies have besmirched your good name then they can enjoy the hospitality of the local nick. Don't worry, I'll see to that.'

'I'm too beautiful for prison,' murmurs Patty in the background.

Rab keeps one hand on Lorenzo and asks one of his friends to take details and check them on the system. After a few minutes, his friend returns and whispers something in his ear.

'A travel agency called Launch, was it?' Rab asks me and I nod. 'Lorenzo alias Larry Maxwell?'

Again I nod. Rab's friend opens the picture that he's had sent and holds it against so-called Laurie. Rab takes the sunglasses and hat off Lorenzo, then compares it again.

'Think they got you, mate.'

The band members apologize to me and offer to buy us drinks. Apparently Lorenzo had just offered to manage them and they were about to hand over some money to secure some recording studio time. I have to admire the guy — I mean he has absolutely no scruples. At one stage I thought the whole debacle with Launch might have been an honest mistake — he was simply out of his depth. It turns out being this type of low life is his calling in life.

Rab calls the local branch and when the police car arrives, they escort Lorenzo into the back seat. Rab asks me if I want to go with them to press charges. I hesitate and try to work out if he's actually committed any crime against me, but aside from being smarmy I don't think he has. I shake my head. 'No, we can deal with his offence against me right here.' I head to the car door, holding out my hand. 'I want my pen back.'

Even now he refuses to do the decent thing, so Rab reaches into Lorenzo's inside pocket and gets out the burgundy award-winner's pen with gold trim.

'I hope this wasn't the treasure you came all this way to find,' says Rab. 'You do realize it's not real gold, don't you?'

'Not to you it isn't.' I put it safely in my bag where it belongs. Despite knowing that Mercury will be OK now, I'm glad Lorenzo will get his comeuppance. Maybe all those people will get their money back, too. It feels like the final piece in the jigsaw.

Up on the stage, Patty's entourage are still going and they shout for her to rejoin them. I feel at peace and now all I want to do is sleep. I tell her to go for it without me but she shakes her head.

'Nah, it's just a bit of fun. It doesn't do it for me like it used to. I just want to get home to Jack and my new career.'

I never thought I'd see the day when she'd say that. Maybe she is ready for Mercury.

Over the remainder of the week, we hop over to Islay and visit the whisky distillery mentioned in Dad's treasure trail clues. From there we head back to the mainland and snake up Applecross Pass before taking in the most glorious scenery on the west coast. Finally, we arrive at Cape Wrath, which Dad described as the '*final crossroad for Viking Norsemen*', a wild and rugged lighthouse at the most north-westerly point of Great Britain.

As we head back with the Highlands in our rear-view mirror, I call my father.

'Thank you — they're going to absolutely love all of this.'

CHAPTER THIRTY-TWO: WE ARE FAMILY

To say that Patty is excited right now would be as inadequate as describing Usain Bolt as 'quite a fast runner'. If she's to be the first to marry on the island, it means we have to get everything ready in just three weeks. She's sitting in my living room telling me her plans and obviously has no intention of compromising because of the timeframes.

'I'd like fireworks on the beach just as the sun goes down,' she says as I sit perched with a notepad and pen making a list of all the practicalities. 'A big heart with P&J in the middle — fizzing away like a big sparkler.'

'Should we start with numbers?' I suggest and receive a wave of dismissal.

'And we should leave the reception on horseback,' she continues, 'galloping along the beach.'

'Can either of you ride a horse?' I ask and get another wave of dismissal.

I pick up the book of flowers Michael bought me when we were first bidding for the resort and try to get Patty to focus on more normal things.

'I've been through this to find out what's going to be in season when we get out there,' I tell her and she takes a quick glance. 'They're all beautiful but I think some are a little too bright for a wedding unless you want bright?'

'You're right,' says Patty. 'I'll go with whatever you think. Isn't the flower choice a duty for the maid of honour?'

'Not usually but I'm happy to do it.' I'll give Michael a call later and get his advice.

'So what do you actually want to do now?' I ask.

'Dress shop.'

Hurrah, sensible notepad tossed aside, we drive to the footballers' wives' part of Cheshire and descend upon the most expensive looking bridal shop we can find. As neither of us is exactly a size eight soap or reality star, I'm expecting the assistants to look us up and down then dismiss us in a scene from *Pretty Woman* kind of way. I have my gold credit card at the ready just in case, but nothing could be further from the truth. A woman of our age comes over, and when she hears we have just three weeks to find the perfect dress for a beach wedding, she gets down to business straight away.

'I can certainly show you the fabrics that work best in that climate but do you have any particular design in mind? Short? Long? Sleeves or sleeveless? White, cream or coloured?'

'Not bright white,' says Patty looking at me for approval. 'Maybe cream or the palest rose colour.'

I nod. The rose colour sounds lovely.

'What do you think, Ange? I don't think I want short.'

'I wouldn't either — something that blows around your ankles in the breeze. Not so long that you have to wear high heels or trip up in the sand though — maybe the length of a maxi dress?'

Both Patty and the assistant nod at my sensible suggestion.

'What about sleeves?' the assistant continues. 'Most ladies our age like to cover up, but for the beach that might not look right.'

'I agree,' I tell Patty. 'How about those sleeves that have just the shoulder cut out. They look quite sexy but hide the worst bits.'

Again Patty nods.

'That would be perfect,' adds the assistant, 'and I have something with the lightest chiffon sleeves dotted with pearl buttons — it's simply beautiful.'

She gets up to look for the right brochure.

'What will you want me to wear?' I ask Patty.

'Well, tell me if this sounds naff but I sort of wanted you to wear something similar to me. We're the same age, best friends and I think it would look lovely.'

'I can't wear a wedding dress on your big day.'

'I know, but if they did this style in that rose colour as well as cream then you could wear the rose — that would suit you better anyway.'

The assistant comes back with the brochure and shows us the dress she has in mind. It is beautiful and the photograph is shot on a beach with a light breeze picking up the model's veil. It doesn't take much of a hard sell after that. The assistant gets the sample dresses from the stock room and we head into the changing room to try them on. I walk out wearing my rose-coloured creation. It's the palest rose I've ever seen and suits my colouring perfectly. I can just imagine the setting sun picking up the delicate layers of fabric. Even if this isn't my day, I get the chance to dress up.

I head out into the shop and wait for Patty to emerge. When she does, the dress has an astounding effect as my best friend simply floats out serenely and elegantly. I smile and give her a round of applause.

'They're perfect,' Patty chokes, the emotion spilling over and even making me cry. We hold hands and look at ourselves in the mirror. Anyone would think it was us getting married.

'You've obviously shared some very special moments,' says the assistant and we simply nod. I'm going back through the years to when Patty was my maid of honour in the early nineties — gosh, that dress was truly awful. I burst out laughing telling Patty what I'm thinking about.

'I'd forgotten about that,' she says. 'Right — off with that gorgeous, tasteful dress! I've got to get you some puff-ball sleeves. I will have my revenge.'

After ordering the dresses we head back to the office and get back to work. We're all going to Patty's wedding, so we're closing the office for a few days and have to let everyone know about it.

At first I was worried that customers would think we'd gone the same way as Lorenzo but the news of his arrest spread quickly and besides which, Patty has become part of the furniture since joining us full time. She shows everyone who comes into the shop the dazzling engagement ring she's sporting so they know the closure is for genuine personal reasons. Patty's wedding also gives us the chance to talk about the new business and to get a feature in our local paper.

'You know, we should be getting vloggers to follow this now,' says Josie, inviting us into her virtual world. I've only just heard of bloggers let alone this new group — I'm beginning to think I'm going to be learning a word a day for the rest of my life. We haven't had time to get the TV channel set up for Patty but Josie isn't going to let the idea die.

'We could post all the preparation for Patty's wedding on Instagram and offer one of the bigger vlogs a live stream of the ceremony. That way all the Mercurians could sort of join in. We could still have that virtual wedding — they just go to the vlog to log in and watch the ceremony. I tell you it could be fabulous.'

Zoe can't get to the wedding because of work commitments, so I love the idea of sharing it with her. She was so excited when she found out about Patty's offer and it would have meant so much if she could have made it in person. Patty is like family to both of us. Fortunately, Patty loves the idea, too.

'If we do that,' she says, 'it would make me feel as if more people were there.'

I glance across at Charlie and he nods me into the back room.

'Did you have any luck?' I ask.

'Sort of,' he says. 'I found a Julian Richard Egerton — it's not a very common name.'

'But that's absolutely brilliant.'

'Hold on,' he continues. 'He died four years ago.'

I deflate. In return for making such a fantastically generous decision to invest in Mercury when we needed it most, I had hoped to do something wonderful for Patty. Before heading off to Scotland I gave Charlie all the information I had on her father with the hope of getting him to her wedding and being able to give her away.

'But there's some potential good news,' adds Charlie, 'she does have brothers.'

He pulls reams of folded printouts from his bag. They're pictures downloaded from social media of tall blond smiling men, the image of my best friend, and their smiling families.

'And nephews and nieces too by the looks of it,' I say, smiling at one of the nieces who is all dressed up in a tutu and feather boa during this obviously formal occasion. I think Patty might get on with her. 'But no sisters.'

It hits me out of the blue: just how relieved I am that Patty doesn't have a little sister out there somewhere. It was my idea to try and track down her family but I'd envisaged a tearful elderly gent taking her hand. I hadn't expected strapping brothers and Patty being an aunty. I'm pleased about that part but so relieved there isn't a sister and I feel terrible for even thinking that. It's just that for the past thirty years, ever since our air-stewardess days, she's been my big sister. Not the kind that behaves sensibly or keeps you out of trouble but the kind who makes you laugh and always looks out for you. And I love her.

'I'm sure she'll still be your big sis even if it turns out she has hundreds of brothers,' says Charlie, kissing me on the top of the head. Again, am I that easy to read?

'How do we know Patty or her brothers would actually want this?' Charlie asks. 'They haven't found each other for all this time and they might be happy with that.'

'I'll ask Jack about Patty,' I say. 'Could you try and contact them to see what they think? If I did it and they said they didn't want to know, I'd be heartbroken for her.'

We nod in agreement at our pact and join the others back in the shop.

* * *

Getting things organized within three weeks means that practically every night we're meeting up to discuss something. Tonight it's everyone's favourite — the food. Peter and Jack have put themselves in charge of the catering and summon all of us to hear their ideas at Peter's house.

'We thought maybe we'd have a barbecue on the beach,' says Jack. 'Fresh fish, prawns with a spicy dipping sauce — that kind of thing.'

Thankfully, Patty shakes her head in horror. 'Not for the actual day,' she tells them. 'You've two women in gorgeous dresses. We don't want to be covered in dipping sauce by the end of the day. And I can't eat without making a mess, which would happen. We should sit inside. There are only a few of us but we could have a very decadent dinner party. The best food, champagne, chandeliers and rose petals — really go to town.'

'And you could have post-ceremony cocktails at Charlie's bar,' I add, picturing the scene. 'Not champagne but something really gorgeous and colourful in keeping with the island.'

I picture myself in the flowing chiffon welcoming people to the resort and placing a flower in their hair.

'These cocktails can't be too alcoholic,' says Charlie. 'We don't want you two finding a stage and belting out Cyndi tunes.'

I protest I don't do that anymore although I obviously can't speak for Patty.

'It shouldn't be all eating and drinking,' says Jack. 'Why don't we do something before we sit down to eat?'

'What about that boat trip?' I suggest, and Peter picks it up immediately.

'You have a late-afternoon ceremony,' he says. 'Then we all walk to the harbour where we board a yacht and have our

242

cocktails. We sail around the island, hopefully seeing some dolphins swimming, and then we come back. Torches light the way to our decadent safari tent — the table is gleaming — all crystal, crisp napkins and an orchid centrepiece. We sit down to champagne and fresh fish, dining until it's dark, then we'll have dancing by our beach bar. The last song you'll hear is 'Perfect Day' and as it finishes, we take that tune to our beds. How does that sound?'

He looks around at us all but none of us speak. I think we're all lost in this vision of perfection. Jack eventually breaks the silence. 'It sounds incredible. Thank you all for making this day so special.'

Charlie's phone beeps and he nods me over to him. We sneak into his study away from the party planners.

'It's Robert,' he says. 'Robert is the eldest brother. He really wants to meet up and says his dad did try to find Patty before he died. They didn't know her surname.'

I can believe that: Patty's mum used a range of stage names and I'm sure there must have been a stage when even Patty couldn't keep track of what her real name was. She was relieved she married Nige and could finally stick to Carmichael.

'What did Jack say?' asks Charlie. 'Does he think she'll be up for it?'

'He thinks so,' I tell him.

'Then let's make it happen.'

At that point, Patty sticks her head around the door. 'What are you two gossiping about?'

I quickly pick up the flower book I've been carrying everywhere. 'We were just having a laugh. Can you imagine what the boys would say if we suggested this for a button hole.'

I'm pointing at a bright red waxy flower with a huge yellow stem poking out of it. The book describes it as heart-shaped but you don't have to be a Georgia O'Keeffe fan to see something rather different in it.

She laughs. 'If I were being polite I'd say they look like alien probes.' She sits down with us and we scroll through page after page of stunning, vibrant flowers. They're dramatic and beautiful but not really bridal.

'I think I've found the one,' I tell her.

I flick to a page I've marked out. On it there's a delicate lilac orchid native to the island.

I read the description: *'The orchid has been held in high regard since ancient times. It symbolizes love, beauty, refinement, thoughtfulness and charm.'*

'That says me,' Patty nods.

'With the exception of the refinement bit,' I say, getting a friendly jab.

* * *

Come the weekend we've arranged for a pre-wedding send-off for Patty and Jack. We could have gone down the traditional hen and stag night but that would have involved a night with my mother in tow and no Dad to keep her in check. We're having a full Mercury family affair at a local pub (gastro, naturally) and I'm rather terrified because Robert and his brother Elliott are joining us as a surprise for Patty. Lord, I hope Jack is right.

They've travelled up from Kent and we've arranged for them to stay in a city-centre hotel. They've never been to Manchester before, so inevitably when we catch up with them they've done a boy's tour of the city taking in the Football Museum, Old Trafford and the Etihad Stadium. Michael would be horrified that they didn't fit in the county cricket ground too. I leave Charlie in charge of them and head over to Patty's. She's at her most glamorous and is quite simply glowing. I'm glad this is how she'll meet her brothers for the first time. Jack and I ask Patty to sit down between us.

'Uh-oh, this looks serious,' she says, the glow fading a little.

'I've done something,' I say, not knowing quite where to start. 'And I hope you'll be happy with it, but I know that there's a chance I've overstepped the mark and interfered.'

'Go on, tell me.'

'After we found those photos in your old house and we spoke about your dad, well, I thought I'd try and find him for you. I asked Charlie to do a search while we were in Scotland.'

Patty swallows. Jack takes her hand and right now I can't judge whether this is going to go well or badly.

'Patty, we did find him . . .'

Her jaw drops but her face lights a little. I shake my head to ease the bad news that's to come.

'I'm truly sorry but he died a few years ago.'

Patty drops her head into her hands. 'Well, I guess that's it,' she says reaching out and squeezing my hand. 'I'm no worse off. Thank you for trying.'

'No, wait, there's more,' I say and Jack moves in to hold her steady. 'Patty you have two brothers.'

She bursts into floods of tears, burying her head into Jack's chest.

'And we've brought them up to Manchester if you want to meet them.'

'Of course I bloody well do,' she snorts, her eyes shining.

We take Patty to the hotel so she can meet her brothers before we go to the restaurant. We all sit quietly in the cab over. I wonder how I'd react to getting the news I've just given Patty. If Mum declared she'd had a secret love child and given it up for adoption before she met Dad? I can't imagine that ever happening, but if I ever found someone to share the burden of her, I'm sure I'd welcome them with open arms. It's not the same though. This is serious.

The cab pulls up at the hotel and Patty takes a deep breath before getting out. We head into the hotel bar and look around. It doesn't take a detective to work out who Robert and Elliott are. The tall Nordic genes that have blessed Patty have obviously been shared around the family. Patty stands looking at them with an anxious smile on her face.

'Hi, there,' she says.

While Robert is replying with a polite 'hi' and an out-stretched hand, Elliott grabs Patty in a bear hug.

'I knew we'd find you one day,' he says through the tears.

'You look a bit different from the photo Dad gave us,' adds Robert, holding out a faded black-and-white picture of a five-year-old Patty on the beach with the Jimmy Dean lookalike we saw back at her house.

CHAPTER THIRTY-THREE: WHITE WEDDING

Time has flown, as it has a tendency to do when there's an awful lot to do in a tiny number of days. Nevertheless, I've checked my notepad time and again and for the life of me, can't think of anything I've forgotten to do.

'Are you happy with everything?' asks Charlie.

'Yes,' I reply. 'Even if we'd had months to pull this together, we couldn't have done it better. Honestly, Charlie, I think this is going to be the most perfect wedding.'

In fact it's looking so perfect that the Mercurians are lining up in their dozens to watch it online. How on earth Josie has pulled this off I don't know, but Patty will have more people watching her take her vows than Will and Kate — OK that bit was a slight exaggeration. Ooh, but what if I get the Pippa Middleton reputation? I take a quick peek at my backside in the mirror — not too bad but I could have done with a few sessions in the gym if I'd thought of it earlier.

I'm collecting the dresses and suits. In fact, I'm making sure everything that has to be worn on the day is checked and double-checked leaving the bride and groom to focus on their holiday clothes. I never thought about it before but the other benefit of an island wedding is that you don't have to pack again for your honeymoon. I'll have to remember to put that in our sales brochures.

I can't help having one side of my brain focused on the business end of this trip, after all we've pulled together something wonderful in three weeks. We have a menu, flowers and a magical yacht trip that we could easily offer time and time again — as long as it all goes well.

The other side of my brain can't wait to see Michael again. He's been out on the island for a month now and although we've spoken every day, it's not the same (oh, hang on a minute, it's not just my brain that's looking forward to seeing him). It hasn't been all sunsets and sea breezes for him. There's been a bit of a storm recently and we wouldn't have been ready without him. During his last call he assured me that everything was in place and ready to host the wedding of the decade.

It's funny how you get used to having someone around and then when they're not there, it's like a piece of you is missing. I've felt like this ever since Michael left. Although I'm with my closest friends, the people I love most in the world, something is definitely missing without him. Getting onto the plane brings it home even more. I should have guessed that any plane travelling to a romantic island is of course going to be full of couples. Even the couples in our group are giddy with excitement. Before boarding, we all go into the lounge for a glass of champagne. Josie and Matt feed each other the raspberry in the glass, Patty and Jack interlink arms to drink from the other's glass, and the two guys simply kiss for longer than is necessary. I toast them and drink my champagne on my own, unnoticed by this loved-up lot. Yep, I'm definitely looking forward to making up for lost time.

Patty and Jack turn left as we board — we've upgraded their seats for the flight. The rest of us turn right and find our row. I'm on the aisle beside Charlie and Peter and after a little glass of wine I relax and feel Peter's shoulders gently rocking with laughter as they both watch an ancient romcom together. I start to fall asleep, imagining that my head is lying on Michael's chest, as it shortly will be.

* * *

Landing after a few hours sitting down in the plane and then the ferry over here, my body feels so stiff, but the first sight of Formentera relaxes every muscle in my body. The sky seems endless. The blue is barely punctuated with picture-perfect clouds. The breeze is warm and as I watch the bougainvillea swaying at the edge of the road, I know Michael will have loved his time here and that we will be back.

The resort more than lives up to my vision of it: Charlie's beach bar stands on the whitest sand — as if someone has just sprinkled icing sugar everywhere. With the candy-coloured tropical flowers and marshmallow clouds, this could be Willy Wonka's second home. As we arrive, Michael rushes out, followed by Lucille and the rest of the team. I run towards him and he picks me up and swirls me around (let a girl dream, please).

'I have missed you so much,' he says, kissing me.

Lucille shakes everyone's hand and then gives me a big hug. 'I've heard so much about you from your wonderful man and now I meet you I can see how he's so in love.' She sounds so genuine and I wonder how I could have been jealous of this lovely woman.

She greets Charlie and Peter like old friends and then turns to Patty and I. 'Ladies, you will be in the main hotel,' she says, 'while all other guests are in the yurts on the beach.'

Lucille reaches out and holds our hands. 'You'll have a truly blissful relaxation before the wedding.'

'I'm happy with that but I think you'll find Angie would rather be on the beach,' says Patty smiling at me. I give her a dig — I guess I'll have to wait a little longer for Michael.

Patty and I are in adjoining rooms with a balcony looking over the bay. Tomorrow we check everything is ready for the wedding, and the day after, the celebrations begin. I lie back on my glorious bed, wondering whether everything is going according to plan downstairs.

After we dine in my room and both retire 'exhausted' I drift off to sleep, having first peaked through our adjoining door to see Patty dreaming peacefully. The real reason Patty and I have been banished to the main hotel is that I have a surprise in store for her, so she can't be allowed to wander around on her own.

I wake up to see the sun rising on the picture-perfect horizon, then bounce out of bed completely refreshed and head down to breakfast. Exotic fruits of every colour greet me and I pile a plate with them, dying to taste everything — especially those I've never seen. I've never been this excited about fruit before. Full of virtue and vitamins I meet up with Lucille and Patty to go through the schedule for tomorrow. She shows me the planting Michael has done over the past few weeks and the safari tents he has built. These are the bridal suites and tomorrow night there's a part of the beach that will be exclusively reserved for the bride and groom. A shiver of excitement flows through my body — this really is wonderful. Behind us, Josie appears with her tablet: she's shooting a video of the preparation day, showing everyone back home where the wedding will take place.

'Is it everything you dreamed it would be?' she asks Patty for the camera.

'It's more than I could ever have dreamed of,' she says. 'Everyone can see how beautiful the island is but when you get here and smell the sea, the air and flowers, when you feel that warm breeze . . . It's just magical. What do you think, Ange?'

'Honestly, I can't imagine anywhere more perfect to marry the one you love,' I say to camera.

With everything in place, there's nothing for us to do but relax. Josie gives me the nod that all is OK and stays with us girls. I'm told the guys are out diving — rather them than me. Lucille doesn't seem to relax at all. She checks up on us frequently but afterwards rushes off to attend to something or the other.

'Are there other guests staying at the moment?' asks Patty.

'Dunno — probably,' I say, trying to sound nonchalant and hiding beneath a wide-brimmed hat that I have balanced over my face.

'We should get out of this sun,' advises Josie. 'Can't have you Poms glowing bright pink on your big day.'

'Not again, anyhow.' I sigh.

Memory of my tanning mishap is all the incentive I need to retire to the beach bar and sample one of its legendary cocktails.

In the distance I see the diving boat coming back.

'I can't wait to hear if Charlie actually got into the water. Shall we go down and meet them?' says Patty.

Josie starts choking on a chunk of pineapple — so it's not the drink that does you damage, it's the fruit that comes with it.

'I thought we'd have a guy-free day,' I say, slapping Josie on the back.

'What about dinner?' Patty asks.

'I've ordered us a private dinner on my balcony — just us three,' says Josie. 'The three lady Mercury Musketeers — I hope that's OK.'

'I'm OK with that,' Patty says. 'It's been one hell of a year. A quiet evening of counting my blessings is probably just what I need.'

Lucille arrives with the flowers for the ceremony: cascading sprays of delicate lilac blooms.

'Do you like them?' I ask Patty as she poses in front of the mirror with hers.

She simply nods, choking back the emotion. 'I adore them.'

Lucille takes them back to be stored until morning and as she leaves, a waiter arrives with our evening meal and a chilled bottle of wine. The three of us sit down and Josie pours. We raise a toast to friends, family and lovers then clink glasses cheerily.

'To those we love, those we have loved and those we have still to get to know,' adds Patty.

The musketeers end the evening very contented with life and looking forward to the big day.

* * *

You know those times when you wake up and for the briefest moment you can't remember what's going to happen today but you know it's important? Well that happened to me this morning. Precisely ten seconds before Patty burst through our adjoining doors and pounced on my bed.

'I'm getting married!'

Ah yes, that's what's happening today.

'Come on, old maid — sorry, maid of honour. We've got to start looking even more gorgeous than we do now.'

I feel like a pampered princess in her high tower as beautician follows hairdresser follows manicurist follows man bearing a tray of champagne. Throughout the morning, Josie films our activities, giving anyone watching a commentary. Our virtual viewers even choose Patty's lipstick colour.

'Julianne or JLO Nude,' says Josie reading out the colour options. 'Vote now.'

Our audience of sixteen decides she should wear JLO Nude.

We slip on our dresses and the flowers arrive. We look at our reflections in the mirror and we're as ready as we can be.

'Are you OK?' I ask Patty. She drains the remains of the champagne from the glass.

'I am. I just wish my brothers could have made it today.'

'Me too. But it was short notice and I'm sure they're watching online.'

I send Josie ahead. Patty and I check each other over one last time and head for the lift. We say nothing as it descends but my heart is pounding — *please let this go well.* The lift bell tings and the automated voice announces that we've reached the ground floor. The doors open slowly and we step out.

This is the surprise I've organized for Patty. I've arranged for Robert and Elliott to be waiting at either side of the lift as we arrive and they'll walk Patty down the aisle. On cue, her brothers step forward and I step aside. Patty's jaw drops and she looks from me to them and back again. Of course we're all grinning like madmen. Then, from further down the corridor, more people start to emerge — her new sisters-in-law, her nephews, and her nieces dressed as flower girls. One of them is still sporting her feather boa.

Robert steps forward. 'We hope you don't mind, but the kids wanted to gatecrash the wedding of their new Aunty.'

The unintended consequences of my actions are that both Patty and I are starting to cry. Fortunately Lucille has had the foresight to make sure the beautician is on hand to fix our blubbering eyes.

'I'll get you back for this,' says Patty smiling through her tears and looking directly behind me. I turn and see Zoe and James heading our way.

'You made it!' I cry. 'Oh I'm so pleased. How did you get the time?'

'It was all a ruse conjured up by this woman . . .' Zoe is nodding at Patty. 'She wanted to surprise you.'

'Thank you, you gorgeous creature,' I say to Patty, squeezing her hand and hoping there aren't any more mascara-ruining moments in the offing. Robert tells us that it's time to begin, so Zoe and James go to their seats beside Mum and Dad while Michael gives me a peck on the cheek and leaves me to join them.

'You look stunning,' he whispers. I squeeze his hand because if I even attempt to speak right now I'm sure all of the happiness I feel right now will burst out in the form of tears.

The curtains open onto a scene from a movie. Honestly, it really could be. A pergola covered in flowers stands at the end of an aisle lined with seashells. The gloriously blue sky and the sea are seriously competing with Patty to be the star attraction and the sunlight shines down on the party from just the right angle. Everyone looks incredibly glamorous rather than blinded by the light. Josie goes ahead of the bride, filming the event and then turns to catch Patty coming down the aisle. I follow behind and when I reach my chair beside Michael I sit and squeeze his hand trying to hold back the tears. The vows begin and they've each written their own. Patty starts.

'. . . *we'll chase every rainbow . . .*'

'Is she quoting *The Sound of Music*?' whispers Zoe and I nod, giggling at my friend. It's Jack's turn next.

'. . . *fall, I will catch you . . .*'

I can't stop myself this time. I burst out laughing and Charlie does the same. Jack and Patty look at us, glad that someone has spotted it. Jack's vows are the lyrics of 'Time After Time', one of Patty's favourite songs.

They are pronounced man and wife. I was expecting a full-on Patty-style crowd-pleasing snog but instead Jack kisses her hand very tenderly and I see Patty swallow back a tear. She takes a deep breath and turns to us.

'Come on, guys. It's time for a party.'

We follow the bride and groom down to the shore where the yacht is waiting to take us on our early-evening cruise. We're served our colourful cocktails as we sail around the island seeing the romantic little coves, the glorious foliage and spectacularly coloured birds that our guests will soon be sharing this paradise with.

'I can't imagine not having this place now,' I say to Charlie.

'Me neither. I think it's going to be very good for us.'

'Well, thanks to the web-stream, we've already got our first booking,' says Josie.

We all drop our jaws in a silent scream and clink glasses. It's fabulous news but this is Patty's day, not Mercury's. The yacht returns to harbour and we disembark. Patty is going to throw her bouquet from the bow. We politely gather around and she throws, directly at me. In a slow-motion moment,

I realize that every other woman has stepped away from the flying flowers, so if I don't reach out to grab it, a stunning arrangement of orchids will land in the water. I reach out and catch it just in time. The wedding party cheer and I blush. I try to give it to one of Patty's young nieces but it seems that even they've been briefed.

'I guess it's your turn next then, boss,' says Josie.

'I'm sure Michael might have something to say about that,' I reply, struggling for words.

'Bring it on,' he says, kissing me.

CHAPTER THIRTY-FOUR: PERFECT DAY

The celebrations go on into the evening. Patty's new family love to show off as much as she does, so there are a few duets taking place. Well if you can't bond over 'You're the One that I Want' what can you bond over?

My mum and dad have already retired to bed when Zoe comes up and says that they're heading up, too.

'It was a wonderful day, Mum,' she says and I nod. It really was. I kiss her goodnight.

'Shall we go up?' asks Michael. 'Leave this lot to their own version of *The X-Factor*?'

Patty's words *be more spontaneous* have been gathering momentum as this lovely day has gone on and I think the time is right. I gather up all my bravado and say, 'Come with me first. There's something I've always wanted to do.'

We sneak away from the table and then through the hotel, giggling like school children. The front door creaks as we try to open it quietly and then we run along the beach as if escaping from the crowds. The moon and stars are lighting up the beach and the tide is gently lapping against the gleaming white sand. The last cries of birdcall seem louder and more exotic in the quiet of the night.

I walk along until the hotel is out of sight and we're in a little cove that I spotted while out on the yacht earlier today. At this hour, the moon seems to shine on it like a spotlight on a stage. I turn to Michael and kiss him.

'You remember I said in the furniture store that I wanted our first time to be perfect?'

He nods. 'It was memorable at least. I'll never forget Or-Ang-Ina.'

'You can say that again. I'd still love that magical moment. And then I found this place yesterday and well, I thought it would be absolutely perfect for our first time here on the island.' I'm whispering coyly.

I pull Michael towards me and kiss him.

'Our own private *From Here To Eternity*,' he murmurs, stroking my hair and smiling into my eyes.

We lie down on the sand and I run my hands down the muscles in his back. He nibbles my neck.

Ouch that bite was a bit sharp.

Ouch, so was that.

'That's not actually you, is it?' I cry, sitting up and brushing the sand off my body.

'No it isn't, something's biting me. I think it might be sand flies.' He leaps up and pulls his shirt off.

At that point a heron or gull of some sort takes fright from all the commotion. It swoops from the cliffs down over the sea, nearly taking my head off and leaving a healthy deposit on my hair.

'Oh, no!' I yell, not wanting to leave it there but not wanting to touch it.

'Angie, watch out,' yells Michael, pointing to the sea.

Too late. A small gathering wave smacks me right in the face. I sit there in my beautiful chiffon dress, covered in bird poo and soaking wet. Behind me, Michael just starts laughing. Soon he's uncontrollably doubled up with laughter. I look at him as he stands there wearing half a shirt, scratching away on our perfect island paradise. What do we look like? I start laughing, too, and we put our arms around each other to make our way to the hotel. He takes off his shirt properly to wrap around me as the night breeze turns chilly.

'I'm sorry I've gone and done it again. Some perfect night this turned out to be,' I say.

'Oh I don't know,' he says, holding me tightly. 'There's an old saying which goes, "... *at the end of the day, your feet should be dirty, your hair messy and your eyes sparkling*".'

I kiss him.

'Well if that's what it takes, I think we might be very happy together.'

THE END

ACKNOWLEDGEMENTS

I have loved writing the Mercury Travel Club series and hope that you have enjoyed spending time with Angie and Patty. They're like friends to me now and I'd love you to feel the same way too.

There are many episodes across the books that have actually happened in my life so this is a series well and truly inspired by my wonderful friends and family. I'd like to thank them all for giving me so much material to work with!

I've also travelled to many of the places mentioned — including the gorgeous parts of Scotland mentioned in this book. If you ever get the chance, please do go; the library in the woods is quite magical.

Writing a book is a partnership and without the lovely people at Joffe, I wouldn't be able to reach so many readers. In particular I'd like to thank Emma for commissioning the series and Sarah for her editing prowess.

Please do leave a review and if you haven't read the other books in the series, now is your chance!

Happy reading,
Helen x

THE CHOC LIT STORY

Established in 2009, Choc Lit is an independent, award-winning publisher dedicated to creating a delicious selection of quality women's fiction.

We have won 18 awards, including Publisher of the Year and the Romantic Novel of the Year, and have been shortlisted for countless others. In 2023, we were shortlisted for Publisher of the Year by the Romantic Novelists' Association.

All our novels are selected by genuine readers. We are proud to publish talented first-time authors, as well as established writers whose books we love introducing to a new generation of readers.

In 2023, we became a Joffe Books company. Best known for publishing a wide range of commercial fiction, Joffe Books has its roots in women's fiction. Today it is one of the largest independent publishers in the UK.

We love to hear from you, so please email us about absolutely anything bookish at choc-lit@joffebooks.com

If you want to hear about all our bargain new releases, join our mailing list: www.choc-lit.com/contact

ALSO BY HELEN BRIDGETT

SERENITY BAY
Book 1: SUMMER AT SERENITY BAY
Book 2: CHRISTMAS AT SERENITY BAY

PROFESSOR MAXIE REDDICK FILES
Book 1: ONE BY ONE
Book 2: WRONG SORT OF GIRL
Book 3: MY SISTER'S KILLER

THE MERCURY TRAVEL CLUB
Book 1: THE MERCURY TRAVEL CLUB
Book 2: THE HAPPINESS PROJECT
Book 3: THE HIGH LIFE

Milton Keynes UK
Ingram Content Group UK Ltd.
UKHW041951130824
446844UK00005BA/228

9 781781 897270